2010 A.D.

After the Nuclear Spasm, *homo sapiens* was extinct, save for a tiny remnant scattered in small, primitive space colonies. At first Solar Humanity had only one goal: survival. But when the battle for existence was won, humankind began moving outward in slow, multi-generation space ships, and as the millennia passed planet-based civilizations emerged in many star systems.

27,698 A.D.

To these new worlds come the Immortals, beings with strange ties to ancient Earth, beings who seem to live forever, who can travel light years in days—and who use their strange powers to control the existence of ordinary mortals.

On the planet Pentecost, a small group sets out to find and challenge the Immortals. But in the search they themselves are changed: as Immortals, they discover a new threat, not just to themselves, but to the galaxy itself.

Between the Strokes of Night

Charles Sheffield

HEADLINE

To Rose

ISBN 0 7472 3077 3

Printed and bound in Great Britain by
Collins, Glasgow

HEADLINE BOOK PUBLISHING PLC
Headline House
79 Great Titchfield Street
London W1P 7FN

Lying asleep between the strokes of night,
I saw my love lean over my sad bed,
Pale as the duskiest lily's leaf or head . . .
                    —Augustus Swinburne.

Prologue:

Gulf City; New Year 14 (29,872 A.D.)

From the diary of Charlene Bloom:

Today I received word from Pentecost. Wolfgang IV is dead. He was five hundred and four years old, and like his forebears he was respected by the whole planet. A picture of his own grandson came with the message. I looked at it for a long time, but blood thins across six generations. It was impossible, save in my imagination, to recognize any sign of the original (and to me the one-and-only) Wolfgang in this descendant.

My Wolfgang is dead, long dead; but the great wager goes on. On days like this I feel that I am the only person in the Universe who cares about the outcome. If Wolfgang is at last the winner, who but I will know and be here to applaud him? And if I win, who but I will know the cost of victory?

It is significant that I record this death first, before acknowledging the report of a faster-than-light drive from Beacon's World. Gulf City is throbbing with the news, but I have heard the same rumor a hundred—a thousand?—times before. For

28,000 years our struggle to escape the yoke of relativity has continued; still it binds us, as strongly as ever. In public I say that the research must go on even if Beacon's World has nothing, that the faster-than-light drive will be the single most important discovery in human history; but deep within me I deny even the possibility. If the Universe is apprehensible to the human mind, then it must have some final laws. I am not permitted to admit it, but I believe the light-speed limit is one. As humans explore the galaxy, it must be done at a sub-light crawl.

I wish I could believe otherwise. But most of all today I wish that I could spend one hour again with Wolfgang.

"They told me, Heraclitus, they told me you were dead,
They brought me bitter news to hear and bitter tears to shed.
I wept as I remembered, how often you and I
Had tired the sun with talking, and sent him down the sky.

But now that thou art lying, my dear old Carian guest,
A handful of grey ashes, long, long ago at rest.
Still are thy pleasant voices, thy nightingales, awake;
For death he taketh all away; but these he cannot take."

PART I
A.D. 2010

Chapter 1: *The Road to Armageddon*

The snow was drifting down in tiny flakes. Its fall, slow and steady, had added almost four inches of new crystals to the frozen surface. Two feet below, torso curled and nose tucked into thick fur, the great she-bear lay motionless. Walls of translucent ice caverned about the shaggy, light-brown pelt.

The voice came through to the cave as a disembodied thread of sound. "Sodium level still dropping. Looks really bad. Jesus Christ. Try one more cycle."

On the periphery of the cave a flicker of colored light began to blink on and off. The walls shone red, clear blue, then sparkled with dazzling green. A stippling of pure colors rippled a pattern to the beast's closed eyelids.

The bear slept on at the brink of death. Its body temperature held steady, ten degrees above freezing point. The massive heart pumped at a sluggish two beats per minute, the metabolic rate down by a factor of fifty. Breathing was steadily weakening, betrayed now only by the thin layer of ice crystals in the fringe of white beard and around the blunt muzzle.

"No good." The voice held an added urgency. "Still dropping, and we're losing the pulse trace. We have to risk it. Give her a bigger jolt."

The light pattern altered. There was a stab of magenta, a rapid twinkle of sapphire and cyan, then a scattershot of moving saffron and ruby dots on the icy wall. As the rainbow modulated, the bear responded to the signal. Slate-grey eyes flickered in the long, smooth head. The massive chest shuddered.

"That's as far as I dare take it." The second voice was deeper. "We're beginning to get more heart fibrillation."

"Hold the level there. And keep an eye on that rectal temperature. Why is it happening *now*, of all times?" The voice echoed anguished through the thick-walled cavern.

The chamber where the bear lay was fifteen meters across. Through the outer wall ran a spidery filament of fiber optics. It passed beneath the ice to a squat box next to the beast's body. Faint electronic signals came from needles implanted deep in the tough skin, where sensors monitored the ebbing currents of life in the great body. Skin conductivity, heartbeat, blood pressure, saliva, temperature, chemical balances, ion concentrations, eye movements and brain waves were continuously monitored. Coded and amplified in the square box, the signals passed as pulses of light along the optic bundle to a panel of equipment set outside the chamber's wall.

The woman who leaned over the panel outside the chamber was about thirty years old. Her dark hair was cropped short over a high, smooth forehead that now creased with frown lines as she studied the monitors. She was watching one digital read-out as it flickered rapidly through a repeated sequence of values. She was in her stockinged feet, and her toes and feet wriggled nervously as the digital readout values moved faster.

"It's no good. She's still getting worse. Can we reverse it?"

The man next to her shook his head. "Not without killing her faster. Her temperature's down too far already, and she's below our control on brain activity. I'm afraid we're going to lose her." His voice was calm and slow under rigid control. He turned to look at the woman, waiting for an instruction.

She took a long, shuddering breath. "We must *not* lose her. There must be something else to do. Oh my God." She stood up, revealing a supple, willowy build that emphasized the thinness of her stooped shoulders. "Jinx might be in the same condition. Did you check on his enclosure, see how he's doing?"

Wolfgang Gibbs snorted. "Give me credit for something, Charlene. I checked him a few minutes ago. Everything is stable there. I held him four hours behind Dolly here, because I didn't know if this move was a safe one." He shrugged. "I guess we know now. Look at Dolly's EEG. Better accept it, boss woman. We can't do one thing for her."

On the screen in front of them, the pattern of electrical signals from the bear's brain was beginning to flatten. All evidence of spindles was gone, and the residual sinusoid was dropping in amplitude.

The woman shivered, then sighed. "Damn, damn, *damn*." She ran her hand through her dark hair.

"So what now? I can't stay here much longer—JN's meeting starts in less than half an hour. What the hell am I going to tell her? She had such hopes for this one."

She straightened under the other's direct gaze. There was a speculative element to his look that always made her uneasy.

He shrugged again and laughed harshly. "Tell her we never promised miracles." His voice had a flat edge to the vowels that hinted at English as a late-learned second language. "Bears don't hibernate in the same way as other animals do. Even JN will admit that. They sleep a lot, and the body temperature drops, but it's a different metabolic process." There was a beep from the monitor console. "Look out now—she's going."

On the screen in front of them the trace of brain activity was reduced to a single horizontal line. They watched in silence for a full minute, until there was a final, faint shiver from the heart monitor.

The man leaned forward and turned the gain as high as it would go. He grunted. "Nothing. She's gone. Poor old Dolly."

"And what do I tell JN?"

"The truth. She already knows most of it. We've gone farther with Jinx and Dolly than JN had any reason to hope we could. I told you we were into a risky area with the bears, but we kept pushing on."

"I was hoping to keep Jinx under at least another four days. Now, we can't risk it. I'll have to tell JN we're going to wake him up now."

"It's that, or kill him. You saw the monitors." As he spoke, he had already switched to the injection control system for the second experimental chamber, and was carefully increasing the hormonal levels through Jinx's half-ton body mass. "But you're the boss. If you insist on it, I'll hold him under a bit longer."

"No." She was chewing her lip, rocking backwards and forwards in front of the screen. "We can't take the risk. Go ahead, Wolfgang, bring him up all the way. Full consciousness. How long had Dolly been under, total time?"

"One hundred and ninety one hours and fourteen minutes."

She laughed nervously and wriggled her feet back into her shoes. "Well, it's a record for the species. We have that much to comfort us. I have to go. Can you finish all right without me?"

"I'll have to. Don't worry, this is my fourth hour of overtime already today." He smiled sourly, but more to himself than to Charlene. "You know what I think? If JN ever does find a way for a human to stay awake and sane for twenty-four hours a day, first thing she'll do is work people like us triple shifts."

Charlene Bloom smiled at him and nodded, but her mind was already moving on to the dreaded meeting. Head down, she set off through the hangarlike building, her footsteps echoing to the high, corrugated-steel roof. Behind her, Wolfgang watched her depart. His look was a combination of rage and sorrow.

"That's right, Charlene," he grunted under his breath. "You're the boss, so you go off and take the heat. Fair enough. We both deserve it after what we did to poor old Dolly. But you ought to stop kissing JN's ass and tell her she's pushing us too fast. She'd probably put you in charge of paperclips, but serve you right—you should have put your foot down before we lost one."

A hundred yards away along the length of the open floor, Charlene Bloom abruptly turned to stare back at him. He looked startled, raised his hand, and gave an awkward half-wave.

"Reading my thoughts?" He sniffed, turned back to his control console. "Nah. She's just chicken. She'd rather stay here than tell JN what's happened in the last half-hour."

He switched to Jinx's displays. The big brown bear had to be eased back up to consciousness, a fraction of a degree at a time. They couldn't afford to lose another one.

He rubbed at his unshaven chin, scratched absent-mindedly at his crotch, and pored over the telemetry signals. What was the best way? Nobody had real experience at this, not even JN herself.

"Come on, Jinx. Let's do this right. We don't want you in pain when the circulation comes back. Blood sugar first, shall we, then serotonin and potassium balance? That sounds pretty good."

Wolfgang Gibbs wasn't really angry at Charlene—he liked her too well. It was worry about Dolly and Jinx that upset him. He had little patience or respect for many of his superiors. But for the Kodiak bears and the other animal charges, he had a good deal of affection and concern.

Chapter 2:

Charlene Bloom took almost a quarter of an hour to make her way along the length of the main hangar. More than reluctance to attend the impending meeting slowed her steps. Fifty experiments went on in the building, most of them under her administrative control.

In one dim-lit vault a score of domestic cats prowled, sleepless and deranged. A delicate operation had removed part of the reticular formation, the section of the hindbrain that controls sleep. She scanned the records. They had been continuously awake now for eleven hundred and eighty hours—a month and a half. The monitors were at last showing evidence of neurological malfunction. She could reasonably call it feline madness in her monthly report.

Most of the animals now showed no interest in food or sex. A handful had become feral, attacking anything that came near them. But they were all still alive. That was progress. Their last experiment had failed after less than half the time.

Each section of the building held temperature-controlled enclosures. In the next area she came to the rooms where the hibernating rodents and marsupials were housed. She walked slowly past each walled cage, her attention divided between the animals and thoughts of the coming meeting.

Marmots and ground squirrels here, next to the mutated jerboas. Who was running this one? Aston Naugle, if she had it right. Not as organized as Wolfgang Gibbs, and not as hard working—but at least he didn't make the shivers run up and down her spine. She was taller than Wolfgang. *And* his senior by three grades. But there was something about those tawny eyes . . . like one of the animals. He wasn't afraid of the bears, or the big cats—or his superior. A sudden disquieting thought came to her. That look. He would ask her out one evening, she was sure of it. And then?

Suddenly conscious that time was passing, she began to hurry along the next corridor. Her shoes were crippling, but it wouldn't do to be late. These damned shoes—why could she never get any that fitted right, the way other people did? *Mustn't be late.* In the labs since JN had been made Director, unpunctuality was a cardinal sin ("When you delay the start of a meeting, you steal everyone's time to pay for your own lack of efficiency. . . .")

The corridor continued outside the main building, to become a long covered walkway. She took her first look at the mid-morning cloud pattern. It was still trying to rain. What was going on with this crazy weather? Since the climate cycle went haywire, none of the forecasts was worth a thing. There was a low ground mist curling over the hills near Christchurch, and it was hotter than it was ever supposed to be. According to all the reports, the situation was as bad in the northern hemisphere as it was in New Zealand. And the Americans, Europeans, and Soviets were suffering much worse crop failures.

Her mind went back to the first lab. Everything had been designed for less moisture. No wonder the air coolers were snowing on Jinx, the humidity outside must be close to a hundred percent. Maybe they should add a dehumidifier to the system, what they had now was working like a damned snow machine. Should she request that equipment at today's meeting?

The meeting.

Charlene jerked her attention away from the lab experiments. Time to worry about that later. She hurried on. Up a short flight of stairs, a left turn, and she was at C-53, the conference room where the weekly reviews were held. And, thank God, there before JN.

She slipped into her place at the long table, nodding at the others who were already seated; "Catkiller" Cannon from Physiology, de Vries from External Subjects, Beppo Cameron from Pharmacology (daffodil in his buttonhole—where did he get *that* in this wild weather?). The others ignored her and examined their open folders.

Five minutes to eleven. She had a few minutes to review her own statement and to stare for the hundredth time at the framed embroidery on the wall opposite. It had been there as long as she had, and she could close her eyes and recite it by heart.

"Do but consider what an excellent thing sleep is: it is so inestimable a jewel that, if a tyrant would give his crown for an hour's slumber, it cannot be bought: of so beautiful a shape is it, that though a man lie with an Empress, his heart cannot be quiet till he leaves her embracements to be at rest with the

other: yea, so greatly indebted are we to this kinsman of death, that we owe the better tributary, half of our life to him: and there is good cause why we should do so: for sleep is the golden chain that ties health and our bodies together.''—Thomas Dekker.

And underneath the beautifully needle-worked quotation, in Judith Niles' clear, bold cursive, was the recent addition:

Nuts. In this Institute, sleep is the enemy.

Charlene Bloom opened her own folder, leaned back, and eased off her black shoes, one foot tugging at the heel of the other. Eleven o'clock, and no Director. Something was wrong.

At four minutes past eleven, the other door of the conference room opened and Judith Niles entered followed by her secretary. Late—and she looked angry. Peering past her into the adjoining office, Charlene Bloom saw a tall man standing by the desk. He was curly-haired and in his early thirties, pleasant-faced but frowning now at something over on one of the walls.

A stranger. But those wide-set grey eyes seemed vaguely familiar; perhaps from an Institute Newsletter picture?

Judith Niles had remained standing for a moment instead of taking her usual place. Her glance went around the table, checking that all the Department Chiefs were already in position, then she nodded her greeting.

"Good morning. I'm sorry to keep you waiting." Her lips pouted on the final word and held that expression. "We have an unexpected visitor, and I have to meet with him again as soon as this meeting is over." She at last sat down. "Let's begin. Dr. de Vries, would you start? I'm sure everyone is as interested as I am in hearing of the results of your trip. When did you get back?"

Jan de Vries, short and placid, shrugged his shoulders and smiled at the Director. Judith Niles and he saw the world from the same place, half a head lower than most of the staff. Perhaps that was what allowed him to relax with her, in a way that Charlene Bloom found totally impossible.

"Late last night." His voice was soothing, slow and easy as warm syrup. "If you will permit me one moment of tangential comment, the treatment for jet-lag that we pioneered here at the Institute is less than a total success."

Judith Niles never took notes. Her secretary would record every word, and she wanted all her own mind concentrated on the pulse of the meeting. She leaned forward and looked closely at de Vries' face. "I assume you speak from experience?"

He nodded. "I used it on the trip to Pakistan. Today I feel lousy, and the blood tests confirm it. My circadian rhythms are still somewhere between here and Rawalpindi."

The Director looked across at Beppo Cameron and raised her dark eyebrows. "We'd better take another look at the treatment, eh? But what about the main business, Jan? Ahmed Ameer—is he fact or fiction?"

"Regrettably, he is fiction." De Vries opened his notebook. "According to the report we received, Ahmed Ameer never slept more than an hour a night. From the time he was sixteen years old— that's nine years, he's twenty-five now—he swore that he hadn't closed his eyes."

"And the truth?"

He grimaced, rubbed at his thin moustache. "I've got our complete notes here, and they'll go in the file. But I can summarize in one word: exaggeration. In the six days and nights that we were with him, he went two nights with no sleep. One night he slept for four and a quarter hours. For the other three nights he averaged a little more than two and a half hours each."

"Normal health?"

"Looks like it. He doesn't sleep much, but we've had other subjects with less right here in the Institute."

Judith Niles was watching him closely. "But you don't look like a man who wasted a week on a wild-goose chase. What's the rest of it?"

"My perceptive superior." De Vries looked angelic. "You are quite right. On the way out I went through Ankara to check out a long shot—another one of the rumors from the Cairo labs, about a monk who keeps a vigil over the sacred relics of Saint Stephen. A vestment was stolen while he was on duty two years ago, and after that he supposedly swore he would never sleep again."

"Well?" Judith Niles tensed as she waited for his answer.

"Not quite—but closer than we've ever come before." De Vries was all sly satisfaction. "Would you believe an average total daily sleep of *twenty-nine minutes*? And he doesn't sit in a chair and nod off for the odd few minutes when nobody's looking. We had him hooked up to a telemetry unit for eleven days. We have the fullest biochemical tests that we could make. You'll see my full report as soon as someone can transcribe it for you."

"I want it today. Tell Joyce Savin that it's top priority." Judith Niles gave de Vries a little nod of approval. "Anything else?"

"Nothing good enough to tell. I'll have my complete report for you tomorrow."

He winked across the table at Charlene. And she'll never read it, said his expression. The Director depended on her staff to keep track of the details. No one ever knew how much time she would spend on any particular staff report. Sometimes the smallest element of data would engage her attention for days, at other times major projects would run unstudied for months.

Judith Niles took a quick look at her watch. "Dr. Bloom, you're next. Keep it as short as possible—I'd like to squeeze our visitor in before lunch if we can."

But at my back I always hear, Time's winged chariot hurrying near. . . . Charlene gritted her teeth. JN was obsessed with sleep and time. And most of what Charlene could offer was bad news. She bent her head over her notebook, reluctant to begin.

"We just lost one of the Kodiaks," she said abruptly. There was a rustle of movement as everyone at the long table sat up straighter. Charlene kept her head bowed. "Gibbs took Dolly down to a few degrees above freezing and tried to maintain a positive level of brain activity."

Now there was a charged silence in the room. Charlene swallowed, felt the lump in her throat, and hurried on. "The procedure is the same as I described in last week's report for the Review Committee. But this time we couldn't stabilize. The brain wave patterns were hunting, seeking new stable levels, and there were spurious alpha thresholds. When we started to bring the temperature back up all the body functions just went to hell. Oscillations everywhere. I brought the output listings with me, and if you want to see them I'll pass them round."

"Later." Judith Niles' expression was a mixture of concentration and anger. Charlene knew the look. The Director expected everyone—everything—to share her drive towards Zero Sleep. Dolly had failed them. JN's face had turned pale, but her voice was calm and factual.

"Gibbs, you said? Wolfgang Gibbs. He's the heavy-set fellow with curly hair? Did he handle the descent and ascent operations himself?"

"Yes. But I have no reason to question his competence—"

"Nor do I, I'm not suggesting that. I've read his reports. He's good." Judith Niles made a gesture to the secretary at her side. "Were there any other anomalies that you consider significant?"

"There was one." Charlene Bloom took a deep breath and turned to a new page of her notebook. "When we were about fifteen degrees above freezing, the brain wave patterns hit a very stable form. And Wolfgang Gibbs noticed one very odd thing about them. They seemed to be the same profile as the brain rhythms at normal temperature, just stretched out in time."

She paused. At the end of the table, Judith Niles had suddenly jerked upright.

"*How similar?*"

"We didn't run it through the computer yet. To the eye they were identical—but fifty times as slow as usual."

For a fraction of a second Charlene thought she saw a look flicker between Judith Niles and Jan de Vries, then the Director was staring at her with full intensity. "That's something I want to see for myself. Later today Dr. de Vries and I will come out to the hangar and take a look at this project. But let's run over it in a little more detail now, when we're all here. How long did you hold the stable phase, and what was the lowest body temperature? And what about tryptophan settings?"

Below table level, Charlene rubbed her hands along the side of her skirt. They were in for a digging session, she just knew it. Her hands were beginning to tremble, and she could feel new sweat on her palms. Was she well-prepared? She'd know in a few minutes. With the Director in the mood for detail, the visitor to the Institute might be in for a long wait.

Chapter 3:

For Hans Gibbs it was turning into a long and confusing day.

When first suggested, a Downside visit to the U.N. Institute for Neurology in Christchurch had sounded like the perfect break from routine. He would have a week in full earth gravity instead of the quarter-gee of PSS-One. He would gain a batch of exercise credits, and he needed all he could scrape together. He'd be able to pick up a few things Downside that were seldom shuttled up as cargo—how long since anyone on PSS-One had tasted an oyster? And even though Christchurch was down in New Zealand, away from the political action centers, he'd be able to form his own impressions on recent world tensions. There were lots of charges and counter-accusations flying about, but chances are it was more of the same old bluster that the Downsiders mislabelled as diplomacy.

Best of all, he could spend a couple of evenings with randy old Wolfgang. The last time they'd been out on the town together, his cousin had still been married. That had put a crimp on things (but less than it should have—one reason maybe why Wolfgang wasn't married now?)

The trip down had been a disaster. Not the Shuttle flight, of course; that had been a couple of hours of relaxation, a smooth re-entry followed by activation of the turbofans and a long powered coast to Aussieport in northern New Guinea. The landing had been precisely on schedule. But that was the last thing that went according to plan.

The Australian spaceport, servicing Australia, New Zealand and Micronesia, normally prided itself on informality and excitement. According to legend, a visitor could find within a few kilometers of the port every one of the world's conventional vices, plus a few of the unconventional ones (cannibalism had been part of native life in New Guinea long after it had disappeared elsewhere).

Today all informality had disappeared. The port had been filled with grim-faced officials, intent on checking every item of his baggage, documents, travel plans, and reason for arrival. He had been subjected to four hours of questioning. Did he have relatives in Japan or the United States? Did he have sympathies with the Food Distribution Movement? What were his views on the Australian Isolationist Party? Tell us, in detail, of any new synthetic food manufacturing processes developed for the outbound arcologies.

Plenty was happening there, as he readily admitted, but he was saved by simple ignorance. Sure, there were new methods for synthetics, good ones, but he didn't know anything about them— wouldn't be *permitted* to know about them; they carried a high level of commercial secrecy.

His first gift for Wolfgang—a pure two-carat gemstone, manufactured in the orbiting autoclave on PSS-One—was retained for examination. It would, he was curtly informed, be sent along to his lodgings at the Institute if it passed inspection. His other gift was confiscated with no promise of return. Seeds developed in space might contaminate some element of Australasian flora.

His patience had run out at that point. The seeds were *sterile*, he pointed out. He had brought them along only as a novelty, for their odd shapes and colors.

"What the hell has happened to you guys?" he complained. "It's not the first time I've been here. I'm a regular—just take a look at those visas. What do you think I'm going to do, break into Cornwall House and have a go at the First Lady?"

They looked back at him stonily, evaluating his remark, then went on with the questioning. He didn't try any more backchat. Two years ago the frantic sex life of the Premier's wife had been everybody's favorite subject. Now it didn't rate a blink. If much of Earth were like this, the climatic changes must be producing worse effects than anyone in the well-to-do nations was willing to admit. The less lucky ones spoke of it willingly enough, pleading for help at endless and unproductive sessions of the United Nations.

When he was finally allowed to close his luggage and go on his way, the fast transport to Christchurch had already left. He was stuck with a Mach-One pond-hopper, turning an hour's flight to a six-hour marathon. At every stop the baggage and document inspection was repeated.

By the time they made the last landing he was angry, hungry, and tired out. The entry formalities at Christchurch seemed to go on forever, but he recognized that they were perfunctory compared with those at Aussieport—it seemed he had already been asked every question in the world, and his answers passed on to the centralized Australasian data banks.

When he finally reached the Institute and was shown to Judith Niles' big office it was one o'clock in the morning according to his internal body clock, though local time was well before noon. He swallowed a stimulant—one originally developed right here in the Institute—and looked around him at the office fittings.

On one wall was a personal sleep chart, of exactly the same type that he used himself. She was averaging a little less than six hours a night, plus a brief lunchtime nap every other day. He moved to the bookcase. The predictable works were there: Dement and Oswald and Colquhoun, on sleep; the Fisher-Koral text on mammalian hibernation; Williams' case histories of healthy insomniacs. The crash course he had received on PSS-One had skimmed through them all, though the library up there was not designed for storage of paper copies like these.

The old monograph by Bremer was new to him. Unpublished work on the brain-stem experiments? That seemed unlikely—Moruzzi had picked the bones clean there, back in the 1940's. But what about that red file next to it, "Revised Analysis"?

He reached out to take it from the case, then hesitated. It wouldn't do to get off on the wrong foot with Judith Niles—this meeting was an important one. Better wait and ask her permission.

He rubbed at his eyes and turned from the bookcase to look at the pictures on the wall opposite the window. He had been well briefed, but the more he could learn by personal observation, the less impossible this job would be.

Plenty of framed photographs there, taken with Presidents and Prime Ministers and businessmen. In pride of place was a picture of a grey-haired man with a big chin and rimless glasses. On its lower border, hand-written, were the words: Roger Morton Niles, 1921-1988. Judith's father? Almost certainly, but there was something curiously impersonal about the addition of *dates* to a father's picture. There was a definite family resemblance, mainly in the steady eyes and high cheekbones. He compared the picture of Roger Morton Niles with a nearby photograph of Judith Niles shaking hands with an aged Indian woman.

Strange. The biographical written descriptions didn't match at all with the person who had swept through the office on her way to her staff meeting and given him the briefest and most abstracted of greetings. Still less did it match the woman pictured here. Based on her position and accomplishments he had expected someone in her forties or fifties, a real Iron Maiden. But Judith Niles couldn't be more than middle thirties. Nice looking, too. She was a fraction too thin in the face, with very serious eyes and forehead; but she made up for that with well-defined, curving cheekbones, a clear complexion, and a beautiful mouth. And there was something in her expression . . . or was it his imagination? Didn't she have that look—

"Mr. Gibbs?" The voice from behind made him grunt and spin around. A secretary had appeared at the open doorway while he was daydreaming his way through the wall photographs.

Thank Heaven that minds were still unreadable. How ludicrous his current train of thought would seem to an observer—here he was, flown in for a confidential and highly crucial meeting with the Director of the Institute, and inside two minutes he was evaluating her as a sex object.

He turned around with a little smile on his face. The secretary was staring at him, her eyebrows raised. "Sorry if I startled you, Mr. Gibbs, but the staff meeting is over and the Director can see you now. She suggests that you might prefer to talk over lunch, rather than meeting here. That way you'll have more time."

He hesitated. "My business with the Director—"

"Is private? Yes, she says that she understands the need for privacy. There is a quiet room off the main dining-room, it will be just you and the Director."

"Fine. Lead the way." He began to rehearse his arguments as she preceded him along a dingy, off-white corridor.

The dining-room was hardly private—he could see a hundred ways it could be bugged. But it did offer at least superficial isolation from other ears. He would have to take the risk. If anyone recorded them, it would almost certainly be for Judith Niles' own benefit, and would go no farther. He blinked his eyes as he entered. The overhead light, like every light he had seen in the Institute, was over-poweringly bright. If darkness were the ally of sleep, Judith Niles apparently would not tolerate its presence.

She was waiting for him at the long table, quietly marking entries on an output listing. As he sat down she at once folded the sheet and spoke without any pause for conventional introduction.

"I took the liberty of ordering for both of us. There is a limited choice, and I thought we could use the time." She leaned back and smiled. "I have my own agenda, but since you came to see us I think you are entitled to the first shot."

"Shot?" He pulled his chair closer to the table. "You're misreading our motives. But I'll be pleased to talk first. And let me get something out of the way that may save us embarrassment later. My cousin, Wolfgang, works for you here at the Institute."

"I wondered at the coincidence of name."

And did you follow up with a check on us? thought Hans Gibbs. He nodded, and went on. "Wolfgang is completely loyal to you, just as I work for and am loyal to Salter Wherry. I gather that you've never met him?"

Judith Niles looked up at him from under lowered brows. "I don't know anyone who has—but everybody has heard of him, and of Salter Station."

"Then you know he has substantial resources. Through them we can find out rather a lot about the Institute, and the work that goes on here. I want you to know that although Wolfgang and I have talked generalities from time to time about the work here, none of my specific information, or that of anyone else in our organization, came from him."

She shrugged in a noncommittal way. "All right. But now you have me intrigued. What do you think you know about us that's so surprising? We're a publicly funded agency. Our records are open information."

"True. But that means you are restricted in the budget available to you. Just today, for example, you have learned of additional budget cuts because of the crisis in U.N. finances."

Her expression showed her astonishment. "How

in the name of Morpheus can you possibly know that? I only found out a couple of hours ago, and I was told the decision had just been made."

"Let me postpone answering that, if you don't mind, until we've covered a couple of other things. I know you've had money problems. Worse still, there are restrictions—ones you find hard to accept—on the experiments that you are permitted to perform."

The lower lip pushed forward a little, and her expression became guarded. "Now I don't think I follow you. Care to be more specific?"

"With your permission I'll defer discussing that too, for the moment. I hope you'll first permit me a few minutes on another subject. It may seem unrelated to budgets and experimental freedom, but I promise you it is relevant. Take a quick look at this, then I'll explain exactly why I'm here."

He passed a flat black cylinder across to her. "Look into the end of it. It's a video recorder— don't worry about focus, the hologram phases are adjusted for a perceived focal plane six feet from the eye. Just let your eyes relax."

She wrinkled her brow questioningly, put her unbroken bread roll back on her plate, and lifted the cylinder to her right eye. "How do I work it?"

"Press the button on the left side. It takes a couple of seconds before the picture comes."

He sat silent, waiting as a waitress in a green uniform placed bowls of murky brown soup in front of each of them.

"I don't see anything at all," Judith Niles said after a few seconds. "There's nothing I can focus on—oh, wait a minute. . . ."

The jet-black curtain before her took on faint detail as her eyes adjusted to the low light level.

There was a backdrop of stars, with a long, spindly structure in the foreground lit by reflected sunlight. At first she had no sense of scale, but as the field of view slowly shifted out along the spidernet of girders other scene elements began to provide clues. A space tug lay along one of the long beams, its stubby body half-hidden by the metal. Farther down, she could see a life-capsule, clamped like a tiny mushroom button in the corner of a massive cross-tie. The construction was big, stretching hundreds of kilometers away to a distant end-boom.

The camera swung on down, until the limb of the sunlit Earth appeared in the field of view.

"You're seeing the view from one of the standard monitors," said Hans Gibbs. "There are twenty of them on the Station. They operate twenty-four hours a day, with routine surveys of everything that goes on. That camera concentrates mostly on the new construction on the lower boom. You know that we're making a seven-hundred kilometer experimental cantilever on PSS-One? —Salter Station, most people down here apparently call it, though Salter Wherry likes to point out that it was the first of many, so PSS-One is a better name. Anyway, we don't need that extension cantilever for the present arcologies, but we're sure we'll use it someday soon."

"Uh-uh." Judith did not move her eyes from the viewing socket. The camera was zooming in, closing steadily on an area at the very end of the boom where two small dots had become visible. She realized that she was seeing a high-magnification close-up from a small part of the camera field. As the dots grew in size, the image had begun to develop a slight graininess as the limit of useful resolution was reached. She could make out the limbs on each of the space suits, and the lines that secured the suits to the thin girders.

"Installing one of the experimental antennas," said Hans Gibbs' voice. He obviously knew exactly what point the display in front of her had reached. "Those two are a long way from the center of mass of the Station—four hundred kilometers below it. Salter Station is in six hour orbit, ten thousand kilometers up. Orbital velocity at that altitude is forty-eight eighty meters a second, but the end of the boom is travelling at only forty-seven sixty meters a second. See the slight tension in those lines? Those two aren't quite in freefall. They feel about a hundredth of a gee. Not much, but enough to make a difference."

Judith Niles drew in a deep breath but did not speak.

"Watch the one on the left," said Hans Gibbs quietly.

There was enough detail in the image to see exactly what was happening. The lines that secured one of the two suited figures had been released, so that a new position on the girder could be achieved. A thin aerial had opened up, stretching far out past the end of the boom. The left-most figure began to drift slowly along the length of the aerial, a securing bracket held in its right glove. It was obvious that there would be another tether point within reach along the girder, where the securing line could be attached. The suit moved very slowly, rotating a little as it went. The second figure was crouched over another part of the metal network, attaching a second brace for the aerial.

"In thirty seconds, you drift away by nearly fifty

meters," said Hans Gibbs quietly. His companion sat as still as a statue.

The realization grew by tiny fractions, so that there was never one moment where the senses could suddenly say, "Trouble." The figure was within reach of the tether point. It was still moving, inching along, certainly close enough for an outstretched arm to make the connection. Five seconds more, and that contact had been missed. Now it would be necessary to use the suit controls, to apply the small thrust needed to move back to contact range. Judith Niles suddenly found herself willing the suit thrustors to come on, willing the second figure to look up, to see what she was seeing. The gap grew. A few feet, thirty meters, the length of the thin aerial. The suit had begun to turn around more rapidly on its axis. It was passing the last point of contact with the structure.

"Oh, no." The words were a murmur of complaint. Judith Niles was breathing heavily. After a few more seconds of silence she gave another little murmur and jerked her body rigidly upright. "Oh, no. Why doesn't he do something? *Why doesn't he grab the aerial!*"

Hans Gibbs reached forward and gently took the cylinder away from her eye. "I think you've seen enough. You saw the beginning of the fall?"

"Yes. Was it a simulation?"

"I'm afraid not. It was real. What do you think that you saw?"

"Construction for the boom on Salter Station—on PSS-One. And they were two of the workers, rigging an antenna section."

"Right. What else?"

"The one farther out on the boom just let go his hold, without waiting to see that he had a line secured. He didn't even look. He drifted away. By the time the other one saw, he was too far away to reach."

"Too far away for anything to reach. Do you realize what would happen next?"

Neither of them took any interest in the food before them. Judith Niles nodded slowly. "Re-entry? If you couldn't reach him he'd start re-entry?"

Hans Gibbs looked at her in surprise, then laughed. "Well, that might happen—if we waited for a few million years. But Salter Station is in a pretty high orbit, re-entry's not what we worry about. Those suits have only enough air for six hours. If we have no ship ready, anybody who loses contact with the station and can't get back with the limited reaction mass in the suit thrustors dies—asphyxiates. It was a woman in that suit, by the way, not a man. She was lucky. The camera was on her, so we could compute an exact trajectory and pick her up with an hour to spare. But she'll probably never be psychologically ready to work outside again. And others haven't been so lucky. We've lost thirty people in three months."

"But *why*? Why did she let go? Why didn't the other worker warn her?"

"He tried—we all tried." Hans Gibbs tucked the little recorder back into its plastic case. "She didn't hear us for the same reason that she released her hold. It's a reason that should really interest you, and the reason why I'm here at your Institute. In one word: narcolepsy. *She fell asleep.* She didn't wake up until after we caught her, fifty kilometers away from the boom. The other worker saw what had happened long before that, but he didn't have the reaction mass to go out and back. All he could do was watch and yell at her through the suit radio. He couldn't wake her."

Hans Gibbs pushed his half-full plate away from him.

"I know there's a desperate food shortage around most of the world, and it's a sin not to clear your dish. But neither one of us seems to be eating much. Can we continue this conversation back in your office?"

Chapter 4:

It was early evening before Judith Niles picked up the phone and asked Jan de Vries to join her in her office. While she waited for him she stood by the window, staring out across the garden that flanked the south side of the Institute. The lawns were increasingly unkempt, with the flower beds near the old brick wall showing patches of weeds.

"Midnight oil again? Where's your dinner date, Judith?" said a voice behind her.

She started. De Vries had entered the open office door without knocking, quiet as a cat.

She turned. "Close the door, Jan. You won't believe this, but I did have an offer of dinner. A wild offer, with all the old-fashioned trimmings—he suggested Oysters Rockefeller, veal *cordon bleu*, wine, and the moonlit Avon River. Oysters and wine! My God, you can tell that he's from way out in space. He honestly believed we'd be able to *buy* that sort of food, without a contract or a special dispensation. He doesn't know much about the real situation. One of the scary things about all the government propaganda is that it works so well. He had no idea how bad things are, even here in New Zealand—and we're the lucky ones. Oysters! Damn it, I'd give my virginity for a dozen oysters. Might as well hope to be served roast beef."

Her voice was longing, and it carried no trace of the usual authority. She sat down at her desk, eased off her shoes, and lolled back in her chair, lifting her bare feet to rest them on an open desk drawer.

"Far too late for any of that, my dear," said Jan de Vries. "Roast beef, good wine, oysters—or virginity, for that matter. For most of us they've fled with the snows of yesteryear. But I'm just as impressed by the other implications of his offer. Only somebody out of touch with the climate changes and literally out of this world would want to look at that ghastly river—not when it's eighty-seven degrees and ninety percent humidity."

He sat down gracefully, reclining on a big armchair. "But you turned down the invitation? Judith, you disappoint me. It sounds like an offer you couldn't refuse—just to see his expression when he could compare reality with his illusions."

"I might have taken it if Hans Gibbs hadn't made me the *other* offer."

"Indeed?" Jan de Vries touched his lips with a carefully manicured forefinger. "Judith, from one of your strongly heterosexual tastes, those words ring false. I thought you longed for offers like that, attractive beyond all other lures—"

"Stow it, Jan. I've no time for games just now. I want the benefit of your brain. You've met Salter Wherry, right? How much do you know about him?"

"Well, as it happens I know a fair amount. I almost went to work on Salter Station, if you hadn't lured me here I'd probably be there now. There's a certain *je ne sais quoi* to the notion of working for an aged multi-billionaire, especially one whose romantic tastes before he went into seclusion were said to coincide with mine."

"Does he really own Salter Station? Completely?"

"So it is rumored, my dear. That, and half of everything else you care to mention. I could never discover any evidence to the contrary. Since the charming Mr. Gibbs works for Wherry, and you met with him for many hours this afternoon—don't think your long cloistering passed unnoticed, Judith—I wonder why you ask me these things. Why didn't you ask Hans Gibbs your questions about Salter Wherry directly?"

Judith Niles padded back to the window, and stared moodily out at the twilight. "I need to do an independent check. It's important, Jan. I need to know how rich Salter Wherry *really* is. Is he rich enough to let us do what we need to do?"

"According to my own investigations and impressions, he is so rich that the word lacks real meaning. Our budget for next year is a little over eight million, correct? I will check the latest data on him, but even if Salter Wherry is no richer now than he was twenty years ago, this whole Institute could be comfortably supported on the *interest* on Wherry's petty cash account."

"Maybe that's his plan." Judith swung back to face into the room. "Damn it, he certainly timed it well."

"Money troubles again? Remember, I've been away."

"Bad ones. I've had it with our brainless Budget Committee. They want to squeeze us another five percent, and already the place is falling apart around our ears. And we can't keep some of our experiments and results secret indefinitely, much as I'd like to. Charlene and Wolfgang Gibbs are stumbling over the same lead that we found. Wherry couldn't be approaching us at a better time. It could work out perfectly."

"As I have told you many times, Judith, you are a genius. You can maneuver simple innocents like me around like puppets. But you are not—yet—a manipulator to match Salter Wherry. He is the best in the System, and he can call on seventy years of experience. When you think of your own objectives, and your hidden agenda—which I do not even pretend to be privy to—remember that he undoubtedly has a hidden agenda also, with quite different goals. And if you are a genius, he is an undoubted genius also in finance and organization. And he has a reputation of getting his way."

De Vries crossed his legs carefully and adjusted the sharp crease on his trousers. "But from the look on your face I suspect I'm digressing. What's this great offer you want to discuss? Why aren't you off by the great grey-green greasy Avon River, dining on strawberries and cream to the sound of trumpets—or whatever other delights of dalliance the sadly out-of-touch Mr. Gibbs had in mind?"

Judith Niles rubbed delicately at her left eye, as though it was troubling her. "Hans Gibbs brought me an offer. They're having problems on Salter Station. Did you know that?"

"I have heard rumors. The insurance rates for Station personnel have been raised an order of magnitude above those for conventional space operations. But I fail to see any connection with the Institute."

"That's because you don't know what the problems are. Jan, the offer I had today was a simple one. Hans Gibbs came here with authority from Salter Wherry. The budget of the Institute will be quadrupled, with guaranteed funding levels for eight years. In addition, the schedule of experiments that we conduct here will be free from all outside control or interference. So will our hardware and software procurement."

"It sounds like paradise." De Vries stood up and went to stand next to Judith. "Where's the worm in the apple? There must be one."

She smiled at him, and patted his shoulder. "Jan, how did I get along before you joined the Institute? Here's your worm: to get all the good things that Salter Wherry promises, we must satisfy one condition. The key staff of the Institute must relocate—to Salter Station. And we must do our best to crack a problem that has been ruining the arcology construction projects there."

"What! Up into orbit? I hope you didn't agree to it."

"No, not yet. But I might. I have to go up there and see for myself—Hans Gibbs will make the arrangements this weekend." As Jan de Vries became more and more doubtful, Judith looked more relaxed.

"And since I'll be gone, Jan," she went on. "Somebody else has to look at the initial list of key staff members, just in case we decide to do it. I know my own choices for the top people, but I'm not close enough to all the support staff—and we'd need some of them, too. Who are the best ones, and who is willing to go to Salter Station?"

"You sound as though you have made up your mind already."

"No. I just want to think ahead in case it does

happen." She went across to her desk and picked up a handwritten page. "Here's my first selection. Sit down again, and we'll go over it together."

"But—"

"Get Charlene Bloom to help you on this while I'm away."

"Charlene? Look, I know she's good, but can she be objective? She's a mass of insecurity."

"I know. She's too modest. That's why I want her to know she was on my preferred list from the start. While you're at it, take a look at this." She handed him a couple of pages of print-out. "I just ran it out of the historical data banks. It's the statement that Salter Wherry made to the United Nations when he started his industrial space activity, thirty years ago. We need to understand the psychological make-up of the man, and this is a good clue to it."

"Judith, slow down. You're pushing me. I'm not at all sure that I want to—"

"Nor am I. Jan, we may be forced to do this, even if some of us don't like the decision. Things have been absolutely falling apart around here in the past few months, bit by bit."

"I know times are hard—"

"They'll get worse. The way the Institute is getting screwed around, we can't afford to do nothing. If we're being raped we have to fight any way we can; even if it means risking Salter Wherry trying to screw us too."

He took the sheets from her hand, sighing. "All right, all right. If you insist, I'll blunder ahead. Let's all become experts on Salter Wherry and his enterprises. But Judith, must you be so crude? I prefer to avoid these unpleasant suggestions of rape. Why can't we regard this overture as the first touch of Salter Wherry's perfumed hand in our genteel seduction?" He smirked happily. "That makes it all positively appealing; in seduction, my dear, there's so much more scope for *negotiation*."

From the invited address of Salter Wherry to the United Nations General Assembly, following establishment of Salter Station in a stable six-hour orbit around the Earth, and shortly before Wherry withdrew from contact with the general public:

'Nature abhors a vacuum. If there is an open ecological niche, some organism will move to fill it. That's what evolution is all about. Twenty years ago there was a clear emerging crisis in mineral resource supply. Everybody knew that we were heading for shortages of at least twelve key metals. And almost everybody knew that we wouldn't find them in any easily accessible place on Earth. We would be mining fifteen miles down, or at the ocean bottom. I decided it was more logical to mine five thousand miles up. Some of the asteroids are ninety percent metals; what we needed to do was bring them into Earth orbit.

'I approached the U.S. Government first with my proposal for asteroid capture and mining. I had full estimates of costs and probable return on investment, and I would have settled for a five percent contract fee.

'I was told that it was too controversial, that I would run into questions of international ownership of mineral rights. Other countries would want to be included in the project.

'Very well. I came here to the United Nations, and made full disclosure of all my ideas to this group. But after four years of constant debate, and many thousands of hours of my time preparing and presenting additional data, not one line of useful response had been drafted to my proposal. You formed study committees, and committees to study those committees, and that was all you did. You talked.

'Life is short. I happened to have one advantage denied to most people. Back in the 1950's my father had invested his money in computer stocks. I was already very wealthy, and I was frustrated enough to risk it all. You are beginning to see some of the results, in the shape of PSS-One—what the Press seems to prefer to call Salter Station. It will serve as the home for two hundred people, with ease.

'But this is no more than a beginning. Although Nature may abhor a vacuum, modern technology loves one. That, and the microgravity environment. I intend to use them to the full. I will construct a succession of large, permanently-occupied space stations using asteroidal materials. If any nation here today desires to rent space or facilities from me, or buy my products manufactured in space, I will be happy to consider this—at commercial rates. I also invite people from all nations on Earth to join me in those facilities. We are ready to take all the steps necessary for the human race to begin its exploration of our Universe.'

It was past midnight when Jan de Vries had read the full statement twice, then skipped again to the comment with which Salter Wherry had concluded his address. They were words that had become permanently linked to his name, and they had earned him the impotent enmity of every nation on earth:

'The conquest of space is too important an enterprise to be entrusted to governments.'

De Vries shook his head. Salter Wherry was a formidable man, ready to take on world governments—and win. Did Judith have the equipment to play in Wherry's league?

He closed the folder, his chubby face completely serious. A move to Salter Station. It would be fascinating. But the government outrage and hypocrisy over Wherry's actions still continued, undiminished (perhaps increased) by success. The popularity of the arcologies, and the flood of applicants to embark on them, only added fuel to the official anger. If the Institute moved, everyone there would have to understand that the decision to join the Wherry empire would add to the outcry. They would all be branded as 'traitors' by the U.N. official press.

And once they went out, what then? For many of them there would never be a return home. Earth would be lost to them forever.

The building hummed quietly with the subdued murmur of a thousand experiments, going on through the night. Jan de Vries sat in his easy chair for a long time, musing, peering out of the window into the humid night but seeing only the cloudy vision of his own future. Where was it likely to lead? Would he be in space himself, ten years from now? What would it be like out there?

The ideas were difficult to grasp, drifting away from the periphery of his tired brain. He yawned, and rose slowly to his feet. Ten years—it was too far to see. Better think of near-term things: Judith Niles' list, the budget, the still-unfinished trip report. Ten years was infinity, something beyond his span.

Jan de Vries could not possibly have known it, but he had his crystal ball wrongly focused. He should have been looking much farther ahead.

Chapter 5:

"Either I meet with him personally, or there will be no agreement. It's as simple as that, Hans."

"I'm telling you, that's not possible. He doesn't hold face-to-face conferences any more; not here, or down on Earth."

"*You* see him often enough."

"Well, damn it, Judith, I *am* his assistant. Even he has to see a few people. But I have full legal authority to sign for him, if that's a worry. Check with Zurich for any questions on financing. And if you want to look at anything else on the Station, tell me and I'll arrange it."

Hans Gibbs sounded almost pleading. They were sitting in an eighth-gee chamber halfway out from the hub of Salter Station, watching the mining operations on Elmo, a hundred kilometers above them. Electric arcs sparkled and sputtered in random sequence on the surface of the Earth-orbiting asteroid, and loaded cargo buckets were drifting lazily down along the umbilical. From this distance it was a glittering filament of silver, coiling its length down to the station refining center.

Judith Niles pulled her gaze back from the hypnotic sight of the endless bucket chain. She shook her head, and smiled at the man seated across from her.

"Hans, this isn't just me being awkward. And I'm sure that you and I could conclude the deal. It's not something I want for myself, it's for my team down at the Institute. I'm asking them to give up the security of Government jobs and take a flier to a private industry group in an orbital facility."

"Security?" Hans Gibbs glared at her. "Judith, that's pure crap. You *know* it's crap. A job with Salter Wherry is safer than any government position. Your whole group could be wiped out tomorrow if some jackass in the U.N. decided to throw his weight around. And they have plenty of jackasses. And don't give me any nonsense about your budget—Salter Wherry has better and earlier information about that than you do."

"I believe it." She sighed. "I told you, you don't have to convince me, you're preaching to the choir. I've seen our programs twisted and cut and maimed, year after year. But I need to bring twenty key scientists up here with me and I'm telling you how some of them feel. I go back to the Institute and they say to me, 'Did Salter Wherry agree to this?' And I say, 'Well, no. I signed a long-term contract— but I didn't actually *see* him.' Know what they'll say? They'll say that this project is pretty low on Salter Wherry's list of priorities, and maybe we should think again."

"It's *top* priority. Even down on Earth, most people know that he doesn't hold face-to-face meetings."

"I know." She smiled sweetly. "That's why it

will be so impressive to my staff when they hear that I did meet with him. Think about it for a minute."

Judith Niles leaned back and recalled the last conversation with Jan de Vries and Charlene Bloom before she left. *Negotiate hard.* It had been the point they all agreed on. And if it didn't work out? Well, they would live through it. The Institute would continue somehow, even with Government cuts in funding.

Across from her, Hans Gibbs groaned and eased to his feet. In the two days that they had spent together he had been forming his own impressions of the Institute Director, adding to the odd perspective that had come from his cousin at the Institute.

"She's weird, I mean, like she's not shaped yet," Wolfgang had said. "She's pretty old, right?"

Hans glared at him. "Watch it, sonny. She's thirty-seven. Guess that's old if you're still wet behind the ears."

"Right. So she's thirty-seven, and she has a worldwide reputation. But she's like a little kid in some ways." Wolfgang waved his beer glass in a circle in the air. "I mean, you tell me I act like a retard, but she's the one you should talk to. I can't figure her at all. I think maybe when she was younger all her energy went into science and sex. She's just getting around to *learning* the rest of the world."

"Sex?" Hans raised his eyebrows. "I was right, then. Wolf, if *you* say she's sex-mad, she must be something. Been trying to sleep your way to the top, eh? And I thought she was all fixed up with that little man I met yesterday."

"You mean Jan de Vries?" Wolfgang spluttered his laughter through a mouthful of beer. "Cousin

boy, you are all screwed up on *that* one. No chance
of an affair between him and JN, not if you locked
'em up together and fed 'em Spanish Fly for a
year. I like Jan, he's a great guy, but he's got his
own ideas on sex. He makes friends easily with
women, but for his love life he only looks at men."

"But you're sure about her?"

"I'm sure. Not from personal experience, though.
She's not like me. JN's discreet, she *never* plays
bedroom games around the Institute. But she dis-
appears for nights and weekends."

"She could be working."

"Bullshit. It takes one to know one. She's horny
as I am."

Hans shrugged. His own impressions had been
formed back when he first saw her photograph.
"All right, so she's horny as you are. God help her.
But if she's not shaped and still changing, what
will she be like when she *is* shaped?"

Wolfgang Gibbs' face took on a different expression. He was silent for a moment.

"She could be anything," he said at last. "Absolutely anything. Even the cocky ones at the Institute admit it, she's way above them on technical
matters."

"Even you, cousin? Since when? I thought the
mirror on the wall said *you* were smartest of them
all."

Wolfgang had placed his beer glass down on the
window sill. He looked very serious. "Even me,
cousin. Remember what one of France's old gener-
als said when he came out of his first meeting with
Napoleon? 'I knew at once that I had met my
master.' That's how I felt after my first one-on-one
with JN She's a powerhouse. And when she wants
something, she's hard to stop."

"I've met more than one like that. But where does she get her kicks? If we're going to have a deal, I need to understand her motives."

But at that point Wolfgang Gibbs had only shaken his head and picked up his beer again. And now, thought Hans, looking at Judith's unreadable face, we're one-on-one and I'm experiencing the push for myself. An audience with Salter, she says, or no deal. He began to move slowly towards the exit.

"O.K., Judith. I'll try. Salter Wherry is here on the Station, and I have to see him anyway about some other stuff. Give me half an hour—if I can't do anything in that time, I can't do it at all. Wait here, and dial Central Services if you need anything while I'm gone. But don't get your hopes up. The only thing I can tell you is that he wants the Institute up here so bad he can taste it—he says the narcolepsy problem is top priority. Maybe it will make him break his own rule."

Judith Niles was left with her own thoughts. The words of Jan de Vries kept drifting back to her. "Salter Wherry is a manipulator, the best in the System." And now she was hoping to manipulate the system he had created. Wherry didn't know it, but she had little choice. She had her own urgencies. The experiments she wanted to do *couldn't* be conducted down on Earth. If he were to suspect that. . . .

She looked again out of the concave viewing port. Salter Station was powerful evidence of the effectiveness of that manipulative force. From where she was sitting, Elmo was continually visible. It was the first of the Earth-orbit-crossing asteroids to be steered into stable six-hour orbit

around the Earth: but as Salter Wherry had promised the United Nations, the story had not ended
there.

Looking at the panorama of development above
her, Judith Niles was forced to marvel. Wherry's
asteroid mining operations had provided the base
metals to create and then expand Salter Station.
But at the same time, as no more than a by-product,
they also extracted enough platinum, gold, irid-
ium, chromium, and nickel to make up almost half
of the world's supply. Bans against import of products from Salter Station into most countries had
been totally useless. The shipments of metal were
'laundered' through neutral spaceports in the Free
Trade Zones, and at last arrived where they were
needed—fifty percent more expensive than they
would have been on direct purchase.

Wherry's operations were strong enough to with-
stand a challenge from any government, his defense systems rumored to be capable of meeting a
combined Earth attack. The Institute could be
moved here, safe from withering cuts and changes
of direction. But would it be worth it? Only if she
and the rest of the staff had real freedom to pursue
their work. That was the promise that she must
extract from Salter Wherry. And an ironbound legal contract had to go with it. When you dealt
with a master manipulator, you couldn't afford to
leave loopholes.

She lay back in her seat, staring upwards. A
faint glimmer of light caught her eye, drifting past
her field of view. She realized that she was witnessing one of the infrequent transits of *Eleanora*,
the sixth and most ambitious of the giant arcologies.
It was in an orbit nearly a thousand kilometers
higher, and it passed the station only once every

three days. Initially dubbed as "Salter's Folly" by the sceptical media, the *first* arcology had been started fourteen years ago and had grown steadily. Until the great space station was completed, Salter Wherry seemed content to let the original jeering name serve as the official one. Then he had finally renamed it *Amanda*, assisted its population of four thousand to establish themselves there, and apparently lost all interest. His mind was focused on construction of the second arcology, then the third. . . .

Curious, Judith dialled into the Station's central computer and requested a high-resolution image of *Eleanora*. The half-built arcology blinked into full-color display on the screen. The skeleton was finished now, a seven-hundred-meter spherical framework of metal girders. Wall panels were going in over half the structure, so that she could estimate the size of the rooms and the internal corridors that would exist in the final ship. Allowing for power, food, maintenance and recreational areas, the final Ark would comfortably house twelve thousand people—the biggest one yet. And it had more facilities and living-space per person than the average family enjoyed on Earth. Two more arcologies were starting construction in higher orbits, each supposedly even bigger than this one.

Judith stared out of the port, seeing again her own office back at the Institute. The group's move up here (if it happened; Hans Gibbs had been gone a long time) had seemed such a big thing when it was first proposed. Compared with what Salter Wherry was planning for the arcologies, it was nothing. They were designed to be self-sustaining over a period of centuries and more, free-ranging through the Solar System and beyond if they chose to do so, independent even of sunlight. From a kilo or two of water, self-contained fusion plants would provide enough power for years. As a back-up to the recycling systems, each arcology would tow along an asteroid several hundred meters across, to be mined as needed.

Judith shook her head thoughtfully. She swung her chair to look out of the Earthside ports. It was daylight below, and she could see the great smudge that shrouded most of Zaire and central Africa. Parts of the desiccated equatorial rain forest were still ablaze, casting a dark shadow across a third of the continent. The drought-ridden area stretched from the Mediterranean past the Equator, and no one could predict when it would end. It was hard to imagine what life must be like down there, as the climate changes made the old African life styles impossible. And across the Atlantic, the vast Amazon basin was steadily drying, too, becoming the tinder that would flame in just a few more months unless weather patterns changed.

A turn of the head brought *Eleanora* back into view, far above. Down on Earth the arcologies seemed remote, the daydream of one man. But once you were up here, watching the ferry ships swarming between the Station and the distant, twinkling sphere of *Eleanora*. . . .

"Interested in taking that trip?" said Hans Gibbs' voice from behind her. "There's plenty of space available for qualified people, and you'd be a prime candidate for a colonist."

The spell was broken. Judith realized that she had been staring out mindlessly, more fascinated than she had ever expected. She looked around at him questioningly.

"It's yes," he said at once. He shook his head in

a puzzled way. "I'd have bet my liver that he wouldn't even consider seeing you—I told you, Salter Wherry *never* meets with anybody except a few aides these days. So what does he do? He agrees to see you."

"Thank you."

Hans Gibbs laughed. "For Christ's sake, don't thank me. All I did was ask—and I didn't expect anything except a quick refusal. He agreed so quickly, I wasn't ready for it. I started to give him arguments why he should make an exception in this case, then my brain caught up with my mouth. I suppose that proves how little I know him, even after all these years. If you're ready, we can go over right now. His suite is on the other side of Spindletop, directly across from here. Come on, before he changes his mind."

Chapter 6:

Salter Station was built on the general double-wheel plan defined thirty years earlier for a permanent space station.

The upper wheel, Spindletop, was reserved for communications, living, and recreational quarters. It rotated about the fixed spindle that jutted up to it from the lower wheel. With a diameter of four hundred meters, Spindletop had an effective gravity that ran from near-zero at the hub to almost a quarter-gee at the outer circumference. The thicker under-section turned much more slowly, needing close to two hours for a full revolution compared with Spindletop's one-minute rotation period. All the maintenance, construction, power, and agriculture systems resided on the lower wheel.

"And some of the people, too," said Hans Gibbs as they rode the moving cable in towards the hub of Spindletop. "Once they become used to zero-gee, it's a devil of a job to get them up here again. There's a compulsory exercise program, but you wouldn't believe the ways they find to get around it. We have engineers here who couldn't go back down to Earth without a year's conditioning—they spend all their time loafing around Workwheel. They even take their meals down there." He pointed along a metal corridor, twenty meters across, that went away at right angles from their inward passage. "That's the main route between Workwheel and Spindletop. See, we're at the hub now. If we wanted to we could just hang here and drift."

They paused for a few seconds so that Judith could take a good look around her. The central section was a labyrinth of cables, passages, and airlocks.

"It's all pressurized," said Hans Gibbs in answer to Judith's question about the need for interior airlocks. "But different sections have different pressure levels. And of course the locks are there for safety, too. We've never had a blow-out or a bad air loss but it could happen anytime—we can't track all the meteors."

He took her arm as they caught the cable out along another radial passageway of Spindletop. Her muscles tensed slightly beneath his fingers, but she made no comment.

"Have you spent much time in freefall?" he said after a few moments. He turned so that they were facing each other, dropping outwards steadily down the spiralling circular tunnel that led to the edge of Spindletop.

She shook her head. "Enough so that it doesn't trouble me in the stomach any more, but that's about all. I've sometimes thought it might be nice to take a vacation up on Waterway and see how freefall swimming is done; but I'm told it's expensive and I've always been too busy."

"If you come up here to work, you can do it free.

The big fishtanks down on Workwheel are open to swimmers all the time."

He turned his face so that he was no longer looking directly at her before he spoke again. His voice was completely neutral. "There are some other experiences in freefall that you ought to try—really interesting ones. Maybe you can sample them before you go back down to the Institute and tell the others what it's like here."

He felt her arm muscles tighten again in his grasp. "Let's see what happens first with Salter Wherry, shall we?" she said. Her voice was noncommittal, but she sounded slightly amused. "Maybe I'll have to tell them it didn't work out. Or maybe we'll have something to celebrate."

The area they were entering looked substantially different from the parts of Salter Station that Judith had already seen. Instead of metal walls and bulkheads they now passed over soft carpeted floors flanked by elaborate murals. At the door of an antechamber they were met by a young man dressed in a skintight electric-blue uniform. To Judith he looked like a pretty child, no more than thirteen years old. His complexion was soft, without a sign of facial hair.

"He has decided that he will see her alone," he said, in a voice that was not yet fully broken.

Hans Gibbs shrugged, looked at the youth, then at Judith. "I'll wait for you right here. Good luck—and remember, you're holding a card that he wants very badly."

Judith managed a wry smile. "And what he wants, he gets, right? Thanks anyway, I'll see you later."

She followed the young boy in through the curtained entrance. In the reduced gravity his walk lent an elegant, undulating sway to his hips.

Was he accentuating it intentionally? Jan de Vries was probably right about Salter Wherry's personal tastes—it was the sort of detail that he would know. Judith tried to make her own movements as economical and functional as possible as she followed around the curved floor of the chamber and on to another large room, this one with no viewports. The boy in front of her halted. Apparently they had arrived. Judith looked around her in surprise.

Opulence would have been understandable. These were the private living-quarters of a man whose fortune exceeded that of most Earth nations—perhaps all. But *this*?

The room they had entered was bare and ugly. Instead of the drapes and murals of the outer chamber, she was looking at dark walls and simple, plastic-coated floor and ceiling. The furniture was hard upright chairs, a single narrow couch, and an old wooden desk. And there was something else, stranger yet. . . .

Judith had to think for a few seconds before she could pin it down. Something was missing. The room lacked any signs of data terminals or display screens; she could not even see a telephone or television outlet.

But Salter Wherry had System-wide influence and interests. One word from him could bankrupt whole States. He must find the most modern and elaborate communications equipment absolutely essential. . . .

Judith walked over to the desk, ignoring the youth who had brought her in. There was nothing. No terminal, no data links, no modems; not even data cube holders. She was looking at a flat desk top with two buff file folders upon it, and a black book set neatly between them. A Bible.

"Where does he keep all—" she began.

"Videos? Books? Electronic equipment?" It was a different voice behind her. "I have everything that I find necessary."

Salter Wherry had quietly entered through a sliding door to her left. The pictures that she had seen of him showed a man in vigorous middle age, substantial and strongly-built, with a sensuous, fleshy face and prominent nose. But they had been taken thirty years ago, before Salter Wherry became reclusive. Now the man standing in front of Judith Niles was frighteningly frail, with a thin, lined face. Judith looked at him closely as he held out his hands to take both of hers. The aquiline nose was all that had survived of the younger Salter Wherry. Judith found the new version much more impressive. All the softness had been burned away from the man standing in front of her, and what remained had been tempered in the same inner furnace. The eyes dominated the countenance, glowing bright blue in deep sockets.

"All right, Edouard. You will leave us now," said Wherry after a few moments. His voice was gruff and surprisingly deep, not at all an old man's thin tones.

The boy nodded deferentially, but as he turned to leave there was a pout, a condescending look at Judith, and an arrogant sway of his shoulders. Salter Wherry gestured to the narrow couch.

"If it will not make you uncomfortable, I will stand. Long ago I learned that I think better this way."

Judith felt her stomach muscles tighten involuntarily as she sat on the couch. Wherry's intuitive perception of motives was legendary. It might be hard to hide any secret from the probing intellect behind those steady eyes.

She cleared her throat. "I appreciate your willingness to see me."

Salter Wherry nodded slowly. "I assume that your desire was not merely social. And I want you to be assured that the problem your Institute will be addressing is of prime importance to me. We have been obliged to introduce so many new precautions in space construction work that our rate of progress on the new arcologies has become pathetic."

He stood motionless in front of her, quietly waiting.

"It's certainly not social." Judith cleared her throat again. "My staff are asking certain questions. I want to know the answers as much as they do. For example, you have a problem with narcolepsy. We are well qualified to tackle it."

And if I'm right, she thought, *I may have already solved it. Go carefully now, that's not the main point at issue.*

"But why not employ us simply as your consultants?" she said. "Why go to the trouble and expense of hiring an entire Institute, at great cost—"

"At negligible cost, compared with a hundred other enterprises I have up here. You will find me generous with money and other resources. 'Thou shalt not muzzle the ox when he treadeth out the corn.'"

"All right, even without considering the cost. Why create an Institute, when you want to solve a single problem?"

He was gently nodding. "Dr. Niles, you are logical. But permit me to suggest that you see this with the wrong perspective. The problem is too important to me to use you as consultants. I need a *dedicated* attention. If you were to remain on Earth, with your present responsibilities to the United Nations, how much of your time would be devoted to my problem? How much of Dr. Bloom's time, or Dr. Cameron's time, or Dr. de Vries' time? Ten percent? Or twenty percent? But not one hundred and twenty."

"So why not hire a team for the specific problem? The salaries that you offer would attract many of my staff."

"And you yourself?" He gave a curious little smile as she looked pensive. "I thought not. Yet I am told that if anyone will solve it, it will be Judith Niles."

Judith felt the hair on her arms and shoulders tingle into gooseflesh. Salter Wherry was willing to move a multi-million dollar operation into space and make a long-term commitment, merely to ensure her own availability. *Careful!* said the inner voice. *Remember, flattery is a tool that never fails.*

Did he suspect that she would be *obliged* to move some of the experiments into space, if her ideas on the processes of consciousness were correct? And if she knew already what was causing the narcolepsy problem in Salter Wherry's space construction crews, then from his point of view the move of the Institute would be unnecessary. She would be manipulating the master manipulator.

"You appear doubtful," he went on. "Let me offer an additional argument. I know already of your personal indifference to money, and I will not offer it. But what about freedom to experiment?"

He moved over to the desk and picked up one of

the two buff folders. His hand was thin, with long, bony fingers. Judith watched warily as he flipped open the folder and held it out towards her.

"In the past year, there have been seven requests to the U.N. from Dr. Judith Niles to conduct experiments on sleep research, using twelve new drugs that affect metabolic rate. The experiments would be done using human subjects—"

"—all volunteers, as the applications made clear."

"I know. But all rejected. Perhaps because three years ago, you led an experiment that ended disastrously. The recorded statements are quite clear. Using a combination of Tryptophil and a technique of EEG reinforcement and feedback, you succeeded in keeping three volunteers awake, alert, and apparently healthy for more than thirty days. But then there were complications. First there was atrophy of emotional responses, then atrophy of intellect. To quote one critical review of the study, 'Dr. Niles has succeeded not in abolishing the need for sleep, but only in inducing Alzheimer's disease. We do not need more senile dementia.' "

"Damn it, if you know that much, you probably know who wrote that review. It was Dickson, whose application for *identical research*—under worse control conditions—was turned down in favor of mine."

"Indeed I know it," Salter Wherry smiled again. "My point is not to goad you. It is to ask you how long it will be, for whatever reason, before you are allowed to resume experiments with human subjects—even, as you say, with eager volunteers."

Judith clenched her hands together hard. Her face was impassive. Just how much did he know? He was at the very brink of the new research.

"It could be years before such experiments are permitted," she said at last.

"Or it could be forever. Recall that delay is the deadliest form of denial." He was pressing hard, dominating the meeting, and they both knew it. "And recall Ecclesiastes, that to every thing there is a season, and a time to every purpose under Heaven. Your time is now, your purpose here on this station. You should seize the opportunity. On PSS-One you will not be bound by the rules that crippled your Institute on Earth. Here, you will *create* the rules."

Judith looked up at him. She had regained her self control. "You make all the rules here."

Salter Wherry smiled, and for a second the sensuous mouth of the younger man reappeared. "You are misinformed. Let us admit there are certain rules that I insist on. All the rest are negotiable. Tell me what experiments you wish to conduct. I will be amazed if I do not agree to all of them. In writing. If this is the case, will you come here?"

He finally came to sit in a chair opposite.

"Perhaps," she said. "Your offer is more than generous."

"And if we are realistic, we will agree that things are not going well down on Earth? Very well. I will not press you. But I have one more question. You told Hans Gibbs that this meeting was an absolute essential: if there were no face-to-face encounter, there would be no agreement. Most unusual. He told me your reason, that your own credibility with the people who work for you would be diminished if you did not see me. But you and I know that is nonsensical. Your prestige and reputation carry enough weight with your staff to make a meeting with me neither necessary nor relevant. So. Why did you want to meet me?"

Judith paused for a long time before she replied.

Her next remark might anger Salter Wherry to the point where all his interest in relocating the Institute might vanish. But she needed to gain some psychological advantage.

"I was told that you have certain personal tastes and preferences. That you would never, under any circumstances, deal directly with a woman. And that you had also become hopelessly reclusive. Your sexual habits are not my business, but I could not work for anyone with whom personal contact was denied. I could work with you only if we can meet to discuss problems."

"Because you need my inputs?" he said at last. "Let us be realistic. In your work, my contribution would be no more than noise and distraction."

"That is not the point. My relationships demand a certain logic, independent of gender and personality. Otherwise they become unworkable."

He was smiling again. "And you pretend there is logic in your present dealings with the impenetrable U.N. bureaucracy? It is better for your case if I do not pursue that."

He stood up. "You have my word. If you come here, you will have access to me. But as you grow older you will learn that logic is a luxury we must sometimes forego. Most of the human race struggles along without it. You are undeniably a woman—let me destroy another rumor by saying that I find you to be an attractive woman. I am certainly meeting with you, face to face. So much for idle speculation. When you return to Earth, perhaps you will spread the word that many of the 'known facts' about me are simple invention. Though I know it will make no difference to the public's perceptions."

He had paused in front of her, his manner clearly

indicating that the meeting was over. Judith remained seated.

"You asked me one last question," she said. "Why did I insist on this meeting? I have given you an answer. Now I think I have the right to one more question, too."

He nodded. "That is fair."

"Why did you *agree* to see me? According to Hans Gibbs, you would certainly refuse. I believe that the narcolepsy problem is important to you—but is it *that* important? I think not."

Salter Wherry stooped a little, so that the lined face was directly in front of Judith's. He looked very old, and very tired. She could sense the sadness in his eyes, far down beneath the fire and iron. When he at last smiled, those eyes looked dreamy.

"You are an extraordinary person. Few people see a second level of purpose, except for themselves and their own objectives. I refuse to lie to you, and I feel sure that your own motives sit deeper than we have reached in this meeting. So you should believe me when I say this. Today, you and your staff would find my other motives difficult to accept. Therefore, I will not offer them. But someday you will know my reasons."

He paused for a long moment, then added softly: "And now that I have met you, I think that you will approve of them."

He turned and was heading for the doorway before Judith could frame a reply. The interview with Salter Wherry was over.

Chapter 7:

"Earth has been regarded for centuries as a giant self-regulating machine, absorbing all changes, great and small, and diluting their effects until they become invisible on a global scale. Mankind has taken that stability for granted. Careless of consequences, we have watched as forests were cleared, lakes poisoned, rivers dammed and diverted, mountains leveled, whole plains dug out for their mineral and fuel content. And nothing disastrous happened. Earth tolerated the insults, and always she restored the status quo.

"Always—until now. Until finally some hidden critical point has been passed. The move away from a steady state is signalled in many ways: by increasing ocean temperatures, by drought and flood, by widespread loss of topsoil, by massive crop failure, and by the collapse of worldwide fishing industries.

"Many solutions have been proposed. But none of them can even be attempted now. All of them call for some practice of conservation, for the reversing of certain changes. That is impossible. With a world population approaching eight billion, all margin for *experiment has long disappeared. As resources grow scarcer, pressure to produce grows and grows. The richest nations practise an increased level of isolationism and caution, the poor ones are at the point of absolute desperation. The materials produced in space are no more than a trickle, where a flood is called for.*

"I offer naught for your comfort. The world is ready to explode, and I see no way to avoid that explosion. What I offer you is only a chance for some of your children...."

"Still at it?" said Jan de Vries. He had activated the videophone connection between the offices. At the sound of his voice Judith Niles put down the slim transcript.

"I'm ready to quit. I don't think I want to read any more. Did you take a look at this?"

De Vries nodded. "It is not difficult to see why Salter Wherry lacks popularity in the esteemed halls of the United Nations. His recruiting campaign for the space colonies is certainly effective, but he doesn't paint an encouraging picture of the world's future. Let us hope that he is wrong." He moved his index finger along the line of his neat moustache. "The suit is all set. They are ready when you are."

"Who'll do it? I left the final screening with Charlene."

"Wolfgang Gibbs. He's young, and he's fit, and we're agreed that it is not dangerous."

Judith Niles looked thoughtful. "I'm not so sure of that. Vacuum is vacuum—you don't play games with it. Tell them to get him ready. I'm on my way over."

When she arrived the final lab preparation was

complete. Emergency resuscitation equipment stood in banks along the walls. In the middle, seated on a long table in a sealed chamber, Wolfgang Gibbs was adjusting the gloves of the space suit. Charlene Bloom was by his side, obsessively checking the helmet. She straightened up as Judith Niles entered the room.

"Are you sure this is the same design as they're using now on Salter Station?" she said. "I think I see small differences in the seals."

Niles nodded. "The schematics we had were not quite right. We checked. According to Hans Gibbs this is the one in use now. All hooked up?"

Wolfgang turned and stared at her. His face was pale through the faceplate. "Ready when you are," he said over the suit radio.

Charlene placed her head close to the helmet. "Scared?" she said, in a low voice.

"Give you one guess." He smiled at her through the narrow faceplate. "Jelly in my guts. Now I know what the test animals must feel like. Let's get on with it. You get out of here and let's take the pressure down."

As he spoke the overhead lights flickered, faded, then slowly came back up to full power.

"Jesus!" said Charlene. "That's three brownouts in two hours." She looked at the other woman. "Should we go ahead, JN? It looks as though there's something horribly wrong with the grid."

"Blow-outs in the China link," said Judith Niles. "Cameron checked this afternoon, and he says it will get worse. They expect China may drop out completely in a week or so—they're above capacity, and their equipment is old. So there's no point in delaying here. We have our own stand-by system, and that's in good shape."

"So let's get on with it," said Gibbs. To Charlene Bloom's horror he reached and gave a sly rub along her thigh with one gloved hand, on the side hidden from Judith Niles.

She jerked away from him and shook her head fiercely. She had told Wolfgang over and over—private life must *never* get tangled up with their work.

"So you're telling me you want to stop?" he had said.

She had paused, turning her head to look at his bare, tanned shoulder. "You know I don't. But don't you be horrible, either. I know you have a reputation at the Institute, and I'm not asking about that. But remember this is the first time for me for . . . well, for anything like this."

He had turned to look down at her face, with an expression in his eyes that made her shiver all over. "For me, too."

Liar, she had been about to say. Then she looked at him again. He appeared completely serious. She had very much wanted to believe him—still wanted to believe him; but *not now*, not when JN was watching, even if he was staring at her so intently through the suit's faceplate. . . .

Charlene turned away briskly and stepped out of the chamber. "Sealed, and reducing," she said. She tried to keep her eyes on the gauges and away from Wolfgang.

The pressure was calibrated in kilos per square centimeter, and also as barometric altitude. The two women watched in silence as the green readouts flickered down through their first reduction.

"Three kilometers equivalent height," said Charlene. "Are you feeling all right, Wolfgang?"

He grunted. "No problem." His voice sounded

much more relaxed than she felt. "According to my readings we have a balance of internal and external pressure. Correct?"

"Right. You're on pure oxygen now. Any tightness at the suit's joints, or any feelings of dizziness? Move your arms, legs, and neck, and see how it feels."

He lifted his left arm and waggled the fingers in the suit. "*Morituri te salutamus.* I'm feeling fine."

"Very good. Who's been teaching *you* Latin?" As soon as she said it Charlene felt a blush starting to rise from the back of her neck. What would JN think? Charlene was the only one at the Institute who liked to spice up her reports with Latin tags. "Five kilometers," she said hurriedly. "We're getting a change of scale."

The readouts automatically adjusted to a finer gradation, moving from kilograms to grams per square centimeter. The pressure was reducing very slowly now, at a reduced rate controlled by Charlene. It was another twenty minutes before the chamber value was quivering down at zero. The barometric altitude, after rising steadily to a hundred kilometers, now refused to go any higher.

"Anything new?" Judith Niles had moved to stand with her face close to the chamber window.

"Nothing bad." Gibbs moved his head slowly from side to side. "You were right about the neck seals—I can feel a bit of pressure now, as though the suit bulges in a little bit there."

"That's the new design, they introduced it about a year ago. It's a better seal, but not so comfortable. The bulge is caused by the outside pressure drop, making an inward wrinkle in the seal. You'll get used to it. Any feelings of drowsiness?"

"Not a bit."

"Right. Start moving the blocks, and talk while you do it. Set your own pace."

Wolfgang, clumsy because of the unfamiliar gloves, began to move a heap of colored plastic blocks from one chest-high stand to another. "Haven't done anything like this since I was eighteen months old. Used to seem harder then. Get them all moved correctly, and I get a handful of raisins, right?"

Neither woman spoke as he carefully moved blocks. He was finished in less than a minute.

"Still feeling all right?" said Judith Niles when the task was done.

"Perfectly fine. No aches and pains, no sleepiness. Still have that bit of pressure in my neck, but all the other joints are very comfortable. Shall I switch to the cameras?"

"Whenever you're ready."

Gibbs nodded. The faceplate of the suit slowly darkened. His face became a dark grey and slowly faded from view as the plate achieved total opacity. The watchers heard a grumble through the suit radio. "Lousy color in here. If my TV didn't perform better than this I'd turn it in for service."

The suited figure turned slowly to point its forward viewing camera to look through the chamber window. "Charlene, you've turned green."

"I feel it. We'll worry about camera color balance later. Can you move the blocks again? And keep talking as you do it, just the way you did last time."

"Piece of cake." The bulky figure began to move the blocks slowly back to their original stand. "Reminds me of the work that they used to give you in the army when you were doing basic training. Supposed to tire us out and keep us out of trouble.

First you move the pile of dirt over here, then when you were finished somebody else would move it back. Then you would—"

It happened with startling suddenness. There was no drowsy trailing off of speech. At one moment the suited figure was working efficiently, his matter-of-fact tones clear over the suit radio. Then they were looking in at a silent, motionless statue, frozen with a red block stretched out in one gloved hand.

Charlene Bloom gave a cry of alarm, while Judith Niles took a long, shivering breath. "That's it. No cause for panic, Charlene, it's what we were expecting. Start bringing the pressure up—*slowly*. We don't want a problem there. I'll make sure the bed is ready. My guess is that he'll be out for at least half an hour."

She moved over to the phone. Behind her, Charlene stared wide-eyed at Wolfgang Gibbs' unconscious figure. She had to fight the temptation to bring the pressure instantly to sealevel, and rush into the chamber herself.

Jan de Vries was waiting in her office, calmly reading a file marked *Confidential—Director Only*. He looked up as she came in.

"How is he?"

"Recovered. He was out for nearly an hour, and he remembers nothing of the whole episode. So far as Wolfgang is concerned, he didn't even begin the tests with the suit on video." Judith Niles did not sit down, but instead paced back and forth in front of the chair where Jan de Vries was sitting. "No after effects now, and full alertness."

"So your hypothesis is correct. You predicted what would happen, and the subject performed exactly as required." De Vries slapped the file closed. "Everything can now proceed precisely as you planned. We will move the Institute to orbit, spend a month or two in supposed problem analysis, and then hand Salter Wherry the solution to his major problem; after which we will be in a position to pursue our own researches, as the Institute's new contract explicitly permits. Wonderful. The manipulation is complete, exactly as designed." His mouth twisted in a grimace. "So, my dear, where is the jubilation? You do not have the air of one whose plans approach fruition."

"I'm not satisfied—not at all." Judith Niles paused, looking quizzically down at the diminutive figure of de Vries in the depths of the big armchair. "Listen to this sequence, then tell me what you think. Item one: a year ago there was a slight change in the type of space suit worn in Salter Station for outside construction work. The new one uses a slightly different set of rings and seals in the neck portion.

"Item two." She checked off on the fingers of her right hand. "For some positions of the head, the new suit causes increased pressure on the wearer's carotid arteries."

"*Slight* pressure?"

"Not that slight—big enough for the wearer to notice. Item three: increased pressure within the carotid arteries can cause momentary blackouts.

"Item four: when a suit is on normal visual operation, the blackout is momentary, too brief to be noticed. But when the suit is on remote and using TV cameras instead of faceplate viewing, the scanning rates on the TV give a feedback to the brain that reinforces the blackout. Result: narcolepsy. The wearer will not break out of the cycle unless there is some external interruption. How does that sound to you?"

De Vries sat silent for a few moments, then nodded. "Plausible—more than plausible, almost certainly correct."

"All right. I agree. So here's item five." She closed her fist. "All of this has been known for forty years. The increased pressure in the carotids is a classical cause of narcolepsy. The brain wave reinforcement is a standard positive feedback mechanism. What does all that say to you?"

De Vries leaned far back, gazing up at the ceiling. He shook his head. "Judith, put in those terms I see where you are heading—but I must admit that it would not have occurred to me if you had not waved it in front of my nose."

Judith Niles regarded him grimly. "Be specific, Jan. What's wrong with it?"

"It's too *simple*. When you set the explanation out on a plate, as you just did, it's clear that we should not be needed to solve the problem. Remember, you told me you thought you knew the answer when you *first* looked at the suits and the case histories. All the medics on Salter Station had to do was a minimal amount of background reading, and a few well-designed experiments. At the very least they would have noticed the correlation between the new suits and the onset of the problem."

"Exactly. So why didn't they?" Judith Niles stopped her pacing and stood in front of de Vries. "Even if they didn't catch on as fast as we would here at the Institute, they should have deduced it after a while. Jan, I'm very worried. We *have* to go up to Salter Station. Our own experiments require it, and anyway I've burned too many bridges here in the past few days to stop now. But I feel that things are out of control."

She suddenly lifted her left hand and began to rub gently at her eye, her forehead wrinkled.

Jan de Vries looked concerned. "What's wrong, Judith? Headache?"

She shook her head. "Not any sort I've ever had before. But I'm getting blurring from this eye— very offputting. Not quite seeing double, but not far from that. Odd feeling."

De Vries frowned. "Don't take chances. Even if it is no more than the strain of too much work, let a specialist take a look at it." De Vries did not say it, but he was astonished. Never since he had known her had Judith Niles shown any sign of strain and fatigue, no matter what pressures she had worked under, no matter how she forced herself along.

"I'll be all right," she said. "Sorry, Jan, what were you saying?"

"I agree with you that things may be out of control." The little man wriggled forward in the armchair so that he could stand up. "And let me give you, as Salter Wherry quoted in his speech on the space colonies, 'naught for your comfort.' I've been doing the follow-up work you asked for on Salter Wherry. Did you know that most of his expenditures are not on development of the ar-cologies at all? They go into two other areas: efficient, spaceborne fusion drives, and robots. He is rumored to be many years ahead of anyone else in those areas. I believe it. But what do our projects have to do with either of those research endeav-ors? If you can see the connection, I beg enlighten-ment. And then there is the question of the breadth of Wherry's influence, and his sources of wealth. Do you remember my telling you that insurance rates for Station personnel have gone up greatly in the past year?"

"Yes. Because of the increased accident rate."

"So we had assumed. But this afternoon I obtained and examined the financial statements of Global Insurance—the organization which issues the policies for Salter Station personnel. It turns out that a single individual owns more than eighty percent of the stock of Global, and exercises complete control over corporate actions." De Vries smiled grimly. "You are permitted one guess as to the identity of that individual. Then, my dear Judith, we should perhaps discuss who is manipulating whom."

Chapter 8:

The fish were nervous. Moving in regular array, they darted to and fro through the fronds of weed that curled across Workwheel's great tanks. As the schools of fish turned in the cloudy water their silvery scales caught the green-tinged sunlight, filling the interior with flashes of brilliance.

The two human figures, naked except for light breathing masks, swam slowly around the perimeter of the tank, driving the fish along before them. The outer edge of the wheel was a filled lattice of transparent plastic, admitting perpetual day to the four-hundred-meter cylinder. Far above, near the hollow central axle, oxygenation pumps sent a faint thrumming through the sluggishly moving liquid.

The female figure swooped without warning down to the clear honeycombed plastic of the outer wall, kicked off hard from it, and surged upwards towards Workwheel center. The other, taken by surprise, followed her a second later. He overtook her halfway to the axle and reached out to grasp her calf, but she wriggled away and headed off in a new direction, still slanting towards the surface.

Again he pursued, and this time as he neared her he reached out to grasp both her ankles. His fingers closed, and at that instant the tableau suddenly froze. Two nude sculptures, their muscles tensed, hung in the water among the motionless fishes.

Salter Wherry looked closely at the video display for a few seconds, then carefully moved it along several frames. It was difficult to see the expressions clearly in the recording, and he zoomed in on Judith Niles' face for a high-mag close-up. Even with the mask on, her face contrasted with her taut muscles. She looked totally relaxed, though Hans Gibbs was gripping her firmly around the ankles. After a few moments of study Wherry skipped forward, a few frames at a time, watching the changing expressions as the nude bodies moved together, embraced, then slowly rose. Entwined, they moved to meet the broad concave meniscus of the water surface near the axle of the wheel.

Salter Wherry watched their actions calmly in the darkness of the control room. Always, regardless of the couple's embraces, his attention rested on Judith Niles' face. At last he leaned forward and pressed another key on the console in front of him. The scene changed to a brilliantly lit interior. Now it was Judith Niles standing alone in Wherry's office on Spindletop, just next door from the hidden studio, waiting for her first meeting with him. Again his attention was on her face. One minute more, another press of a key, and Wherry was seeing her as she stood after their first meeting. He grunted in dissatisfaction. The hidden cameras were carefully placed, but they could not offer views from all angles, and this time a full face view was denied him.

He moved on. The next shots had come from the inside of the Institute itself, down on Earth. First preparations were under way for the move to Salter Station. The cameras showed experimental animals being carefully housed in well-ventilated crates for upward shipment. This time Salter Wherry seemed pleased. There was a hint of satisfaction in the blue eyes as he cut to the receiving network for his daily global status report.

Salter Station's observing network tapped all open news channels around the globe, plus a number of sources that national governments would have been shocked to see so routinely cracked. Ground reports were supplemented and confirmed by the station's spy satellite network, the hundred polar-orbiting spacecraft that permitted a constant detailed look at events anywhere on the globe.

Salter Wherry now began his daily routine, switching with long practice between different data sources. As the mood struck him, he cut back to earlier events of the past year, then moved forward again to the present. Patiently, he tacked his way to and fro across the face of the globe, sometimes a thousand miles above the surface, sometimes through a hand-held camera on an open street, occasionally with video taken inside government buildings or within private homes. The images flooded in.

—*East Africa.* The four-thousand-mile flow of the Nile northward to the Mediterranean showed a river shrunk and diminished by unremitting drought. The Sudan was parched desert, the great agricultural systems along the river all vanished. Khartoum, at the confluence of the Blue Nile and the White Nile, was no more than cindered buildings. The cameras swept north, high above the muddy river. Close to the Mediterranean, Cairo was a ghost town where packs of hungry dogs patrolled the dusty streets. The nilometer on Roda Island stood far out above the river's trickling flow. Water supply and sewage systems had failed long since. Now, only the flies were energetic in the monstrous noon heat.

—*Alaska*. The long southern coastline was shrouded in perpetual fogs, marking the meeting of warm and cold currents. Inland, the warming peninsula was suddenly bursting with new life. The permafrost had melted. Rampant vegetation was rising to clog the muskeg swamps, and clouds of mosquito and black fly buzzed and swirled above the soft surface. The population, at first delighted by the warming trend, was now struggling to hold its own against the rising tide of plant and animal life. All day long, aircraft loaded with pesticides sprayed tens of thousands of square kilometers. They enjoyed little success.

—*London*. The steadily melting icecaps had been raising the sealevel, slowly, inexorably, a few inches a year. The tides were lapping now at the top of the seawalls, pressing inward all the way from Gravesend to Waterloo Bridge. Cameras in the streets caught lines of volunteer workers continuing their long toil with sandbags and concrete buttresses. Wading through ankle-deep water, they fought the daily battle with high tide. The work went on quietly, even cheerfully. Morale was good.

—*Java*. The chain of volcanoes along the island, as though in sympathy with the globe's extreme weather, had woken a week earlier to malignant life. Many of the hundred million people packed onto the island had sought flight, north across the shallow waters of the Java Sea. The spaceborne

cameras picked out every detail of the frail boats,
heavily overloaded, as they headed for Borneo and
Sumatra.

But not only the land was seismically active.
When the *tsunami* struck, not a boat remained
afloat. The sixty-foot tidal wave that hit Jakarta
and the whole northern shore of Java ensured that
those who had remained on land fared little better
than their seagoing relatives. Today the cameras
picked up isolated clusters of survivors as they
were gathered by rescue teams and shipped to
mountain camps in the central highlands.

—*Moscow*. Reports from the main agricultural
oblasts were coming in to the central planning
office. A stone-faced calm was being maintained
there, as word arrived of wheat and barley crops
withered and brown, of rice and rye failure, and of
steadily rising winds that ripped away dry topsoil
and carried it pulverized high into the atmosphere.

Salter Wherry crouched motionless over his console, steadily absorbing new information, collating
it with old. Only his mouth and eyes seemed alive.
After the scenes from Moscow, he finally switched
to the interior of the United Nations building. The
formal ritual in the crowded chamber could not
hide the undercurrents of anger and tension wash-
ing in from the stressed world outside. The ambas-
sador from the Soviet Union, face stern and intense,
was concluding his prepared speech.

"What we are seeing in the world today is not
an accident of nature, not the mere vicissitudes of
planetary weather at work. We are seeing deliberate modification of climate, changes directed
against the Soviet Union and our friends by other
nations. The time for reticence in naming these
nations is past. My country is the victim of economic warfare. We cannot permit—"

Wherry jabbed impatiently at the keyboard. He was frowning, bright eyes shadowed by heavy eyebrows. After a few seconds *Eleanora* appeared on the screen in front of him, a silver ovoid framed against the backdrop of stars and a sunlit earth. He held it there while he called out printed schedules and status reports for construction. The curving lines of geodesic support girders on the outer hull had disappeared, covered by bright exterior panels. Final electrical systems were being installed, together with the power sources and the hydroponic tanks; the vast water cylinder was already full.

Wherry skipped to views of the other arcologies. The most distant, *Amanda*, blinked in as a grainy and indistinct image. It was now almost three million miles away from earth, spiralling slowly outward in the plane of the ecliptic. In eight years, unless some new trajectory were adopted, the colony ship would have wound its way out to the orbit of Mars. Already the scientists on board were talking about the possibility of a small manned station on Phobos, and consulting with Salter Station on the available resources for the project.

Salter Wherry flicked off the viewing screen and sat motionless for many minutes. At last he keyed in another sequence. The face of Hans Gibbs, hair tousled, appeared.

"Hans, do you have the schedule for shipping the Neurological Institute staff there with you?"

"Not in front of me. Hold on a minute and I'll get it."

"No need for that. I'll tell you what I want you to do. The schedule calls for everything to be up here seventy-seven days from now."

"Right. Judith Niles grumbled at that, but we're on time so far."

"Hans, it won't do. I don't think we have that long. It's going to hell, and it's skidding there fast. I think I understand international politics pretty well, but today I couldn't even guess which country will go crazy first. They're all candidates. I want you to work up a revised schedule that will have everything from the Institute—people, animals, and equipment—here inside thirty days. Tell Muncie I want him to do the same thing for anything we need to finish *Eleanora*, in the same timetable."

Hans Gibbs suddenly looked much more awake. "Thirty days! No way, the permits alone will take us that long."

"Don't worry about permits. Let me take care of those. You start working the shipping arrangements. Fast. Cost is irrelevant. You hear me?" Salter Wherry smiled. "*Irrelevant*. Now, Hans, how often do you hear me say that about the cost of anything? Thirty days. You have thirty days."

Hans Gibbs shrugged. "I'll try. But apart from permits, we have to worry about launch availability. If that goes sour—"

He paused, and swore. The connection was gone. Hans was talking to a blank screen.

Chapter 9:

Wolfgang Gibbs closed his eyes and leaned his head forward to touch the cool metal of the console. His face was white, and shone with sweat. After a few seconds he swallowed hard, sat upright, took a deep breath, and made another try. He hit the key sequence for a coded message, waiting until the unit in front of him signalled acceptance.

"Well, Charlene—" he had to clear his throat again "—I promised you a report as soon as I could get round to it. I've just screwed up the transmission sequence three times in a row, so if this one doesn't work I'll call it a day. I originally thought I'd be sending to you right after I got here—shows what an optimist I am! Still, here we go, one more time. If you hear puking noises in the middle of the recording, don't worry. That's just me, losing my liver and lungs again."

He coughed harshly. "Hans says that only one person in fifty has as bad a reaction to freefall as I do, so with luck you'll be all right. And they say even I should feel better in a couple more days. I can't wait. Anyway, that's enough moaning, let me get to work.

"Most of the trip up was a breeze. We had everything tied down tight, so nothing could shake loose, and Cameron had all the animals souped up to their eyebrows with sedatives. Pity he couldn't do the same for me. When we hit freefall everything was all right at first, though my stomach felt as if it had moved about a foot upwards. But I was coping with it, not too bad. Then we began moving the animals into their permanent quarters here. They didn't like it, and they showed their annoyance the only way they could. I'm telling you, we'd better not move again in a hurry. They don't pay enough for me to wallow along through a cloud of free-floating-animal puke and animal crap everyday of the week. Wall-to-wall yucky. It was about then that I started to feel I was going to lose my breakfast. And then I *did* lose it—then the previous day's lunch and dinner, and I still feel as though I'll never eat again.

"O.K. Guess that's not what you want to hear, is it? Let me get back to the real stuff. I'll dress it up properly for the lab reports, but here's where we stand."

Wolfgang paused for a moment as another wave of nausea swept over him. He had made his way to the outermost corridor of Spindletop, where the effective gravity was highest, and a quarter-gee was almost enough to bring his stomach in line; but if he allowed himself to look down, he was gazing *out* at infinity, standing on a rotating sea of stars that swirled steadily beneath his feet. And that was enough to start him off again.

He looked straight ahead, steadfastly refusing to

allow his glance to stray towards any of the ports. The turning knot in his stomach slowly loosened.

"I guess the cats came through in worst shape," he said at last. "They're all alive, but we'll have a hell of a time sorting out how much of their troubles are caused by the trip up here, and how much is progressive deterioration in their experimental condition. We lost a couple of sloths—don't know why yet, but looks like it may be a drug-induced cardiac arrest. Cannon warned about that before we started, but nobody had any bright ideas how to prevent it. The other small mammals all seem in pretty good shape, and we had no real trouble moving them to their quarters. That *wasn't* true with the Kodiaks, though." He managed to smile into the camera. "They're big mothers. Thank God we don't have any experiments going on with elephants. You had to be here to see what a job we had with old Jinx. Great fat monster. We'd tug and heave on him for a while, and feel he wasn't moving, then after we finally got him drifting in the right direction we'd find we couldn't stop him. I was nearly flattened against one of the walls. It's a good thing the people on the station are used to handling big masses in space, or I never would have made it.

"I'll cut out the tales of woe. We finally got him in place, 'nuff said, up near the hub of Workwheel. It's a horrible place—no gravity to speak of. I don't know how low, but less than a hundredth of a gee for sure. Hans says that in a month or two I'll enjoy it there, but now just thinking about it makes me sick. But I'll say one thing for the crews here, they know how to build. All the tanks and the supporting equipment we asked for were ready and in place—and it all worked. A couple of hours ago I gave Jinx the treatment, and I have him stabilized now in Mode Two hibernation pattern. You'll get all the detailed logs with the official transmission, and all the video, too. But I thought you'd like to see something at once, so I'm going to run a clip for you right in with this. Here, see what you think of Jinx."

Wolfgang took a long, deep breath and pressed the calling sequence. He did it slowly and painfully, with the fragile and exaggerated care of an old, old man. His fingers stumbled several times, but at last he had a correct pattern entered. He leaned back and massaged his midriff as a copy of the recorded video was displayed before him and simultaneously sent down as a signal to Earth.

Jinx was shown at center screen. The bear was sitting upright on a bed of soft shavings, sniffing curiously at a massive chunk of fish protein held in his front paws. His long black tongue came out and licked tentatively at the flaky surface. The bear's movements were a little jerky, but well-controlled and accurate. Wolfgang watched with approval as Jinx took a neat bite, chewed thoughtfully, then placed the rest of the protein block down on the shavings. When the mouthful was swallowed Jinx yawned and scratched peacefully at a fur-free patch on his left side. The implanted sensors there lay close to the surface of the skin, and it was still a little sensitive. After a few seconds more he picked up the fishy slab and the monstrous jaws began to nibble around it contentedly.

"Looks good, eh?" said Wolfgang. "You'll see more when you get the full coverage later, but let me give you the bottom line now. We saw the first signs of this in those last experiments in Christchurch, and what JN had been predicting all along seems to hold up exactly. We hit the correct drug protocols right away this time. Jinx's body temperature was seven degrees above freezing in that segment of video. His heart rate was one beat per minute—and still is. I estimate that his metabolic rate is down by a factor of about eighty. He's slow, but he's sure as hell not hibernating—look at him chew on that slab. What you're seeing is speeded up, by a factor of sixty-eight over real time. The trickiest piece so far was finding something that Jinx is willing to eat. You know how picky he is. Seems like things feel different to him now, and he doesn't like it. We got the consistency right after about twenty tries, and he seems to be feeding normally."

Wolfgang rubbed ruefully at his midsection. "Lucky old Jinx. That's more than I can say for myself. Best of all, his condition seems to be completely stable. I checked all the indicators a few minutes ago. I think we could hold him there for a month if we had to, maybe more."

He cut back from the picture of the bear to real-time transmission. "That's the report from this end, Charlene. Now I can relax. But I can't wait for you and the others to get up here. I don't know how biassed the news coverage is that comes here to Salter Station, but we hear of trouble everywhere back on Earth. Cold wars, hot wars, and mouthing off in all directions. Did you know it hit sixty-two Celsius yesterday in Baluchistan? That's nearly a hundred and forty-four Fahrenheit. They must be dying in droves. And did you get the reports from the U.N. Security Council? There's talk of closing all national air space, and Hans is having real problems scheduling Shuttle flights up—

not just the usual red tape, either. He's meeting blank walls. He's been told there will be an indefinite suspension of all flights, from all spaceports, until the Earth situation normalizes again. And who knows when that will be? Wherry's experts say the changes are here to stay—we've caused them ourselves with the fossil fuel programs."

His hand moved towards the key that would end transmission, then paused. He looked uncertainly at the screen. "Hey, Hans told me one other thing I really didn't want to hear. Dammit, I wish I knew just how secure this line is, but I'll say it anyway. If it's not common knowledge down at the Institute, Charlene, please keep it to yourself. It's about JN. Did you know that she's been taking a whole battery of neurological tests over at Christchurch Central? CAT scans, radio-isotope tracers, air bubble tracers, the works. They've been probing her brain sixteen different ways. I hope she didn't do something crazy back there, like using herself as a test subject for Institute experiments. Maybe you can check it out? I'd like to be sure she's all right. Don't ask me how Hans knew all this—the information they have up here about Earthside doings amazes me. I guess that's all for now."

Wolfgang pressed the key carefully and leaned back. Transmission terminated, and the circuit was broken.

He closed his eyes. That hadn't been as bad as he expected. It definitely helped to have something good to concentrate on, to take your thoughts away from feeling nauseated. Think of something good. A sudden and startling memory of Charlene came to his mind, her long limbs and willowy body bending above him, and her dark hair falling loosely about his forehead. He grunted. Christ! If he could have thoughts like that, he must definitely be on the mend. Next thing you know he'd be able to face food again.

Maybe it was time for another test.

Wolfgang slowly steeled himself, then turned his head and looked out of the port. Now Spindletop was pointing down towards Earth, and he was facing an endless drop to the sunlit hemisphere beneath. Salter Station was flying over the brown wedge of the Indian subcontinent, with the greener oval of Sri Lanka just visible at its foot.

He gasped. As he watched the scene seemed to spin and warp beneath him, twisting through a strange and surrealistic mapping. He gritted his teeth and held on tight to the console edge. After thirty unpleasant seconds he could force himself to a different perspective. It was Earth's blue-and-white surface, mottled with brown-green markings, that was airy and insubstantial; it was Salter Station that was *real*, tangible, solid. That was it. Cling to that thought. He was slowly able to relax his grip on the table in front of him.

It would be all right. Everything was relative. If Jinx could adapt to his new life, comfortable with a body temperature down near freezing, surely Wolfgang could become at ease with the much smaller changes produced by the move to Salter Station. Better forget self-pity, and get back to work.

Ignoring the twinges from his long-suffering stomach, Wolfgang forced himself to look out again as the station swept towards the Atlantic and the majestic curve of the day-night terminator.

Three more days, then the Institute staff would

be on their way here. And if the news reports were correct, it was just in time. In their fury and endless feuding, the governments of Earth seemed all set to block the road to space itself.

Chapter 10: *The End of the World*

Hans Gibbs had sent his cousin the briefest, uninformative message from the main control room. "Get your ass over here. On the double, or you'll miss something you'll never see again."

Wolfgang and Charlene were in the middle of first inventory when that message came over the intercom. He looked at her and signed off the terminal at once. "Come on."

"What, right now?" Charlene shook her head protestingly. "We're just getting started. I promised Cameron we'd have this place organized and ready to go to work when they got here. We only have a few more hours."

"I know. But I know Hans, too. He always understates. It must be something special. Let's go, we'll finish this later."

He took her hand and began to pull her along, showing off his hard-won experience with low gee. Charlene had been on Salter Station less than twenty-four hours, the second person to make full transfer from the Institute. It seemed grossly unfair to Wolfgang that she hadn't suffered even one moment of freefall sickness. But at least she didn't have his facility yet for easy movement. He tugged her and spun her, adjusting linear and angular momentum. After a few moments Charlene realized that she should move as little as possible, and let him drag her along as a fixed-geometry dead weight. They glided rapidly along the helical corridor that led to the central control area.

Hans was waiting for them when they arrived, his attention on a display screen showing Earth at screen center. The image was being provided from a geostationary observing satellite, 22,000 miles up, so the whole globe showed as a ball that filled most of the screen.

"You won't see anything ship-sized from this distance," Hans said. "So we have to fake it. If we want to see spacecraft, the computer generates the graphics for them and merges it all into the display. Watch, now. I'm taking us into that mode. The action will start in a couple of minutes."

Charlene and Wolfgang stood behind him as Hans casually keyed in a short command sequence, then leaned back in his chair. The display screen remained quiet, showing Europe, Asia and Africa as a half-lit disk under medium cloud cover. The seconds stretched on, for what seemed like forever.

"Well?" said Wolfgang at last. "We're here. Where's the action?"

He leaned forward. As he did so, the display changed. Suddenly, from six different points on the hemisphere, tiny sparks of red light appeared. First it was half a dozen of them, easy to track. But within a few minutes there were more, rising like fireflies out of the hazy globe beneath. Each one began the slow tilt to the east that showed they were heading for orbit. Soon they were almost too numerous to count.

"See the one on the left?" said Hans. "That's from Aussieport. Most of your staff will be on that; Judith, and de Vries, and Cannon. They'll be here in an hour and a half."

"Holy hell." Charlene was frowning, shaking her head. "Those *can't* be ships. There aren't that many in the whole world."

She was too absorbed by the scene in front of her to catch Hans Gibbs' familiar reference to the Institute Director, but Wolfgang had given his cousin a quick and knowing look.

"Charlene's right," said Hans. He looked satisfied at her startled reaction. "If you only consider the Shuttles and other reuseables, there aren't that many ships. But I ran out of time. Salter Wherry told me to get everything up here, people and supplies, and to hell with the cost. He's the boss, and it was his money. The way things have been going, if I'd waited any longer we'd never have been allowed to bring up what we need. What you're seeing now is the biggest outflow of people and equipment you'll ever see. I took launch options on every expendable launch vehicle I could find, anywhere in the world. Watch now, there's more to come."

A second wave had begun, this time showing as fiery orange. At the same time, other flashing red points were creeping round the Earth's dark rim. Launches made from the invisible hemisphere were coming into view.

Hans touched another key, and a set of flashing green points appeared on the display, these in higher orbit.

"Those are our stations, everything in the Wherry

Empire except the arcologies—they're too far out
to show at this scale. In another half-hour you'll
see how most of the launches begin to converge on
the stations. We'll be faced with multiple rendezvous and docking up here, continuously for the next
thirty-six hours."

"But how do you know where the ships are?"
Charlene was wide-eyed, hypnotized by the swirl
of bright sparks. "Is it all calculated from lift-off
data?"

"Better than that." Hans jerked a thumb at another of the screens, off to the side. "Our reconnaissance satellites track everything that's launched,
all the time. Thermal infrared signals for the launch
phase, synthetic aperture radar after that. Software converts range and range-rate data to position, and plots it on the display. Wherry put the
observation and tracking system in a few years ago,
when he was afraid some madman down on Earth
might try a sneak attack on one of his Stations.
But it's ideal for this use."

A third wave was beginning. All around the equator, a new necklace of dazzling blue specks was
expanding away from the Earth's surface. The
planet was girdled by a multi-colored confusion of
spiralling points of light.

"For God's sake." Wolfgang dropped any pre-
tence of nonchalance. "Just how many of these *are*
there? I've counted over forty, and I've not even
been trying to track the ones launched in the Amer-
ican hemisphere."

"Two hundred and six spacecraft, all shapes and
sizes, and most of them not designed for the sort of
docking ports we have available here. The count
for launches shows on that readout over there."

Hans waved a hand at a display, but his attention was all on the screen.

"It's going to be a nightmare," he said cheerfully. "We have to match them all up when they get here. Matter of fact, we won't even try to bring all of them all the way. Lots of 'em will stay in low orbit, and we'll send the tugs down to transfer cargo. I didn't have time to worry about extra thrust to bring them up here. We had enough trouble getting some of that junk into orbit at all."

A fourth wave had begun. But now the screen was too confusing to follow. The points of light were converging, and the limited resolution of the display screen made many appear close to collision, even though miles of space separated them. The two men seemed hypnotized, staring at the bright carousel of orbiting ships. Charlene went to the viewport and looked directly down towards Earth. There was nothing to be seen. The ships were far too small to show against the giant crescent of the planet. She shook her head, and turned to face the launch count readout. The total was ticking higher, skipping ahead in little bursts as orbital velocity was confirmed for the ships in a new group.

Hans had moved back from the control console, and the three stood side by side, motionless. The room remained totally silent for several minutes except for the soft beep of the counters.

"Nearly there," said Charlene at last. She was still watching the ship count. "Two hundred and three. Four. Five. One more to go. There. Two hundred and six. Should we be applauding?"

She smiled at Wolfgang, who absent-mindedly squeezed her hand. Then she casually turned back to the counter. She stared at it for a second, suddenly not sure what she was seeing.

"Hey! Hans, I thought you said the total was two hundred and six? The readout shows two hundred and fourteen now, and it's still going."

"What!" Hans swivelled his head to look, the rest of his body turning the other way to give low-gee compensation for the movement. "It can't be. I scrounged every ship that would fly. There's no way...."

His voice faded. On the screen, a fountain of bright points of light was spouting upwards. It centered on an area of southeast Asia. As they watched, a speaker by the console stuttered and burst to life.

"Hans! Full alert." The voice was harsh and strained, but Wolfgang recognized the note of authority. It was Salter Wherry. "Bring up our defense systems. Monitors show launch of missiles from west China. No trajectory information yet. Could be headed for America or the Soviet Union, some could be coming our way. Too soon to tell. I've thrown the switch here. You confirm action stations. I'll be in central control in one minute."

In spite of its tone of agonized strain, the voice had made its staccato statements so fast that the sentences ran into one stream of orders. Hans Gibbs did not even attempt a reply. He was off his seat and over to another console instantly. A plastic seal was removed and the lever behind it pulled out before Wolfgang or Charlene could move.

"What's happening?" cried Charlene.

"Don't know." Hans sounded as though he were choking. "But look at the screen—and the count. Those have to be missile launches. We can't afford to take a chance on where they're heading."

The readout was going insane, digits flickering too fast to read. The launch count was up over four hundred. As it escalated higher, Salter Wherry came stumbling into the control room.

It was his arrival, in person, that made Charlene aware of the real seriousness of the situation. Here was a man who rarely met with anyone, who prized his privacy above any wealth, who hated exposure to strangers. And he was there in the control room, oblivious to the presence of Charlene and Wolfgang.

She stared at him curiously. Was this the living legend, the master architect of Solar System development? She knew he was very old. But he looked more than old. His face was white and haggard, like a stretched-out death mask, and his thin hands were trembling.

"The fools," he said softly. His voice was a croaking whisper. "Oh, the fools, the damned, damned, *damned* fools. I've been afraid of this, but I didn't really believe it would ever happen in my lifetime. Do you have our defenses up?"

"In position," said Hans harshly. "We're protected. But what about the ships that are on their way here? They'll be blown apart if they're on a rendezvous trajectory with us."

Charlene stared at him mindlessly for a second. Then she understood. "The ships? My God, the whole Institute staff are on their way up here. You can't use your missile defense on them—you can't do it!"

Wherry glared at her, seeming to notice the strangers in the control room for the first time. "Even the fastest of our ships won't be here for an hour," he said.

He sank to a chair, his breath wheezing in his throat. He coughed and leaned back. His skin looked dry and white, like crumbling dough. "By then it will all be over, one way or another. The attack missiles have high accelerations. If they're aimed at us, they'll be here in twenty minutes. If they're not, it will be over anyway. Hans, flag our position on the display."

Under Hans Gibbs' keyboard control, the position of Salter Station appeared on the screen as a glowing white circle. Hans studied the whole display for a few moments, head cocked to one side.

"I don't think they're coming this way," he said. "They're heading for the eastern Soviet Union and the United States, for a guess. What's happening?"

Wherry was sitting, head down. "See what you can catch on radio communications." He cleared his throat, the breath wheezing in his larynx. "We've always been worried that somebody would try a sneak first strike, wipe out the others' retaliatory power. That's what we're seeing. Some madman took advantage of the high level of our launch activity—so much going on, it would take anyone a while to realize an attack was being made."

Hans had cut in a radio frequency scan. "Radio silence from China. Look at the screen. Those will be United States missiles. The counterattack. We knew a pre-emptive first strike wouldn't work, and it didn't."

A dense cluster of points of fire was sweeping up over the north pole. At the same time, a new starburst was rising from eastern Siberia. The launch readout had gone insane, emitting a series of high-pitched squeaks as individual launches became too frequent to be marked as a separate beep from the counter. Over two thousand missile launches had been recorded in less than three minutes.

"Couldn't work. Couldn't work," said Salter

Wherry softly. "First strike never would—it always leaves something to hit back."

His head slumped down. For the first time, Charlene had the thought that she might be seeing something more than old age and worry. "Wolfgang! Give me a hand."

She moved to Wherry's side and placed her hand under his chin, lifting his head. His eyes were bleary, as though some translucent film covered them. At her touch he feebly raised his right hand to grip hers. It was icy cold, and his other hand clutched at his chest.

"Couldn't work. Couldn't." The voice was a rough whisper. "It's the end, end of the world, end of everything."

"He's having a heart attack." Charlene leaned over to lift him, but Wolfgang was there before her.

"Hans. You could do this better than we can, but you'd better stay here—we have to know what's going on. Alert the medical facility, tell them we think it's a heart attack. Ask them if we should move him, or if they want to treat him here—and if they want him at the facility, tell me how to get him there."

Charlene helped to lift Wherry from the seat. She did it as gently as she could, while some part of her brain stood back astonished and watched Wolfgang and Hans. There had been a strange and sudden change in their relationship in the past few minutes. Hans was still older, more senior, and more experienced. But as events became more confused and depressing, he seemed to dwindle, while Wolfgang just became more forceful and determined. At the moment there was no question as to who was in control. Hans was following Wolfgang's orders without hesitation. He was at the console, ear mike on, and his fingers were flying across the array of keys.

"Leave Wherry here," he said after a few seconds. "Med Center says Olivia Ferranti will be right over. Lay him flat, then don't move him, don't try any treatment unless he stops breathing— they'll bring portable resuscitation equipment with them."

"Right." Wolfgang gesture i to Charlene, and between them they carefully lowered Salter Wherry to the floor, supporting his head on Wolfgang's jacket. He lay quiet for a moment, then made an effort to lift himself.

"Don't move," said Charlene.

There was a tiny sideways movement of his head. "Displays." Wherry's voice was a rustling whisper. "Have to see the displays. Reconnaissance. Cities."

Hans had turned to watch them. He nodded. "I've already asked for that. Major cities. What else?"

"Can you reach the ship with the Institute senior staff on board?" asked Wolfgang. "We have to talk to JN. They're well clear of the atmosphere, but I don't know if they're line-of-sight from here."

"Doesn't matter." Hans turned back to the console. "We can go through relays. I'll try to reach them. We'll have to use another channel for that. I'll feed them in to the screen behind you."

He set to work at the keyboard. He was the only one with enough to occupy him completely. Charlene and Wolfgang stood by feeling helpless. Salter Wherry, after his effort to raise his head, lay motionless. He looked drained of all blood, with livid face and hands bent into withered claws. His breath gargled deep in his throat, the only sound that broke the urgent beep of new launches. The sparks were no longer concentrated in a band around the Earth's equator. Now they covered the globe like a bright net, drawn tighter in the northern hemisphere and over the pole.

Olivia Ferranti arrived just as the reconnaissance satellite images appeared on the screen. The doctor took one startled look at the blue-white blossoming explosion that had been Moscow, then ignored it and knelt beside her patient. Her assistant rapidly connected electrodes from the portable unit to Salter Wherry's bared chest, and took an ominous-looking saw and scalpel from a sterilized carrying case.

"Transmissions from the ship you want coming in," said Hans. "Who do you want?"

"JN," said Wolfgang. "Charlene, you'd better talk to her. Tell them to move away from a rendezvous trajectory until our missile defense goes off here. They'll be safe anywhere—"

His words were lost in a huge burst of noise from the communications units.

"Damnation." Hans Gibbs rapidly reduced the volume to a tolerable level. "I was afraid of that. Some of the thermonuclear explosions are at the edge of the atmosphere. We're getting ElectroMagnetic Pulse effects, and that's wiping out the signals. We're safe enough, all the Wherry system was hardened long ago. I'm not sure about that ship. I'm going to try a laser channel, hope they're hardened against EMP, and hope we're line-of-sight at the moment."

The reconnaissance screens told a chilling story. Every few seconds the detailed display shifted to show a new explosion. There was no time to identify each city before it vanished forever in the glow of hydrogen fusion. Only the day or night conditions of the image told the watchers in which hemisphere the missiles were arriving. It was impossible to estimate the damage or the loss of life before a new scene was crowding onto the screens. Salter Wherry was right, the hope of a pre-emptive first strike had proved an empty one.

Wolfgang and Charlene stood together in front of the biggest screen. It still showed the view from geostationary orbit. Again the display was sparking with bright flickers of light, but this time they were not the result of computer simulation. They were explosions, multiple warhead, multi-megaton. The whole hemisphere was riddled with dark pocks of cloud, as buildings, bridges, roads, houses, plants, animals and human beings were vaporized and carried high into the stratosphere.

"Hamburg." Wolfgang whispered the word, almost to himself. "See, that was Hamburg. My sister was there. Husband and kids, too."

Charlene did not speak. She squeezed his hand, much harder than she realized. The explosions went on and on, in a ghastly silence of display that almost seemed worse than any noise. Did she wish the screen showed an image of North America? Or would she rather not know what had happened there? With all her relatives in Chicago and Washington, there seemed no hope for any of them.

She turned around. On the floor, a mask had been placed over the lower part of Salter Wherry's face. Ferranti had opened Wherry's dark shirt, and was doing something that Charlene preferred not to look at too closely to his chest. The assistant was preparing a light-wheeled trolley to carry a human.

Dead, or alive? Charlene was shocked to see that Wherry was fully conscious, and that his eyes were swivelling to follow each of the displays. There was an intensity to his expression that could have been heart stimulants, but at least that dreadful glazed and filmy look was gone.

Charlene followed Wherry's look to the screen at the back of the room. A fuzzy image was building there, with a distorting pattern of green herringbone noise overlaid upon it. As the picture steadied and cleared, she realized that she was looking at Jan de Vries. He was sitting in a Shuttle seat, a pile of papers on his lap. He looked thoroughly nauseated. And he was crying.

"Dr. de Vries—Jan." Charlene didn't know if he could hear her or see her, but she had to cry out to him. "Don't try to rendezvous. We're operating a missile defense system here."

He jerked upright at her voice. "Charlene? I can hear you, but our vision system's not working. Can you see me?"

"Yes." As soon as she said the word, Charlene regretted it. Jan de Vries was dishevelled, there was a smear of vomit along his coat, and his eyes were red with weeping. For a man who was so careful to be well-groomed always, his present condition must be humiliating. "Jan, did you hear what I said?" she hurried on. "Don't let them try to rendezvous."

"We know." De Vries rubbed at his eyes with his fingers. "That message came in before anything else. We're in a holding orbit until we're sure it's safe to approach Salter Station."

"Jan, did you see any of it? It's terrible, the world is exploding."

"I know." De Vries spoke clearly, almost absently. Somehow Charlene had the impression that his mind was elsewhere.

"I have to talk to a doctor on Salter Station," he went on. "I would have done it before launch, but there was just too much confusion. Can you find me one?"

"There's one here—Salter Wherry had a heart attack, and she's looking after him."

"Well, will you bring the doctor to the communicator? It is imperative that I talk with her about the medical facilities on Salter Station. There is an urgent need for certain drugs and surgical equipment—" Jan de Vries suddenly paused, looked perplexed, and shook his head. "I'm sorry, Charlene. I hear you, but I am having difficulty in concentrating on more than one thing just now. You said that Wherry had a heart attack. When?"

"When the war started."

"A bad attack?"

"I think so. I don't know." Charlene couldn't answer that question, not with Salter Wherry gazing mutely at her. "Dr. Ferranti, do you have time to talk for a few moments with Dr. de Vries?"

The other woman looked up at her coldly from her position by Wherry. "No. I've got my hands more than full here. But tell me the question, and I'll see if I can give you a quick answer."

"Thank you," said de Vries humbly. "I'll be brief. Back on Earth there are—or were—four hospitals equipped to perform complete parietal resection, with partial removal and internal stitching of the anterior commissure. It needs special tools and a complicated pre- and post-operative drug protocol. I would like to know if such an operation could be performed with the medical facilities available at Salter Station's Med Center."

"What the hell is he going on about?" asked Hans in a gruff whisper over his shoulder to Wolfgang. "The world's going up in flames, and he's playing shop talk about hospitals."

Wolfgang gestured to Hans to keep quiet. Jan de Vries had stated many times that he was unencumbered in the world, an orphan with no living relatives, and no close friends. His griefs should not be for lost family or loved ones. But Wolfgang could see the look on de Vries' face, and something there spoke of personal tragedy more than any general Armageddon. A strange suspicion whispered into Wolfgang's mind.

Dr. Ferranti finally turned her head to stare at de Vries' image. "We don't have the equipment. And seeing that—" she jerked her head at the main display "—I guess we'll never have it."

Salter Station's orbit had steadily taken it farther west, to the sunlit side of Earth. Now they looked directly down on the Atlantic Ocean. The tiny dark ulcers on the Earth's face had spread and merged. Most of Europe was totally obscured by a smoky pall, lit from within by lightning flashes and surface fire-storms. The east coast of the United States should have been coming into view, but it was hidden by a continuous roiling mass of dust and cloud.

And the missiles were still being launched to seek their targets. As enemy missiles hit and vanished from the displays, new bright specks rose like the Phoenix from the seething turmoil that had been the United States, setting their paths over the pole towards Asia. The guiding hands that controlled them might be dead, but their instructions had long since been established in the control computers. If no one lived to stop it, the nuclear rain would fall until all arsenals were empty.

"Can you put together a facility for the operation?" asked de Vries at last. Unable to see the displays himself, he did not realize that everyone in the central control room was paralyzed by the scene of a dying Earth. His question was an urgent one, but no one would reply. Since the beginning of the day everything in de Vries' world had taken place in a slow dream, as though everything had already been running down before its final end.

"Can you build one?" he repeated.

Ferranti shivered, and finally replied. "If we wanted to we might be able to build a makeshift system to do the job—but it would take us at least five years. We'd be bootstrapping all the way, making equipment to make equipment."

She looked down again at Salter Wherry, and at once lost interest in talking further to de Vries. Wherry's breathing was shallower, and he was trembling. He appeared to be unconscious.

"Come on," she said to her assistant. "I didn't want to move him yet, but we have no choice. We have to take him back to the center. At once, or he'll be gone."

With Wolfgang's help, Wherry was carefully lifted on to the light-weight carrier. He still wore the breathing mask over his lower face. As he was lowered into position, his eyes opened. The pupils were dilated, the irises rimmed with yellowish-white. The eyeballs were sunk back and dark-rimmed. Wolfgang looked down into them and saw death there.

He began to straighten up, but somehow the frail hand found the strength to grip his sleeve.

"You are with the Institute?" The words were faint and muffled.

"Yes." It was a surprise to find that Wherry was still able to speak.

"Come with me."

The weak voice could still command. Wolfgang nodded, then hesitated as Ferranti prepared to wheel Wherry slowly away. Charlene was speaking to de Vries again, asking the question that Wolfgang himself had wanted to ask.

"Jan," she was saying. "We've tried to reach Niles. Where is she?"

"She is here. On this ship." De Vries put his hands to his eyes. "She's unconscious. I didn't want her to come. I wanted her to wait, build up her strength, have the operation, then follow us. She insisted on coming. And she was right. But back on Earth, she could have been helped. Now. . . ."

Wolfgang struggled to make sense of de Vries' words. But the frail hand was again on Wolfgang's arm, and the thread of voice was speaking again. "Come. Now. Must talk *now*."

Wolfgang hesitated for a second, then reluctantly followed the stretcher out of the control room.

Salter Wherry turned his head towards Wolfgang, and a dry tongue moved over the pale lips. "Stand close."

"Don't try to talk," said Ferranti.

Wherry ignored her. "Must give message. Must tell Niles what is to be done. You listening?"

"I'm listening." Wolfgang nodded. "Go ahead, I'll make sure that she gets the message."

"Tell her I know she saw through narcolepsy. Thought she might—too simple for her. Want her to know reason—real reason—why had to have her here."

There was a long pause. Wherry's eyes closed. Wolfgang thought that he had lapsed into unconsciousness, but when the old voice spoke again it sounded stronger and more coherent.

"I had my own reasons for needing her here—and she had hers for coming. I don't know what they were; I want her to know mine. And I want her to carry plan out here. I hoped we wouldn't blow ourselves up down there, but I had to prepare for worst. Just in time, eh?" There was a wheezing groan, that Wolfgang realized was a laugh. "Story of my life. Just in time. 'Nother day, we'd have been too late."

He moved his arm feebly as Ferranti took it to make an injection. "No sedatives. Hurts—in my chest—but I can stand that. You, boy." The eyes burned into Wolfgang. "Lean close. Can't talk much more. Tell you my dream, want you to tell Niles to make it hers."

Wolfgang stooped over the frail body. There was a long pause.

"Genesis. You remember Genesis?" Wherry's voice was fading, indistinct. "Have to do what Genesis says. 'Be fruitful and multiply.' Fruitful, and multiply."

Wolfgang looked quickly at Ferranti. "He's rambling."

"Not rambling." There was a faint edge of irritability still in the weak voice. "Listen. Made arcologies to go long way—seed universe. Be fruitful, and multiply. See? Self-sustaining, run thousand years—ten thousand. But can't do it. We're weak link. Fight, change minds, change societies, kill leaders, break down systems. Damned fools. Never last thousand years, not even hundred."

They had reached the Med Center, and Wherry was being lifted onto a table all prepared for emergency operations. A needle was sliding into his left arm, while a battery of bright lights went on all around them.

Wherry rolled his head with a last effort to face Wolfgang. "Tell Niles. Want her to develop suspended animation. That's why need Institute on station." The breathing mask had been removed, and there was a travesty of a smile on the tortured face. "Thought once I might be first experiment. See stars for myself. Sorry won't be that way. But tell her. Tell her. Cold sleep . . . end of everything . . . sleep. . . ."

Ferranti was at Wolfgang's side. "He's under," she said. "We want you out of here—we're going to operate now."

"Can you save him?"

"I don't think so. This is the third attack." She bit her lip. For the first time, Wolfgang noticed her large, luminous eyes and sad mouth. "Last time it was a patch-up job, but we hoped it would last longer than this. One chance in ten, no more. Less unless we start at once."

Wolfgang nodded. "Good luck."

He made his way slowly back along the corridors. They were deserted, everyone on the station had retreated with their thoughts. Wolfgang, usually impervious to fatigue, felt drained and beaten. The explosions on Earth rose unbidden in his mind, a collage of destruction with Jan de Vries' sad face overlaid on it. The morning optimism and the joking inventory of supplies with Charlene felt weeks away.

He finally came to the control room. Hans was alone there, watching the displays. He seemed in a shocked trance, but he roused himself at Wolfgang's voice.

"The missile defense system has been turned off.

They were too busy with themselves—down there—
to waste their time on us. Your ships will start
docking any time now."

"What's the situation. . . ." Wolfgang nodded his
head at the screen, where the big display showed
the smudged and raddled face of Earth.

"Awful. No radio or television signals are coming out—or if they're trying, they're lost in the
static. We tried for an estimate of released energy,
just a few minutes ago. Thirty thousand mega-
tons." Hans sighed. "Four tons of TNT for every
person on the planet. There's night now, all over
Earth—sunlight can't penetrate the dust clouds."

"How many casualties?"

"Two billion, three billion?" Hans shook his head.
"It's not over yet. The climate changes will get the
rest."

"*Everyone?* Everyone on Earth?"

Hans did not reply. He sat hunched at the console, staring at the screen. The whole face of the
planet was one dark smear. After a few seconds
Wolfgang continued back to his own quarters. Hans
and the others were right. Soon the ships would be
docking, but before that there was the need for
solitude and silent grief.

Charlene was waiting for him in a darkened
room. He went and took her in his arms. For several minutes they sat in silence, holding each other
close. The pace of events had been so fast for many
hours that they had been numbed, and only now
did their awful significance begin to sink home.
For Charlene in particular, less than twenty-four
hours away from Earth and the Neurological Institute, everything had a feeling of unreality. Soon,
she felt, the spell would break and she would return to the familiar and comfortable world of ex-

periments, progress reports, and weekly staff meetings.

Wolfgang stirred in her arms. She lifted his hand and rubbed it along her cheek.

"What's the news on JN?" he said at last. "I didn't like the look of de Vries."

Charlene shivered in the darkness. "Bad as it could be. Jan met with her this morning, when she had the final lab test results. She has a rapidly-growing and malignant brain tumor—even worse than we'd feared."

"Inoperable?"

"That's the worst part—that's what Jan de Vries was asking about. There is an operation and associated chemotherapy program, one that's been successful four cases out of five. But only a handful of places and people could perform it. There's no way to do it on Salter Station—you heard Ferranti, it would take five years development."

"How long does she have?"

"Two or three months, no more." Charlene had held back her feelings through the day, but now she was quietly weeping. "Maybe less—the acceleration at launch knocked her unconscious, and that's a bad sign. It was only three-gee. And every facility that could have done the operation, back on Earth, is dust. Wolfgang, she's doomed. We can't operate here, and she can't go back there."

He was again silent for a while, rocking Charlene back and forward gently in his arms. "This morning we seemed at the beginning of everything," he said. "Twelve hours later, and now it's the end. Wherry said it: the end of everything. I didn't tell you this, but he's dying, too. I feel sure of it. He gave me a message for JN, to work on cold sleep for the arcologies. I promised to deliver it to her, and I will. But now it doesn't matter."

"They're all gone," said Charlene softly. "Earth, Judith Niles, Salter Wherry. What's left?"

Wolfgang was silent for a long time. In the darkness, feeling his body warm against her, Charlene wondered if he had really heard her. They were both beginning to drowse off, as nervous exhaustion drained away all energy. She felt too weak to move.

Finally Wolfgang grunted and stirred. He took a long, shivering breath.

"We're left," he said. "We're still here. And the animals, they're here too. Somebody has to look after them. They can't be left to starve."

He rested his head again on her shoulder. "Let's just stay here, try to sleep a little. Then we can go and feed old Jinx."

His words were broken and indistinct, fading into sleep. "Some things have to go on; even after the end of the world."

Chapter 11:

For almost four hours there had been no conversation. Each of the three white-garbed figures was absorbed with their particular duties, and the gauze masks imposed an added isolation and anonymity. The air in the chamber was freezingly cold. The workers rubbed at their chilled hands, but they were reluctant to wear thermal gloves and risk decreased dexterity.

The woman on the table had been unconscious throughout. Her breathing was so shallow that the monitor's reassurance was necessary to tell of her survival and stable condition. Electrodes and catheters ran into her abdomen, chest cavity, nose, eyes, spinal column, and skull. A thick tube had been connected to a major artery in the groin, ready to pump blood to the chemical exchange device that stood by the table.

All was ready. But now there was hesitation. The three checked the vital signs one more time, then by unspoken agreement went outside the chamber and removed their masks. For a few seconds they looked at each other in silence.

"Should we really go through with it?" said Charlene abruptly. "I mean, with the uncertainties and the risks—we have no experience with a human. Zero. And I'm not sure how any of the drug amounts should be adjusted for different body mass and body chemistry. . . ."

"What action would you suggest, my dear?" Jan de Vries had been the one who opposed the idea most vehemently when it was first proposed, but now he seemed quite calm and resigned. "Bring her body temperature back to normal? Try to wake her? If that is your suggestion, propose it to us. But *you* must be the one, not I, to face her and explain why we did not accede to her explicit wishes."

"But what if it doesn't work?" Charlene's voice was shaking. "Look at our record. It's so risky. We've had Jinx in that mode for only three weeks, that's all."

"And you argue that your experience with the bear is not applicable?"

"Who knows? There could be a hundred significant differences—body mass, pre-existing antigens, drug reactions. And some a lot more improbable than that. For all we know, it works for Jinx because of some *previous* drug used in our experiments with him. Remember, when we did the same sort of protocol with Dolly, it killed her. We need to try other tests, other animals—we need more time."

"We all know that." Wolfgang Gibbs didn't share de Vries' fatalist calm, or Charlene's nervous vacillation. He seemed to have an objective interest in the new experiment. "Look at it this way, Charlene. If we can move JN into Mode Two in the next few hours, one of two things will happen. If she stays stable and regains consciousness, that's fine. We'll try to communicate with her and find out how she feels. If we get her into Mode Two and she's *not* stable, we can try to bring her back to normal. If we succeed we'll have the chance to try again. If we fail, she'll die. That's what you're worried about. But if we don't *try* to stabilize in Mode Two, she's dead anyway—remember the diagnosis. She'll be gone in less than three months, and we can't change that. Ask it this way: if it were you on that table, what would you want us to do?"

Charlene bit her lip. There was a dreadful temptation to do nothing, to leave JN with her body temperature down close to freezing while they deliberated. But the temperature in the chamber was still dropping. Within the next half hour they had to bring Judith Niles back up to consciousness, or try for Mode Two.

"What's the latest report on Jinx?" Charlene said abruptly.

"He's fine."

"Right. Then I say, let's go ahead. Waiting won't help anything."

If the other two were startled at the sudden change of attitude, neither mentioned it. They adjusted their masks and went back at once into the chamber. Already the temperature inside had dropped another degree. The monitors recorded a pulse rate for Judith Niles of four beats a minute, and the chilled blood was driven sluggishly through narrowed veins.

The final stage began. It would be carried out under computer control, with the humans merely there to provide an override if things went wrong. Jan de Vries initiated the control sequence. Then he went across to the still figure on the table and gently placed the palm of his hand on her cold forehead.

"Good luck, Judith. We'll do our best. And we'll be communicating with you—God willing—when you get there."

He stood looking at her face for a long time. The carefully-measured drug injections and massive transfusion of chemically-changed blood had already begun. Now the monitors showed strange patterns, steady periods alternating with abrupt changes in pulse rate, skin conductivity, ion balances, and nervous system activity. Oscilloscope displays showed unpredictable peaks and valleys of brain rhythms, as cycles of waves rose, fell, and merged.

Even to the experienced eyes of the watchers, everything on the monitors looked odd and unfamiliar. And yet that was no surprise. As she had requested, Judith Niles was embarked on a strange journey. She would be exploring a region where blood was close to freezing, where the body's chemical reactions proceeded at a fraction of their usual rates, where only a few hibernating animals and no human had ever ventured and returned to life.

The frozen heart slowed further, and the blood drifted lazy along cold arteries and veins. The body on the table suddenly shuddered and twitched, then was quiet again. The monitors fluttered a warning.

But there would be no going back now. The search was on. In the next few hours, Judith Niles would be engaged in a desperate quest. She had to find a new plateau of physiological stability, down where no human had ever gone before; and her only guide was the uncertain trail left by one Kodiak bear.

PART II

A.D. 27,698

"Any sufficiently advanced technology is indistinguishable from magic"—Proverbial, attributed to the pre-Flight philosopher/writer Isaac (?) Clarke, 1984(?)-2100(?) (Old Calendar); Central Record Library, Pentecost. (Bubble memory defective; this section of records unreliable)

Chapter 12: *Pentecost*

The last shivering swimmer had emerged from the underground river, and now it would be possible to assemble the final results. Peron Turco pulled the warm cape closer about his shoulders and looked back and forth along the line.

There they stood. Four months of preliminary selection had winnowed them down to a bare hundred, from the many thousands who had entered the original trials. And in the next twenty minutes it would be reduced again, to a jubilant twenty-five.

Everyone was muddied, grimy, and bone-weary. The final trial had been murderous, pushing minds and bodies to the limit. The four-mile underwater swim in total darkness, fighting chilling currents through a labyrinth of connecting caves, had been physically demanding. But the mind pressure, knowing that the oxygen supply would last for only five hours, had been much worse. Most of the contestants were slumped now on the stone flags, warming themselves in the bright sunlight, rubbing sore muscles and sipping sugar drinks. It would be a little while before the scores could be tallied, but already their attention was turning from the noisy crowds to the huge display that formed one outer wall of the colosseum.

Peron shielded his eyes against Cassay's morning brilliance and studied each face in turn along the long line. By now he knew where the real competition lay, and from their expressions he sought to gauge his own chances. Lum was at the far end, squatting cross-legged. He was eating fruit, and he looked bored and sweaty. Somehow Pentecost's hot summer had left his skin untouched. He stood out with a winter's paleness against the others.

Ten days ago Peron had met him and dismissed Lum as soft and overweight, a crudely-built and oafish youth who had reached the final hundred contestants by a freakish accident. Now he knew better. The fat was mostly muscle, and when necessary Lum could move with an incredible grace and speed; and the fat face and piggy eyes hid a first-rate brain and formidable imagination. Peron had revised his assessment three times, each one upwards. Now he felt sure that Lum would be somewhere high in the final twenty-five.

And so would the girl Elissa, three positions to the left. Peron had marked her early as formidable competition. She had started ten minutes ahead of him in the first trial, when they made the night journey through the middle of Villasylvia, the most difficult and dangerous forest on the surface of Pentecost.

Peron had been very confident. He had been ʳⁱsed in wooded country. He was strong and ag- and his sense of direction was better than any- ᵤₙe he had ever met. After two hours, when he had failed to overtake Elissa, he was convinced that the dark-skinned girl had gone astray and was lost in the dangerous depths of Villasylvia. He had felt mildly sorry on her behalf, because before they began she had smiled and wished him luck; but most of his attention was on avoiding the darters and night-lappers that ruled the nightwoods.

He had made splendid time, striking a lucky path that took him back to base without any detours or backtracking. It had come as a great shock to reach home and find her there well before him, fresh and cheerful, and humming to herself as she cooked her breakfast.

Now Elissa turned to look at him while he was still staring along the line at her. She grinned, and he quickly averted his eyes. If Elissa didn't finish among the winners, that would be bad news for Peron, too; because he was convinced that wherever they placed, she would rank somewhere above him.

He looked back at the board. The markers were going up on the great display, showing the names of the remaining contestants. Peron counted them as they were posted. Only seventy-two. The last round of trials had been fiercely difficult, enough to eliminate over a quarter of the finalists completely. No Planetfest celebration for them. They would already be headed back to their home towns, too disappointed to wait and find out who the lucky winners might be.

Peron frowned and looked again along the line of finalists. Where was Sy? Surely he hadn't failed to finish? No, there he was, lounging a few yards behind the others. As usual, he was easy to miss—he blended inconspicuously into any scene, so that it had taken Peron a while to notice him. He shouldn't have been difficult to pick out, with his black hair,

bright grey eyes, and slightly deformed left fore-
arm. But he was somehow difficult to *see*. He could
sink into the background, quietly observing everything with the cynical and smug expression that
Peron found so irritating—perhaps because he suspected that Sy really *was* superior? Certainly, on
anything that called for mental powers he had
effortlessly outperformed Peron (and everyone else,
according to Peron's rough assessment); and where
physical agility or strength was needed, Sy somehow found a way to compensate for his weakened
arm. It was a mystery how he did it. He was never
in the first rank for the most physical of the trials,
but given his handicap he was much higher than
anyone could believe.

Now Sy was ignoring the display and concentrating all his attention on his fellow contestants,
clearly evaluating their condition. Peron had the
sudden suspicion that Sy already knew he was in
the top twenty-five and was looking ahead, laying
his plans for the off-planet tests that would determine the final ten winners.

Peron wished he could feel that much confidence.
He was sure (wasn't he?) that he was in the top
thirty. He *hoped* he was in the top twenty, and in
his dreams he saw himself as high as fourth or
fifth. But with contestants drawn from the whole
planet, and the competition of such a high cali-
ber. . . .

The crowd roared. At last! The scores were finally appearing. The displays were assembled
slowly and painstakingly. The judges conferred in
great secrecy, knowing that the results would be
propagated instantly over the entire planet, and
that a mistake would ruin their reputations; and
the individuals responsible for the displays had

been influenced by the same obsession with care and accuracy. Everything was checked and re-checked before it went onto the board.

Peron had watched recordings of recent Planet-fests, over and over, but this one was different and more elaborate. Trials were held every four years. Usually the prizes were high positions in the government of Pentecost, and maybe a chance to see the Fifty Worlds. But the twenty-year games, like this one, had a whole new level of significance. There were still the usual prizes, certainly. But they were not the real reward. There was that rumored bigger prize: a possible opportunity to meet and work with the Immortals.

And what did *that* mean? Who were the Immortals? No one could say. No one that Peron knew had ever seen one, ever met one. They were the ultimate mystery figures, the ones who lived forever, the ones who came back every generation to bring knowledge from the stars. Stars that they were said to reach in a few days—in conflict with everything that the scientists of Pentecost believed about the laws of the Universe.

Peron was still musing on that when the roar of the crowd, separated from the contestants by a substantial barricade and rows of armed guards, brought him to full attention. The first winner, in twenty-fifth place, had just been announced. It was a girl, Rosanne. Peron remembered her from the Long Walk across Talimantor Desert, when the two of them had formed a temporary alliance to search for underground water. She was a cheerful, tireless girl, just over the minimum age limit of sixteen, and now she was holding her hand to her chest, pretending to stagger and faint with relief because she had just made the cutoff.

All the other contestants now looked at the board with a new intensity. The method of announcement was well established by custom, but there was not a trial participant who did not wish it could be done differently. From the crowd's point of view, it was very satisfying to announce the winners in ascending order, so that the name of the final top contestant was given last of all. But during the trials, every competitor formed a rough idea of his or her chances by direct comparison with the opposition. It was easy to be wrong by five places, but errors larger than that were unlikely. Deep inside, a competitor knew if he were down in ninetieth place. Even so, hope always remained. But as the names gradually were announced, and twenty-fourth, twenty-third, and twenty-second position were taken, most contestants were filled with an increasing gloom, panic, or wild surmise. Could they possibly have placed so high? Or, more likely, were they already eliminated?

The announcements went on steadily, slowly, relentlessly. Twentieth position. Seventeen. Fourteen.

Number ten had been reached: Wilmer. He was a tall, thin youth whose head was completely hairless. Either he shaved it daily, or he was prematurely bald. He was always hungry and always awake. The rest of them had joked about it—Wilmer cheated, he refused to go to sleep until everyone else had nodded off. Then he slept *faster* than other people, which wasn't fair. Wilmer took it all good-naturedly. He could afford to. Needing hours less sleep than the others, he could spend more time preparing for the next trial.

Now he lay back on the stones and closed his

eyes. He had always said that when this stage of the trials was over he would sleep for ten days solid.

The list advanced to number five. It was Sy. The dark-haired youth appeared to be as cool as ever, with no visible sign of pleasure or relief. He was standing with his head slightly inclined, cradling his weak left elbow in his right hand and not looking at anyone else.

Peron felt his own stomach tightening. He had passed the positions he expected to occupy, now he was in a region where only his wildest hopes had taken him.

Number four: Elissa. She whooped with delight. Peron knew he should feel pleased, but he had no room in him now for pleasure. He clasped his hands tightly together to stop them shaking, and waited. The display was static, never changing. The colosseum seemed to be full of a terrible silence, though he knew the crowd must be cheering wildly.

Number three. The letters went up slowly. P-e-r-o-n o-f T-u-r-c-a-n-t-a. He felt his lungs relax in a long, tortured gasp. He had been unconsciously holding his breath for many seconds. He had done it! Third place. *Third place!* No one from his region had ever placed so high, not in four hundred years of Planetfest games.

Peron heard the rest of the results, but they scarcely registered. He was overwhelmed with pleasure and relief. Some part of his mind puzzled when the second place winner, Kallen, was announced, because he hardly recognized the name. He wondered how they could have passed through so many difficult trials together without ever having spoken to each other. But everything—the crowd, the colosseum, the other contestants—seemed miles away, mirages in the bright yellow sunlight.

The last name appeared, and there was a final huge roar from the crowd. Lum! Lum of Minacta had won first place! No one would begrudge him his triumph, but he would be a sad disappointment to all the parents who urged their sons and daughters to live good lives so that they could be the winner of the Games. Who would want to be a winner, if it meant growing up big, meaty, and coarse-looking like this year's?

There was a commotion at the end of the line. Two of the girls near to Lum had given him a hug, then tried to lift him onto their shoulders to carry him forward in triumph towards the crowd. After a few moments it became obvious that he was too heavy. Lum leaned forward, grabbed one girl in each arm and lifted them up. They perched, one on each shoulder, as he strode forward to the barricade. He held up his hands and did a quick pirouette, while the crowd went berserk.

"Come on, misery!" The voice came from Peron's side. It was Elissa, who grabbed his arm as he turned to face her. "You look as though you're going to sleep. Let's get in and celebrate—we're *winners*! We should act like it."

Before he could object she was dragging him forward to join the others. The party was beginning. Winners and losers, everyone had lost their fatigue. Now that the contest was over, and the bets had been decided, the crowd would treat them all as winners. Which they were. They had survived the most gruelling tests that Planetfest could provide. And now they would celebrate until Cassay went down in the sky, until only the feeble red light of Cassby was left to lead them to their dormitories.

Planetfest was over for another four years. Few people ever stopped to think that the final winner had not yet been selected. The last trials took place off-planet, away from the high publicity, far away where no announcements were made. The contestants knew the truth: a tougher, unknown phase still lay ahead, where the only prize would be knowledge of victory. But the cash prizes, the celebrations by whole provinces, the public applause, and the generous family pensions were not based on off-planet results. So to most of the inhabitants of Pentecost—to almost everyone but the finalists themselves—the planetary games were over for another four years.

And Lum's name, Lum of Minacta, stood above all others.

Chapter 13:

"I'm sure you feel you've been through a lot. Well, it's my job to tell you that hard times are just beginning. Take a word from Eliya Gilby, you've seen *nothing*. Compared with the off-planet tests, the crappy Planetfest games are for kiddies."

The speaker was a thin, grey-haired man dressed in the black leather and glittering brass of a System Guard. His face wore a sardonic smile that could be read equally as pity, contempt, or dyspepsia. He was unable to stand still as he spoke. He paced in front of the silent group, and all the time his hands were also in motion, pulling at his belt, adjusting his collar, or rubbing at bloodshot eyes.

The Planetfest winners who made up his audience were in much better shape. The offers of drinks, drugs, and stimulants from the celebrating well-wishers had been numerous, but years of preparation for the trials had taught the contestants self-control. And a quiet sleep until almost midday, without having to plan for the next trial, had been a restorative and a luxury. They looked at each other as the guard was speaking, and exchanged secret smiles. Captain Gilby was in terrible condition. He had refused no offers of free drinks, by the look of it. There was no doubt that he was hung over—and badly—from a night's long revelry.

Captain Gilby moved his head from side to side, very slowly. He grunted, sighed, and cleared his throat. "Bloody hell. All right, here we go. It's my job to try to explain the Fifty Worlds to you. But I can tell you now, there's no real way you'll know what they're like until you've been there for yourself. Take my word for it, I've made six trips off planet, with six lots of you winners, all over the Cass system. And everybody tells me when they see the real thing that my pictures are useless. And I agree. But my bosses won't listen to that, so today that's what you get. Pictures. They won't give you more than a faint idea, but they're *all* you'll get until next week."

He sniffed, bent forward slowly and carefully, and lifted up a large, flat case. "Let's take a look at a few pictures of Barchan, in near to Cassay. There's a hell-hole for you, if you want my opinion. I suppose it's too much to hope that any of you already know something about it?"

Wilmer looked around him, then raised a tentative hand. "I do."

Gilby stared at him. "Do you now? Mind telling me how, since that sort of knowledge shouldn't be public down on Pentecost."

"My uncle was a Planetfest winner, twelve years ago. Last year I asked him about the off-planet trials."

"Before you even started on the first round for Planetfest! Cocky little bastard, aren't you? So tell us all about Barchan."

"Sand dunes, just like the picture shows. Primitive vegetable life, no animals, not much atmosphere. And hot as blazes except at the poles. Hot as melted lead." Wilmer hesitated, then added: "Not my choice for a trial. If it's held there it will mean hotsuits all the time."

"Now then, no trying to influence the others," said Gilby mildly. While Wilmer had been talking a tray of hot drinks had arrived, and the captain was eyeing it longingly. "But the rest of what you say is right enough. Hot enough to boil your balls off in two minutes, if your suit fails. And if you *have* balls. Barchan is only a hundred and twenty million kilometers from Cassay. Let's look at another one, a bit farther out. This is Gimperstand. Know anything about it?"

Gilby was holding up two pictures. One showed a space view of a greenish-brown ball, the other a lush jungle of incredibly tangled vines. Wilmer shook his head, and no one else seemed ready to speak.

"And you probably don't want to. It's officially Gimperstand, but the unofficial name we have for it is *Stinker*. And it deserves it. There's an atmosphere. It's a little thin, but in principle it's breathable. I've tried it. Two breaths make you run off and puke. It's something one of the vines releases, and it makes night-lapper shit smell like honeysuckle. A real stinkeroo. One whiff of it will knock you flat."

He held the pictures out delicately at armslength, then dropped them back into the case.

"We have a lot of ground to cover, but I don't think we'll do it all right now. For a start, I don't think you lot can absorb much at a time. And for a second, I want one of those drinks or I'll fall down right here." He walked over to the tray and grinned unpleasantly at his audience. "I'm glad it's you doing the trial, not me. We've got some monsters out there in the Cass System. You've seen the official planet names in school, but that's not what people who've been there call them. And their names are a lot more accurate. There's Bedlam, and Boom-Boom, and Imshi, and Glug, and Firedance, and Fuzzball. And when we get to the Outer System, it's even worse. We've got to take a look at Goneagain, and Jellyroll, and Whistlestop, then Whoosh, Pinto, Dimples, Camel, and Crater. They're not called the Fifty Worlds for nothing, and every one can be a death trap." He picked up a flask, took a tentative sip, and gave his audience another sadistic grin. "Don't you think your worries are over. By the time the off-planet tests are done you'll be wishing that you'd gone back home today with the losers."

The whole afternoon had been devoted to briefings, by Gilby and others. Then came news conferences and meetings with the VIP's from each winner's home area. It was late evening before they had any time to themselves, or even time for food. Peron had found a quiet place in a corner of the food area and was eating alone. But he was more than pleased when Elissa carried a tray over and seated herself opposite him uninvited.

"Unless you're hiding away for a good reason, I thought I'd join you. I've already talked to Lum and to Kallen, now I want to pay my respects to you."

"You're working down the whole list of winners, in order?"

She laughed. "Of course. Doesn't everyone? No,

I was just joking. I'm interested in you, so I thought it would be nice to eat dinner together—unless you really are hiding away?"

"I'm not. I'm brooding. I've just been sitting here and thinking how damnably rude everybody has been today. It started this morning with Captain Gilby, and I just assumed it was his hangover. But it's been getting *worse*. We're polite to everyone, and people we meet—complete strangers, most of them—treat us like dirt."

"Of course they do," said Elissa. "Better get used to it. They don't mean any harm. But see, we're the Planetfest winners, names in lights, and that makes us a big deal. A lot of people have to keep telling themselves that we're not all that great, that they're just as good as we are. And one way they convince themselves of that is by putting us down."

"I'm sure you're right." Peron looked at Elissa with respect. "But I wouldn't have thought that way. You know, this is going to sound stupid, but I still can't believe that I came higher than you in the rankings. You did better than me in everything. And I think you think better. I mean, more perceptively. I mean, you're—"

"If you're getting ready to ask me to go out for a walk," said Elissa, "there are more direct ways." She leaned forward and put her hand on Peron's arm. "All you have to do is say it. You're the exact opposite of Sy. He thinks everybody else is some sort of trained ape. But you always undervalue yourself. That's rare for a winner in Planetfest. Most people are like me, pushy. And as for Lum—"

"And as for Lum—" echoed a voice behind her. "What about him? Something nice, I hope."

It was Lum, and he had with him Kallen, the second place winner.

"Good. It's convenient to find you two together," he said. He hoisted one huge thigh and buttock to perch on the corner of their table, threatening to overturn the whole thing. "Do you feel up to another interview tonight? The Planetfest organizers would like to meet with the top five."

"First things first, Lum," said Elissa. "Peron, you have to meet the mystery man. This is Mario Kallen."

"Hello." Peron stood up to take the hand of the second place winner, and found he was grasping empty air. Kallen was blushing a bright red, and looking away.

"Pleased to meet you." The voice was a whisper, deep in the throat. Peron looked at Kallen again, and noticed for the first time the red lines of scar tissue on his Adam's apple.

"Let's all sit down," said Lum cheerfully. "We have an hour yet before the interview, and I want to tell you what Kallen has been telling me, about Planetfest."

"Don't you have to find Sy, too?" asked Elissa.

"I already did. He told me to go to blazes, said he didn't want any fool interviews." Lum pulled back the bench so that he and Kallen could sit down. "He's an interesting case, old Sy. I don't know how he could do so well with that injured arm, but he certainly didn't get any extra points from the judges for tact and diplomacy."

Elissa winked at Peron. Nor does Lum, said her smile. She turned innocently back to the other two.

"I've thought of nothing but Planetfest for two years. But I'd like to hear something new."

"You will," said Lum grimly. "Go on, Kallen."

Kallen sat for a moment, rubbing his hands together. He again turned red with embarrassment. "I thought of nothing but Planetfest, too," he said at last, in that throaty, pained voice. Then he hesitated, and looked helplessly from one person to the next. What had been difficult to tell to one person was impossible to tell to three.

"How about if I say it, and you tell me when I get it wrong?" said Lum quickly. "That way I'll have a chance to see if my understanding is correct."

Kallen nodded gratefully. He smiled in a sheepish fashion at Elissa, then looked away to the corner of the room.

"I suspect we all did the same sort of thing when we started out in the trials," said Lum. "Once I knew I was going to be involved, I set out to discover everything I could about the Planetfest games—when they started, how they're organized, and so on. I'd heard all the vague legends—about the Gossameres, and the Immortals, and Pipistrelle, and Skydown, and the Kermel Objects. And S-space, and N-space. I wanted to know what they were all about, or at least get the best rumors I could."

Peron and Elissa nodded assent. It was exactly what they had done themselves.

"But Kallen's case was a little different. He was legally old enough—just—for the *previous* games. He was born on the exact cutoff date, right at midnight. And he went through all the preliminary rounds then. He aced them."

Kallen blushed a brighter red. "Never said that at all," he whispered.

"I know. But it's true. Anyway, that's when he had his accident. A carriage wheel broke apart as it went past him, and a piece of a spoke speared his throat. It cost him his vocal chords, and it took him out of circulation for almost a year. And of course it killed off all his hopes for the trials. That looked like the end of it, except that Kallen was born in border country, between two planetary time zones. He found out his birth was recorded twice, in two different zones. According to one zone he was an hour younger. Still young enough to try again, in *this* trial. So he applied again, and here he is.

"But before the trials began this time, he was very curious to catch up on the results of the last one. He remembered the people who had competed, and he was pretty sure, from his own experiences, who the winners would be. He checked, and sure enough he was right. The top twenty-five had seven people that he remembered. And in the off-planet tests, three of those had finished in the final ten. They had gone through the preliminary rounds with Kallen, and they'd all become pretty good friends."

Peron and Elissa were listening, but they were both beginning to look a little puzzled. It hardly seemed that Kallen's tale held any surprises.

Lum had caught the look that passed between them. "Wait a bit longer before you yawn off," he said. "You'll find something to keep you awake in a minute. I did.

"He tried to get in touch with them, but not one of them had gone back to their home region. According to their families, they were all working in big jobs for the government, and they all sent messages and pictures home. Kallen saw the videos, and it was the same three people he remembered. And the messages replied to questions from their families, so they couldn't be old videos, stored and sent later. But they never came home themselves, not in four years. They had stayed off-planet. They were out there, somewhere in the Fifty Worlds.''

Kallen lifted his hand. "Don't assume that," he whispered. "I don't assume that."

"Quite right. Let's just say they *might* be somewhere in the Cass System. Or they could be even farther away. Anyway, at that point, Kallen got nosy. He checked back to the previous Planetfest, the one before he was involved. With over a billion people on Pentecost, the odds that you'll know a finalist personally are pretty small. But you know the old idea, we're only three people away from anybody. You'll know somebody who'll know somebody who'll know the person you want to get to. Kallen started looking—he's persistent, I found that out the hard way in the Seventh Trial, when we were both lost in The Maze. And he finally found somebody who had been knocked out in the preliminary trials from the earlier 'Fest, but who was a friend of a winner. And *that* winner had never been home since the off-planet trials.''

Lum paused and stared at Peron, who was nodding his head vigorously. "You don't seem very surprised. Are you telling me you know all this?''

"No. But I had a similar experience. I tried to reach a former winner from our region, and I got the run-around. She was supposed to be off-planet, and unavailable, but she'd be happy to answer written questions. And she did, eventually, and sent a video with it. Kallen, are you suggesting that none of the off-planet winners comes back to Pentecost? That doesn't seem to make much sense. Why would they want to stay away?''

Kallen shrugged.

"No reason that we can think of," said Lum. "Let me give you the rest of it. When Kallen went through the preliminaries on the previous Planet-fest, there was a contestant called Sorrel. He never came first in any trial, but he was always high enough to make the cutoff for the next round. He was easy-going, and popular, and he seemed to hit it off well with the guards, but he never got any publicity from the government media. Three other things: he never seemed to need much sleep; he tended to know bits and pieces of information that others didn't—because a cousin of his had been a finalist in a previous 'Fest. And he was completely bald. That make you think of anybody we know?"

"Wilmer," said Elissa and Peron in unison.

"But he can't be," went on Elissa. "He couldn't compete twice. He wouldn't be allowed to, unless he was a freak like Kallen—oh, don't look like *that*, you know what I mean, he'd have to be born at just the right time at exactly where two zones meet."

"Didn't compete—twice," said Kallen softly.

"Sorrel and Wilmer don't look anything like each other," added Lum. "Kallen is absolutely sure they are two different people. Wilmer didn't compete twice."

"Or even once?" said Peron thoughtfully. "We travelled back together after the Polar Trial. And I couldn't get a word out of him about the way he'd handled the glacier crossing and crevasses. He just grinned at me. I thought at the time, he's so cool and fresh, it's hard to believe he's just spent four-teen hours stretched to the limit."

"I agree," said Lum. "After I heard what Kallen had to say I had the same feeling. Wilmer's not a real contestant at all. He's a plant. I don't think he took part in any of the trials—no one saw him *during* them, only before and after. The question is, why put an outside observer in with the contestants?—and a completely bald one, at that, which makes him easy to remember."

"My father told me before I entered," said Peron. "There's more to Planetfest than the government wants to tell. He hates the government of Pentecost, and he didn't want me to take part in these trials. He says we've lived for the past four hundred and fifty years at a standstill, without real progress, ever since Planetfest began. But I didn't take much notice. He lives for underground politics, and since I was ten years old I've expected that one day he'll be arrested. Now you seem to be agreeing with him, the 'Fest had things in it that we've never been told about."

"But it doesn't answer Lum's question," said Elissa. She was tracing patterns in water droplets on the table top, but now and again her eyes did a quick survey of the room to see if anyone was watching them.

"Not yet," agreed Peron. "But give me a minute, and let me tell you the way my father would see it. First, Wilmer. Suppose he is a government plant. Then he is observing us for a definite reason. My father would say, there's no point in his presence if it has no effect on the Planetfest trial results. So that suggests the results are being tampered with— so that the right people win. But I just don't believe that. Too many people are involved in the evaluation and judging. So it has to be a little more subtle. Somebody wants to know how the winners will behave when faced with certain facts. And that's consistent with Kallen's other observation: something that we haven't been told about yet happens to Planetfest winners. Maybe not to all of them, but at least to some of them."

The other three were silent for a long time. They were looking at Peron expectantly. He finally realized that they were simply waiting. He remained silent himself, until at last Lum glanced at his watch.

"Five minutes more, then we have to go." His voice was respectful. "Carry on, Maestro, keep going and tell us the rest. I'm sure you're right so far. I'm beginning to feel less and less entitled to that number one rating."

Peron looked intently at each of the others. Elissa's eyes were downcast, staring thoughtfully at the table. Kallen and Lum were both visibly excited.

"First of all," Peron said. "If we know of *one* government plant in the group, there could be others. So we don't say anything to anyone, unless we're absolutely sure of the other contestant. That means people we knew before, or people we've worked with on trials who couldn't be fake competitors. What about Sy?"

Kallen shook his head. "He is a genuine competitor," he whispered. "And an amazing one. I spent time with him during some of the trials. He is much more intelligent and resourceful than any of us, but because of that withered arm he sees the world through a distorting mirror. We should tell him—though it will confirm all his worst suspicions about people."

It was Kallen's longest speech to the group. He seemed to realize that, and smiled at Elissa in an embarrassed way.

"All right, Sy is in," said Lum. "What else, Peron?"

It was disconcerting to be treated as an authority. Peron chewed at a fingernail, and thought hard.

"We don't have to do anything at all," he said at last. "Except keep our eyes open and our mouths shut. You see, it's obvious from what Kallen told you that at some point we *will* learn the mystery of the off-planet trials. The earlier winners must have been told. So we'll be told, too, and we'll find out what happens to the winners after the off-planet contest is over. There's no suggestion that anything bad happens to us—just that something is going on that the government doesn't want the public to know. I tend to agree with my father, that in itself is a bad thing. But until we know what it is, we can't disagree with it. So it's simple: for the moment we try to define how many of our group of twenty-five we can really trust. And from now on we question everything that we're told."

"You think we should even discuss this with others?" Lum stood up. "My preference is to tell no one else at all."

"We need all the eyes and ears we can find," said Peron. "We'll be careful."

They moved as a group to the exit, not speaking again until they were outside the food hall and heading for the Planetfest communication headquarters.

Lum and Kallen walked on ahead, leaving Peron and Elissa to stroll side by side through the chilly autumn air. Little Moon had already risen, and off near the horizon the red fire of Cassby threw long, ochre shadows across the deepening twilight.

Elissa stopped and looked up at the sky. It was

clear, and the stars were slowly appearing through the dusk.

"We'll be up there in a few days," said Peron. He took her arm in his. "We'll see the Fifty Worlds, and maybe we'll see The Ship. I've dreamed of that since I was four years old."

"I know. So have I. My aunt doesn't even believe there is a Ship. She says we've been here on Pentecost forever."

"What did you tell her?"

"Nothing. For someone with that view, logic is irrelevant—she'll believe what she chooses, regardless of evidence. Her religion says God placed us here on Pentecost, and for her that's the end of the argument."

"And you?" Peron was aware that she had moved in very close to him. "What do you think?"

"You know what I think. I'm cursed with a logical mind, and a lot of curiosity. That's why I'm taking a good look. Once we go up there, away from the planet, the sky will all be changed." She sighed. "When I used to think about going off-planet, back when I was little, it almost seemed the same as going to heaven. I thought that everything would be different there. No controls, no security officers, no guards, everything clear and simple. Now it's going to be another horrible contest."

Peron nodded. "That's why they won't let us be contestants after we're twenty years old. To do your best in the 'Fest, it's fatal if you question what you're doing too much. The trials need an uncluttered mind."

"Which we'll never have again. We've left the cradle, and there's no going back. Let's hope we'll find compensations." She took his hand and ran her fingertips gently over the palm. "Come on, let's get the interview over. Then you can take me for that walk—the one you were all ready to ask me about when Lum arrived."

Chapter 14:

For most of the journey up Captain Gilby had
harangued them incessantly. He had pointed out
the features of the ship, dwelling in detail on the
things that could go wrong during the ascent phase;
he had told them, again and again, that freefall
sickness was all psychological, to the point where
they would go to any lengths to vomit in private;
and he had asked each of the twenty-five to point
out their own region of Pentecost as the orbit carried them over it, sniffing contemptuously at their
failures. Recognizing a familiar land area from
space turned out to be harder than any of them
had anticipated. Cloud cover, haze, and oblique
angle changed all the usual elements of identifica-
tion.

But finally, when the spacecraft was nine thousand kilometers above Pentecost and approaching
The Ship, Gilby fell silent. This was a case where
he had learned to let the event itself overwhelm
the contestants, without his assistance.

The craft that had carried them up from the
surface of Pentecost was bigger than anyone had

expected. A vessel capable of carrying thirty people did not sound particularly large, even knowing in principle how much capacity was needed for fuel. The reality had rendered them speechless. They would ride to space at the top of a mammoth obelisk, towering twenty stories high above the flat plain of the Talimantor Desert.

Now they were facing another change of scale. The Ship had first appeared on the screens as a point of light, far above and ahead of them. As they slowly closed with it, and features became visible, the dimensions could be seen if not comprehended. They were looking at an irregular ovoid, a swollen ball covered with pimples, hair and scratches, like a diseased and mottled fruit. Closer approach brought more details. Each of the small nipples on the underside was a complete docking facility, capable of receiving a vessel the size of the one they rode in; the thin, hair-fine protrusions on the side were landing towers; the regular scratches were composed of a multitude of fine dots, each of them an entry port to the hull.

All conversation had ceased. They all realized the significance of the moment. They were looking at The Ship, the mystical, almost mythical structure that had carried their ancestors across the void from Earth, from a place that was so far away in time and space that it was beyond imagining.

"Take a good look at it," said Gilby at last. His lecture was continuing, but his voice had a different tone. "That was the only home of your ancestors for fifteen thousand years—three times as long as we've lived on Pentecost. The Ship roamed from system to system, never finding anywhere that could be a new home. It visited forty-nine suns and a hundred planets, and everywhere it was frozen, dead worlds, or burning deserts. Cass was the fiftieth system, and they found Pentecost. It was right to support human life. Paradise, eh? Do you know what happened then?"

They all remained silent, overwhelmed by the swelling presence of The Ship as it filled the screen in front of them.

"They argued," said Gilby. He paused in his fidgeting with his shoulder strap to touch his gunbelt. "They squabbled in The Ship, over whether or not they should leave it and land on Pentecost. The Ship was home, and half the people didn't want to leave it. It took two hundred years before the final transfer down took place and The Ship was left deserted. The final act was to move it to a high orbit, where it could circle Pentecost forever."

They had approached within a couple of kilometers, and were spiralling slowly around the shining hull. There was a burred, matte finish to the surface, the evidence of eons of meteor impact and the scouring of interstellar dust.

"Any chance we can all go on board?" asked Wilmer. Like a small child, he had pressed his nose to the transparent port.

Gilby smiled. "It's a shrine. No visitors allowed. The original travellers stated only one situation in which The Ship could be opened up to use again. It's not one we care to think about. The Ship will be re-opened and refurbished if nuclear weapons are ever used on Pentecost."

He pointed to the port. "Look out there now, and fix it in your memories. You won't see this again."

As he spoke they felt a steadily increasing acceleration pressing them back into the seats. The

Ship moved past their spacecraft, fell behind, and dwindled rapidly in size. They were heading farther out, out to the sprawling menagerie of planets that moved around and beyond Cassay and together made up the Fifty Worlds.

Seen through the best Earth telescopes, the system of Eta Cassiopeiae had been no more than twin points of light. It appeared as a striking red-and-gold binary, a glittering topaz-and-garnet jewel less than twenty light-years away from Sol. No amount of magnification by Earth observers could give any structural detail of the stellar components. But to the multiple sensors of *Eleanora*, curving on a slowing trajectory towards the brighter component of Cassiopeia-A, a system of bewildering complexity had revealed itself.

Cassiopeia-A is a yellow-gold star, stellar type GO V. It is a little brighter and more massive than Sol. Its companion is a red dwarf, lighter and only one twenty-fifth as luminous.

Dense, rust-red, and metal-poor, Cassiopeia-B keeps its distance from the bright partner. It never approaches closer than ten billion kilometers. Seen from the planets near Cass-A, the weak, rusted cinder of the companion appears far too feeble to have any influence. But the gravitational field is a long-range force. Gravitational effects of Cass-B had profound influence on the whole system. The planetary family that evolved around Eta Cassiopeiae is a whole zoo, with a bewildering variety of specimens.

Over fifty worlds reel and gyrate around the star pair. Their orbits are at all inclinations and eccentricities. The planets within a few hundred million kilometers of Cass-A exhibit orbital regularity and stable cycles, with well-defined orbital periods and near-circular orbits. But the outer worlds show no such uniformity. Some follow paths with both Cass-A and Cass-B as foci, and their years can last for many Earth centuries. Others, locked into resonances with both primaries, weave complicated curves through space, never repeating the pattern. Sometimes they will journey in lonely isolation, billions of kilometers from either star; sometimes they dip in close to the searing surface of Cass-A.

The travellers on *Eleanora* had concluded that a close encounter of a major planet was also the cause of the system's complexity. Millions of years earlier, a gas giant had come too close. It had skirted the very photosphere of Cass-A. First the volatile gases were evaporated away; then irresistible tidal forces caused disruption of the remaining core. The *ejecta* from that disintegration had been hurled in all directions, to become parts of the Fifty Worlds.

To the visitors approaching the system, the wild variations of the outer worlds at first seemed to dominate everything. The Cassiopeia binary complex was an unlikely candidate for human attention. Where orbits are wildly varying, life has no chance to develop. Changes are too extreme. Temperatures melt tin, then solidify nitrogen. If it is once established, life is persistent; it can adapt to many extremes. But there is a fragility in the original creation that calls for a long period of tightly-controlled variations.

The automated probes were sent out from *Eleanora*, but only because that was the procedure followed for many centuries. First returns confirmed an impression of scarred and barren worlds, bleak and empty of life. When the electronic reports were beamed back from the probe to Pentecost, they seemed just too good to be true. Here was a stable planetary orbit, close to circular, one hundred and ninety million kilometers from Cass-A. And Pentecost was a real Earth-analog, with native vegetation and animal life, acceptable temperatures, an eighteen degree axial tilt, twenty-two hour day, breathable atmosphere, forty percent ocean cover, a mass that was only ten percent less than Earth, and an orbital period only four percent longer than an Earth year.

It was hard to believe that Pentecost could exist amid the dizzying variations that comprised the Fifty Worlds. But the probes never lied. At last, after eons of travel between the stars, and endless disappointment, humanity had found a new home.

Chapter 15:

The Fifty Worlds held enormous diversity. Peron knew that. They were of all sizes, shapes, orbits, and environments. No two seemed even remotely alike, not even the twins of the doublet planet of Dobelle. And most of them fit poorly anyone's idea of a desirable place to visit, still less as the site for another trial.

And as for Whirlygig. . . .

Peron was approaching it now. He had to land there. Of all of them, he thought gloomily, this one has to be the most alien and baffling.

In the past two months the Planetfest winners had orbited over a dozen worlds. The planets had ranged from depressing to unspeakable. Barchan was a baking, swirling dust-ball, its surface forever invisible behind a scouring screen of wind-borne particles. They were held aloft by a thin, poisonous atmosphere. Gilby had warned them that Barchan would be a terrible choice for a trial (but he had said that about most places!). The dust and sand found its way into everything—including a ship's controls. There was a good chance that a landing on Barchan might be final.

Gimperstand was no better. The contestants had voted not even to look at it, after one of the ship's crew had produced a sample bottle of sap from Stinker's juicy vines. The bottle had been opened for less than two minutes. A full day later the air through the whole ship still *tasted*, like rotting corpses. Air purifier units didn't even touch it.

From a distance, Glug had looked pretty good. The ship's telescopes and scanners showed a green, fertile world, ninety percent cloud-covered. They had actually made a field trip down there, and spent a couple of hours squelching and sticking on the viscous surface. A steady grey rain drifted endlessly down from an ash-dark sky, and the sodden fronds of vegetation all drooped mournfully to touch the gluey soil. Once a boot had been placed firmly, the planet acted as though reluctant ever to release it. It clung lovingly. Walking was a pained sequence of sucking, glutinous steps, dragging the foot upwards inch by inch until it came free with a disgusting gurgle. As Wilmer had put it, once you had pulled your boot out you never wanted to put it back again—except that your *other* boot was steadily sinking in deeper.

Glug was revolting, but Peron thought it would still make the final list. Sy had even voted to make it his first choice! Maybe his complex thought processes had discovered something about Glug that could be turned to his advantage. Lum had pointed it out long ago to Peron and Kallen: Sy did not need an *edge* over others to win; all he needed was a situation that cancelled the handicap of his withered arm. Given that, he would wipe the floor with all of them.

Some of the others had also cast a tentative vote in favor of Glug; for by the time the contestants went there they had already visited some choice specimens:

Boom-Boom—constant volcanic activity and earthquakes; an ambient noise level that seemed to shatter eardrums; foul, sulphurous air and treacherous terrain, where fragile crusts of solidified lava stood above molten slag.

Firedance—only microscopic animal life, and at any time one sixth of the vegetation that covered the whole world was a smoldering, charred mass: the rest was bone-dry and ready to spring to blazing life after any random lightning stroke; ribbons of flame danced and crackled their twisting paths along the surface, changing direction unpredictably and moving far faster than a running human.

Fuzzball—every living thing, every plant or animal that lived under or on the surface, or in the salty seas of Fuzzball, served as a host to a single species of fungal growth; evolutionary adaptation appeared complete, so that the fungus did no harm; but its white, hair-fine tendrils sprouted from every inch of skin, and every animal's ears and nostrils carried their own harvest of delicate, trailing fronds; the prospect had been too much for the contestants, even though Gilby assured them that the fungus could be removed from them completely after leaving the planet. Fuzzball had received zero votes.

Goneagain sounded tolerable; but that little world had been ruled out by simple geometry. Its orbit was wildly eccentric, carrying it tens of billions of kilometers away from Cassay and Cassby. It would not return to the Inner System for another three thousand years.

And then there was Whirlygig. Peron peered ahead through the faceplate of his suit. Three hours to go, then he would be landing there—without a ship. Later (if all went according to plan) he would leave in the same way. Meanwhile, there was not a thing to be done until the moment of grazing impact was reached. Peron—not for the first time—wondered about his velocity calculation. He had checked it ten times, but if he were off by a few meters a second. . . .

He resolutely turned his mind to their earlier travels, and struggled to put Whirlygig out of his thoughts for the next three hours.

There were plenty of other things to think about. For the first two weeks of the journey away from Pentecost, privacy had been impossible for all of them. The shuttle vessel was impressively big, but with thirty people squeezed into a space intended for three crew and cargo, the contestants had been shoulder to shoulder. Not until transfer to the big Inter-System ship, after a short visit to Little Moon, did they have room to spare. And at last Peron had been able to compare notes with the others.

By careful cross-checking that had taken them several days, Lum and Kallen had accounted for all the winners. Wilmer was the only bogus contestant. They had also confirmed Peron's first impression: no one had been with Wilmer in any trial, and he had been suspiciously fresh after all of them. But the reason for his presence among them? No ideas from anyone. And to add to the mystery, Wilmer certainly *had* been with them on all the activities since they lifted off from Pentecost—which had sometimes been dangerous, as well as unpleasant.

Wilmer's innocent request to Gilby that they be

allowed to visit The Ship, along with Gilby's answer, had registered on both Peron and Elissa. Someone wanted the winners to know that The Ship was off-limits. But again, what did it *mean*? How was it connected with the fact that some previous winners of the Planetfest games had not returned to Pentecost?

Peron had bounced the questions off Sy, when they had a few minutes of privacy in the Inter-System ship. Sy had stood motionless, his eyes aloof.

"I don't know why The Ship is off-limits," he said at last. "But I agree with you that Gilby was prompted to tell us that. Let me tell you of a bigger mystery. After the off-planet trials the Immortals will supposedly appear. We are told that they will come from the stars, after a journey that will take just a few days. Do you believe that?"

"I don't know." Sy's question was voicing one of Peron's own worries. "If it is possible to travel faster than light, our theories of the nature of the universe must be wrong."

"That is *possible*," said Sy slowly—with a tone of voice that said clearly, that is quite impossible. "But don't you see the problem? If the Immortals can exceed lightspeed, they must have improved on our theories. And if they are so friendly to us, why do they keep that better theory from us?"

Peron had shaken his head. Anything about the Immortals remained a mystery.

"It is my personal belief that nothing can exceed lightspeed," said Sy at last. "I will mistrust anyone, government or Immortal, man or woman, human or alien, who attempts to tell me otherwise without providing convincing evidence."

And he had moved quietly away, leaving Peron

more puzzled than ever. Conversation with Sy often left that unsettling feeling. Lum had explained it in his offhand way—Sy was just a whole lot smarter than the rest of them. And Elissa had thrown in her own evaluation: Sy was not *smarter*, not if that meant either memory or speed of thought; but he could somehow see problems from a different angle from everyone else, almost as though he were located at a different point in space. His perspective was different, and so his answers were always surprising.

And if he weren't so strange, she had then added irrelevantly to Peron, he would be really attractive; which had of course irritated Peron greatly.

His thoughts moved inevitably back to Elissa and their last night on Pentecost. While Lum and Kallen had been working conscientiously to screen contestants, Peron had been subjected to a pleasant but intense cross-examination. He and Elissa had found a quiet place in the Planetfest gardens. They stretched out on the soft ground cover and stared up at the stars, and Elissa must have asked him a thousand questions. Did he have brothers and sisters? What was his family like? Were they rich? (Peron had laughed at the idea that his father could ever be rich.) What were his hobbies? His favorite foods? Did he have any pets back home? Had he ever been on a ship, across one of Pentecost's salt-water seas? What was his birthdate? *Do you have a girl friend, back in Turcanta?*

No, Peron had said promptly. But then his conscience had troubled him, and he told Elissa the truth. He and Sabrina had been very close for two years, until he had to devote all his time to preparation for the trials. Then she had found someone else.

Elissa didn't bother to disguise her satisfaction. She had quietly taken hold of Peron and begun to make love to him.

"I told you I was pushy," she said. "And you were acting as though you'd never get round to it. Come on—unless you don't want me? I've wanted to do this—and especially *this*—ever since I met you on the forest trial, back in Villasylvia."

They had done things together that Peron had never imagined—and he used to think that he and Sabrina had tried everything. Lovemaking with Elissa added a whole new dimension. They had stayed together through the night, while the fireworks of Planetfest celebrations fountained and burst above them. And by morning they seemed infinitely close, like two people who had been lovers for many months.

But that, thought Peron unhappily, made Elissa's comment about Sy much harder to take. If she thought Sy was attractive—hadn't she said *very* attractive?—did that mean she thought Sy was more interesting than he was? He remembered the last evening on Pentecost as fabulous, but maybe she didn't feel the same way. Except that everything since then suggested that she *did* feel that way, and why would she lie to him?

Peron's suit gave a gentle whistle, bringing him back from his dreaming. He felt irritated with his own train of thought. No denying it, he was feeling *jealous*. It was exactly the kind of mindless romantic mushiness that he despised, the sort of thing for which he had so teased Miria, his younger sister.

He looked straight ahead. No time for dreaming now. Here came Whirlygig, to teach him a lesson in straight thinking. He was within a couple of kilometers of the surface, travelling almost parallel to it but closing too fast for comfort.

Seen through a telescope, Whirlygig was not an interesting object. It was a polished silver ball about two thousand kilometers across, slightly oblate and roughened at the equator. Its high density gave a surface gravity at the poles of a fifth of a gee, a bit more than Earth's Moon. A person in a spacesuit, freefalling straight down to the surface of Whirlygig, would hit at a speed of two kilometers a second—fast enough that the object in the suit afterwards would hardly be recognizable as human.

But that was true for a fall towards any planet in the system, and people did not attempt landings on objects of planetary size without a ship; and the composition of Whirlygig was of no particular interest. The planet had been ignored for a long time, until finally some astronomer took the trouble to examine its rotation rate.

Then interest grew rapidly. Whirlygig was unique. What made it so had happened recently, as geological time is measured. A mere hundred thousand years ago a close planetary encounter had transferred to the body an anomalously high angular momentum. After that event Whirlygig was left spinning madly on its axis, completing a full rotation in only seventy-three minutes. And at that speed, centripetal acceleration on the equator just matched gravitational force. A ship flying in a trajectory that grazed Whirlygig's surface, moving at 1,400 meters per second at closest approach, could soft-land on the planetoid with no impact at all; and a human in a suit, with only the slightest assistance of suit steering jets, could do the same.

But theory and practice, thought Peron, were a long way apart. It was one thing to sit and discuss the problem on the Inter-System ship with the other contestants, and quite another to be racing in towards Whirlygig on a tangential trajectory.

They had drawn lots to see who would be first contestant down. Peron had "won"—Gilby's term, delivered with a sadistic smile. The others, following in pairs, would face a far easier task because of Peron's actions of the next few minutes. *If* he arrived in one piece.

He wondered what they would do if he *didn't* land safely—would they nominate someone else to try again? Or would they abandon the whole idea, and move on to another planet? A contestant in theory had just one shot at the trials (Kallen was a rare exception). But death was an earnest contender in every Planetfest games. The deaths of contestants were never mentioned by the government, and never given one word of publicity in the controlled news media; but everyone who entered the trials knew the truth. Not everyone went home a winner, or even a loser. Some contestants went forever into the shimmering heat of Talimantor Desert, or to a blood-lapped nightdeath in the woods of Villasylvia, or to a frozen tomb in the eternal snows of Capandor Mountains; or (Peron's own secret fear) to a slow asphyxiation in the underwater caverns of Charant River.

He shivered, and peered ahead. Those dangers were past, but death had not been left behind on Pentecost. He would visit Peron just as readily on Whirlygig. The equipment that Peron was hauling along behind him had seemed small when he left the ship, but now four hundred kilos of lines, springs, and pitons felt like a mountain, trailing half a kilometer directly behind him. Uncontrolled, they would envelop him on landing.

The surface felt so close that it seemed he could reach out a suited arm and touch it. He made small attitude adjustments with the suit jets. His velocity was just right for a stable orbit about Whirlygig at surface level. He turned his suit to land feetfirst, and touched, gently as a kiss.

He had landed softly, but at once there was a complication. He found he was at the center of a blinding cloud of dust, pebbles, and rock fragments. Effective gravity here on Whirlygig's equator was near to zero, and the shower of rock and sand was in no hurry to settle or disperse. Working purely by touch, Peron took one of the two pitons he was carrying, placed it vertically on the surface, and primed the charge. His hands were shaking in the gloves. *Must be quick.* Only thirty seconds left to secure a firm hold. Then he would have to be ready for the equipment.

The explosive charge in the top end of the piton exploded, driving the sharp point deep into the planet's surface. Peron tugged it briefly, made sure it was secure, then for double safety primed and set off the second piton. He braced two loops on his suit around the pitons, and looked back towards the moving bundles of equipment.

It seemed impossible. The equipment was still a couple of hundred meters away. The whole landing operation—minutes according to his mental clock—must have been completed in just a few seconds. He had time to examine the bundle of equipment closely, and decide just where he would secure it.

It swung in towards him, drifting down towards the surface. The velocity match had been exact. It was less than five minutes work to place another array of pitons in a parabolic curve along the surface, and set up catapult cables to run around the array. The final web of cables and springs looked fragile, but it would hold and secure anything with less than three hundred meters a second of relative velocity.

Peron made one last examination of his work, then activated the suit phone.

"All set." He hoped his voice was as casual as he would have liked it to be. "Come on in anytime. The catapult is in position."

He took a deep breath. *Halfway.* When they had explored the surface as a group, the catapult would be used to launch all the others away from Whirly-gig; and Peron would be alone again. Then he would make a powered ascent (with fingers crossed) to the safety of the waiting ship.

Chapter 16:

Peron could not recall the exact moment when he knew that he was going to die on Whirlygig. The knowledge had grown exponentially, over perhaps a minute, as his mind rapidly ran through every possible escape and rejected all of them as impossible. Cold certainty had finally replaced hope.

The landing had gone almost perfectly, as the six other contestants assigned to visit Whirlygig sailed in to a smooth encounter with the landing web. Wilmer, paired with Kallen, had proved the exception. He had come barreling in too fast and too high, and only Kallen's hefty pull on their line had brought him low enough to connect with the cables.

He seemed not at all upset by his narrow escape. "Guess you were right, Kallen," he said cheerfully, once he was safely down. "Odd, that. I'd have bet money I had the speed accurate and you had it wrong."

"Be thankful you weren't first man in," said Rosanne severely—she had seen how close Kallen had been to losing his own hold. "If Peron had done that he'd have been in big trouble. And what do you have in *there*? That's probably the mass you didn't allow for in your calculations."

Wilmer held up a green case. "In this? Food. I didn't know how long we'd be here. I've no wish to starve, even if you all don't mind it. And if I *had* been first one in, Rosanne, with my trajectory I'd also have been first one out. At that speed and height I'd have missed Whirlygig altogether. There's a moral in that: better come in too high and fast than low and slow."

He had begun to hop gingerly from one foot to the other, testing his balance. The effective gravity on Whirlygig's equator was not exactly zero, but it was so slight that a tumbling upward leap of hundreds of feet was trivially easy. Everyone had tried it, and soon lost interest. It took minutes for the feather-light float down back to the surface, and one experience of that was enough.

They soon began the careful trek away from Whirlygig's equator, travelling in small groups and heading for the comforting gravity of the polar regions. Only Sy was left behind, making his own solitary and perplexing experiments in motion over the rough terrain.

Progress for everyone was slower than expected. They could fly low over the surface with little effort, using the tiny propulsive units flown in after they were all landed. But Whirlygig's rapid rotation made Coriolis forces a real factor to reckon with, and allowing for them called for constant adjustment to the flight line. The suit computers refused to accept and track a simple north reckoning, and it was easy to stray twenty or thirty degrees off course. After they had been on the way for a couple of hours, Sy caught up and quickly passed them all. He had discovered his own prescription for estimating and compensating for Coriolis effects.

As they flew north the appearance of the land below gradually changed. The equator was all broken, massive rocks, heaped into improbable, gravity-defying arches, spires, and buttresses. A few hundred kilometers farther towards the pole the terrain began to smooth, settling down into a flatter wilderness of rugged boulders. It was not a pleasant landscape, and the temperature was cold enough to freeze mercury. But compared with some of the other worlds, Whirlygig seemed like vacation-land.

The suits had efficient recycling systems, and ample food supplies. The contestants agreed to carry on right to the pole, then rest there for a few hours before returning to the equator and leaving. According to Gilby they would find a sizeable research dome at the north pole, where they would be able to sleep in comfort and remove suits for a few hours. All scientific surveys on Whirlygig had been completed many years earlier, but the dome facilities should still be in working order.

Elissa and Peron had chosen to travel side by side, with their radios set for private conversation. The suit computers would monitor incoming messages and interrupt for anything urgent. Elissa was bubbling over with high spirits and cheerfulness.

"Lots of things to tell you," she said. "I didn't have a chance to talk to you yesterday, you were too busy getting ready for the landing here. But I've spent a lot of time making friends with one of the crew members—Tolider, the short-haired one with the pet tardy."

"That hadn't escaped my attention," said Peron

drily. "I saw you petting it and pretending you liked it, too. Disgusting. Why would anybody want a big, fat, hairy pet worm?"

Elissa laughed. "If I were to tell you what some people want with it, I'd shock your innocent soul. But Tolider just likes it for company, and he looks after it well. Love me, love my tardy, that's what he seems to think. Once he thought I was a tardy-lover, too, he was ready to bare his soul. Now, are you going to spend the next few hours sounding jealous, or do you want to know what he said?"

"Oh, all right." Peron's curiosity was too great to allow him to maintain an aloof tone, and he knew from his own experience how good Elissa was at winkling information out of anyone. "What did he tell you?"

"After he felt comfortable with me we talked about the Immortals. He says they aren't a hoax, or something invented by the government. And they aren't human, or alien, either. He says they are *machines*."

"How does he know?"

"He saw them. He's been working in space for over twenty years, and he remembers the last time the Immortals came. He said something else, too, once I'd softened him up—shut up, Peron—something that he says the government doesn't want anyone down on Pentecost ever to know. He told me because he wanted to warn me, because he feels sorry for me. He says that some of the winners of the Planetfest games who go off-planet are sacrifices to the Immortals. They—that means us—will become machines, themselves."

"Rubbish!"

"I agree, it sounds like it. But he made a lot of good points. You hear about the Immortals, but you never hear a description of one—no stories that they're just like us, or that they're big or little, or have green hair, or six arms. And you tell me: what *does* happen to Planetfest winners when they go off-planet?"

"You know I can't answer that. But we've seen videos of them, after they won the games. How could that happen if they had been converted to machines?"

"I'll tell you what Tolider says—and this is supposed to be common rumor through the whole space division. It's like an old legend that goes back to the time we were first contacted by the Immortals. We know that the computer records on The Ship were destroyed, but there's no real doubt that it left Sol over twenty thousand years ago, and travelled around in space until five thousand years ago when it found Pentecost."

"No one will argue with that, except maybe your old aunt who thinks we've been on Pentecost forever. We were even taught it in school."

"But the old records say that everything on Earth was wiped out, and everyone died in the Great Wars. Suppose that's not true—partly true, but exaggerated. Suppose there were enough people left to start over again, says Tolider, and suppose they survived the bombs and the Long Winter. They wouldn't be starting from scratch, the way we began on Pentecost. They'd be able to breed back quickly—it took us less than five thousand years to grow from The Ship's people to over a billion. Earth would have had at least fifteen thousand years to develop their technology, beyond anything we can imagine, while we were wandering round on The Ship, looking for a home. They would have machines hundreds of generations better than our best computers. Maybe they would have reached the point where the dividing line between organic and inorganic would be blurred. We definitely know they have better computers—did you realize that the Immortals, not Pentecost, control space travel through the Cass System, because their computerized tracking system is enormously better than ours? Sy told me that, and he got it from Gilby. Anyway, that's what Tolider believes: the Immortals are intelligent computers, maybe with biological components, sent here from Earth. There. You're the smart one—so find a hole in that logic."

They flew along in silence as Peron thought it over.

"I don't need to find a logical gap," he said at last. "Tolider's story doesn't fail on logical grounds, it fails on sense. People do things for *reasons*. If Earth had recovered and gone back to space, they might have sent ships out to look for us, sure—and for the other ships that supposedly left at the same time we did. Suppose that's true, and suppose they eventually found us. Then they'd come and tell us we had been discovered. Why would they ever *not* want to tell us? Tolider is repeating old stories. Nothing wrong with that, but you don't expect legends to make sense. Let me ask *you* a question that doesn't depend on myths for an answer. Supposedly we get scientific information from the Immortals, and they drop off a new batch of ideas every twenty years, along with a few rare materials that are in short supply in the Cass System. Right?"

"I think that's definitely true. Tolider says he has actually been involved in the materials transfer. He also says that the government down on

Pentecost is obsessed with control and maintaining the status quo, and that they use new technology to remain in power. That's why we've had a stable, single regime ever since we were contacted by the Immortals, and that's one reason he prefers to stay out in space where there's more freedom."

"He should meet my father—he's been saying for years that the government is run by a bunch of repressive tyrants. But don't you see the problem? The Immortals give us things, and it's a one-way transfer. Nobody, not even a machine, will stand for a one-way trade for four hundred and fifty years. If all they wanted to do was give us information, they could do that using radio signals. But they actually come here. So here's my question: What do the Immortals get from their visits to Pentecost?"

"Some of *us*, if you want to believe Tolider. You and me, that's what the government trades to get new information."

"That makes even less sense if we want to believe Tolider. We winners are a talented group, but we're not *that* special. If Earth had been repopulated to the point where they could explore the stars again, they'd have thousands like us."

"Tolider told me that we *are* an unusual group. Rumor says it's the first time for many games that all the top five in the Planetfest games are 'troublemakers'—he couldn't define the term for me."

"I think I can. We won't take answers without digging for ourselves. That's one reason I feel so comfortable with the rest of you."

"I'll accept that. So let me point out one other thing. You can tell me what it means. The contestant groups for surface visits to Glug and Bedlam and Crater and Camel and the other planets were all some random mixture of all twenty-five winners. But look who's here on Whirlygig: Sy, me, you, Kallen, and Lum—the top five, all 'troublemakers,' plus Rosanne and Wilmer. I think Rosanne would be classed as a wild one, too, difficult to control—your hair would curl if I told you some of the things she's done. And we all wonder about Wilmer. We've been specially *picked* for this trip, and I'm worried about what might happen here."

Peron moved their suits closer together so that he could see her face. He realized she was genuinely worried, not just joking. He reached across to take her suit glove. "Relax, Elissa. You're as bad as Tolider, all wild surmises. They wouldn't bring us all this way to dispose of us on Whirlygig. If we are that much of a nuisance we could have been chucked out of the contest back on Pentecost, and nobody would ever have suspected a thing." He laughed. "Don't worry. Now we've landed we're safe enough on Whirlygig."

They had made good progress. The north pole would soon be in sight. And in less than an hour, Peron would know the falseness of his final words.

The dome was a hemisphere of tough, flexible polymer, roughly twenty meters across. It was located on the exact axis of rotation of the planet. That axis was highly tilted to Whirlygig's orbit plane, so at this time of year the golden sun of Cassay was permanently invisible, hovering down over the other pole. Only the weak companion, Cassby, threw its ruddy glow across the landscape, providing adequate light but little heat. There were no free volatiles on Whirlygig, but the surface temperature at polar midwinter would be cold enough to liquefy methane.

Peron and Elissa had been too engrossed in their conversation to make the best speed from the equator, and they arrived last. The others were already landed, clustered around the dome. Sy Lum and Rosanne were inspecting the entry airlock, without touching any part of the door. Kallen and Wilmer were away around the back, on the opposite side of the dome, looking at something on the wall.

Elissa stepped close to see what Sy was doing. "Problems?"

Lum turned and nodded. "Wondered when you two would get here. Problems. Maybe we won't have a pleasant night out of our suits after all."

Sy was still crouched over by the door. He seemed rather pleased to be faced with the new challenge.

"See, here's how it's *supposed* to work," he said. "There's an airlock with an inner and outer door. The outer door, this one here, has a fail-safe on it, so it won't open when there's any gas pressure in the air-lock. First you have to pump out the lock to near vacuum, and you can do it from outside. That's this control, on the outside wall. When we arrived, there was atmosphere in the airlock, so naturally it wouldn't open. We pumped it out—the pumps work fine—but it *still* won't open."

"Motor failure?" asked Peron.

"Could be. The next step is to try to open it manually. But we want to be sure we know what we're doing. Over on the other side of the dome there's a big patch of black sealant. Suggests there was a meteor impact, and the self-repairing system took care of it. But we don't know what that may have done to the inside until we get there. And we don't know how much damage the mechanical systems may have suffered. Maybe the meteor hit the lock, too. We'll have to get in and find out."

Peron stepped forward to peer at the door. It appeared quite intact. "You're sure there's no pressure now in the airlock?"

"Positive. The gauge there is working. It showed positive pressure when we arrived, and as we pumped it went down to zero."

"So it should be safe enough to open manually," added Lum. "We were preparing to do that when you two arrived. Come on, another pair of hands may help a lot."

The outer door of the lock gave grudgingly, as Sy, Lum, and Peron jerked hard at it. Finally it was about halfway open, almost enough to admit a person.

"My turn now," said Rosanne. "I couldn't be much use in the tugging and heaving part, but I'm thin enough to get in there where you fatties can't, and see what's going on. Give me room."

She came to the lock door, turned sideways, and began to crab carefully into the opening.

Peron was standing just behind her. He heard Sy's warning yell at the same moment as the thought came into his own head. *Idiots! If we know the outer door isn't working right, why assume that the controls for the inner one are any better?*

He leaned forward, took Rosanne around the waist and with one movement propelled her back and sideways, away from the open outer door of the lock. He heard a gasp of surprise and annoyance over her radio as Rosanne skittered away across the silver-and-brown surface. Then before he could follow her, a great force took him and drove him end-over-end across the jagged rocks.

Even as he was jerked and battered inside his

suit, his own thoughts remained quite clear. The inner door seal must have been already broken, ready to fail and hanging on a thread. So long as there was an equalizing pressure in airlock and dome, there was no problem. But once they had pumped down the pressure in the lock, the inner door had tons of air pressure exerted upon it. If it failed, all the dome's gases would be released in one giant blow-out through the lock. And for anyone standing in the way. . . .

Peron was spinning and ricocheting from one rock formation to the next. He felt three separate and shattering collisions, one on the chest, one on the head, and one across his hip. Then, quite suddenly, it was over. He was lying supine on the surface, staring at the ruby orb of Cassby and surprised to find that he was still alive.

The others came crowding round him, helping him to his feet. He was amazed to see that he was almost fifty meters away from the dome. Rosanne had picked herself up and was waving to show that she was all right.

"I'm all right, too," said Peron.

There was a long, strange silence from the others. At last Peron noticed a faint, ominous chill on the lower left side of his abdomen. He looked down. His suit there was dreadfully buckled and splintered from chest to thighs, and over his abdomen it showed white instead of the usual metallic grey.

"Air supply working, but he's lost two tanks." That was Lum, his voice oddly distorted, from behind him. The suit radio had taken a beating, but it still functioned after a fashion.

"No problem, he can share ours."

"Motor controls look all right."

"Food containers gone."

"We can cover for that."

"Oh-oh. Thermal system is out. And most of the suit insulation is stripped from the lower torso."

"That's a worse problem."

His radio's distortion was so bad that Peron found it hard to identify the speakers. He cut to a privacy mode. While they inspected the condition of his equipment, his own mind raced on ahead of them.

Evaluate the options.

Think!

Fourteen hours back to the equator—say that could be shaved to ten hours at maximum speed. A few minutes in the launch catapult, then another six or seven hours to ship rendezvous. Hopeless. Even with full insulation, in these temperatures the suit would protect him for only three or four hours. He'd be dead of hypothermia long before he reached the equator.

Change to a new suit? There was none. They carried spare parts for small suit components, but not for the whole thing.

Think. Bundle him into something that would keep him warm for a long time? Fine—but what? There was nothing.

Take him into the dome, replace the lost atmosphere from tanks, and raise the temperature? Maybe. They could get air in there in less than an hour. But they couldn't generate heat fast enough. He would be able to breathe, and still he'd freeze to death.

Signal for an emergency landing at the pole of Whirlygig by a small ship? It was probably the best hope—but still too slow. Say three or four hours to prepare, then another three before it arrived here. By then Peron would be an icy corpse.

Other ideas? He could find none. His mind ran on, writing its own obituary: Peron of Turcanta, twenty years old, who survived the dunes of Talimantor Desert, the night woods of Villasylvia, the Hendrack Maze, the water caverns of Charant, the Capandor glaciers, the abyssal depths of the Lackro Trench . . . who had lived on, to freeze on Whirlygig. His name would be added to that list of names that the government never mentioned, the unfortunates who died in the off-planet final trials of the Planetfest games.

Peron turned his suit back to general receiving mode.

"We're agreed, then," a clear voice was saying. "Nothing any of us can think of would do it in time?"

The distortion of the damaged radio changed the tone of the voice. Peron came back from his own somber thoughts, and found to his surprise that the speaker was Wilmer.

"Looks that way." That was obviously Lum speaking. "We called the ship and they'll have something on the way as soon as they can, but it will probably be eight hours. Sy did a rough heat loss estimate from the condition of the suit, and calculates that we have a couple of hours to do something—three at the outside."

"Damnation."

My thoughts exactly, said Peron to himself calmly. Damnation. But what's happening to Wilmer? After tagging along as a good-natured mystery and non-contestant through all the games, he's suddenly the dominant figure of the group. The others are actually deferring to him, letting him control them.

Peron had a sudden insight. It was simple shock.

Shock had overwhelmed all of them; but somehow Wilmer and he, Peron, the source of all the concern and the one who was condemned to die, could distance themselves from the emotion. He caught sight of Elissa's horrified face through the faceplate of her suit, and gave her an encouraging smile. Kallen had tears in his eyes, and even Sy had lost that remote look of calm confidence.

"No other ideas?" went on Wilmer. "Right. Give me a hand. Peron, I want to talk to you. The rest of you, I want an atmosphere inside the dome as soon as you can get it. Don't worry about the temperature, I know it will be low and we can handle that."

He was opening the green equipment sack that he had carried with him down to Whirlygig, and examining the array of ampoules, syringes, and electronic tools that lay in neat rows within it. After one long, startled look Sy headed for the dome, but the others stood motionless until Lum's roar: "Let's get to it." As he left he turned to Wilmer, his great hands clenched in their suit gloves. "This is no time to talk, but you'd better know what you're doing. If you don't I'll personally skin you alive when we get back to the ship."

Wilmer didn't bother to answer. Behind the faceplate his face was set in a scowl of concentration.

"Private circuit. You and I have to talk for a couple of minutes," he said to Peron, and waited until the personal suit frequency was confirmed. "All right. How do you rate your chances?"

"As zero."

"Fine. We'll be starting off without any delusions. I assume you're ready to take a risk?"

Peron felt like laughing. "You mean, one that gives me less chance of survival than I have now?"

"A fair answer. I know exactly what I'm going to try to do, but I've never tried it under circumstances remotely like these. I've got the drugs I need, and the environment in the dome won't be too far from the lab conditions. All right?"

"I have absolutely no idea what you are talking about."

"And I don't have the time to explain. Never mind. First, I'm going to give you an injection. It will have to go right in through your suit, but I think the needle will take it and the self-sealing will take care of the puncture. After that we'll get you inside. I think the shoulder seal is best."

Before Peron had time to object Wilmer had moved to his side, and he felt the sharp sting of a needle in his left trapezius muscle.

"Now we have less than a minute before you'll begin to feel dizzy." Wilmer had thrown the hypodermic away and was taking another one out from his case. "Listen closely. I want you to crack all the suit seals so we can easily take it off you when you're unconscious. Don't talk, and just try to go on breathing as shallowly as you can. When you feel you are going under, don't try to fight it. Let it happen. All right?"

The chilly area in the center of his stomach was spreading rapidly to engulf his whole torso. At the same time he had the feeling that the horizon of Whirlygig was retreating steadily from him, becoming farther and farther away. He nodded to Wilmer, and manipulated the control that transferred all suit seals to external access. His own breathing felt harsh and rapid, and he struggled to inhale and exhale slowly and steadily.

"Good man. Sorry I don't have time to explain, but I've never heard of this situation happening before. I'll probably get slaughtered when they find out what I'm trying to do. But you're lucky. I was in bad trouble myself on Whirlygig once, over three hundred years ago. And I remember how I felt." Wilmer gripped his hand. "Good luck, Peron. If you wake up again you'll be over in S-space."

In S-space. If I survive, there'll be one mystery explained, thought Peron. He returned Wilmer's grip.

"I'll need help," said Wilmer. He was back on open circuit. "We have to get Peron out of that suit as soon as the pressure will let us. And he'll be unconscious. Elissa, will you organize the fastest way to do that?"

Peron felt an overpowering and irrational urge to laugh. Wilmer, said a voice inside him, my odd and hairless friend, how you've changed. You were an old tardy-worm down on Pentecost, and now you're transformed into a golden-winged butterfly of authority. Or do I mean a *plant*, a rare exotic form that only blooms when it's off-planet? That question was suddenly important, but he knew he could not provide an answer.

Control had gone. He knew they were at the dome and ready to go inside it, but he could no longer see the door of the lock. Or the stars, or even the ground he stood upon. The scene before him was blinking out, bit by bit. It was like a great jig-saw puzzle, where every piece was black. All he could see was Wilmer, still holding his arm.

So. This is what it's like to die. Not too bad, really. Not bad at all.

The final piece of the puzzle was placed in position. Wilmer disappeared, and the whole world was black.

Chapter 17:

Waking was agony.

It began as only a low murmur of voices, speaking a familiar language but with pitch and intonation so changed that they were barely comprehensible. It was like the voice of a machine. He strained to understand. "... little more asfanol ... even a few more minutes ... until we know what to do with athers (others?) ... heart beat sturdy (steady?) now...."

Then a clearer statement, in an angry and petulant lower voice. "Damned nuisance. Can't do a thing until we have a policy statement. Why that fool had to do what he did ... it will take us a month...."

He was breathing. The air came hot into his lungs, searing the delicate alveoli with every slow breath. He felt it burn across the air-blood barrier, then fiery rivers of oxygen were surging along arteries and capillaries out to every extremity of his body. It was a relentless pain. There was an agony of awakening tissue and returning circulation, accompanied by muscle spasms he could not control.

Peron moved his tongue. As it touched his teeth it felt dry and swollen, too big for his mouth. But when he licked his lips there was a sense of slick, glycerine texture and a taste that puckered the inside of his mouth. He grunted in disgust, but no sound would come from his throat.

"He's awake," said another voice. "Get ready. Peron Turca. Can you open your eyes?"

Peron tried to do it. The lashes felt gummed shut, but by a steady effort he could free them, little by little. He peered upward through slitted eyes and found that he was looking at a pale grey ceiling, curving without seam to meet walls of the same color. Somewhere off to his right there was a steady swishing and pulsing sound.

He turned his head to that side. The neck muscles reluctantly creaked, stretched, and obeyed his mental command. He was lying next to a great mass of medical equipment, monitors, pumps, I/V's, and telemetering units. Numerous tubes and wires ran across to his bared right arm. Others extended to run up his nostrils and down to his lower body. He was naked.

He lifted his head. There was something subtly wrong in making the movement, but it did not feel like an internal problem. It felt rather as though the laws of mechanics had been changed, so that although he was clearly not in freefall, neither was he moving under any normal form of gravity.

And something was wrong with his eyes. Badly wrong. He could see, but everything was blurred and indistinct, with edges poorly defined and with all colors muted to pastel shades.

Peron turned his head to the left. Next to the

table on which he was lying sat a woman. She was middle-aged, frowning, and looking at him with obvious disapproval. Her face had a smooth, baby-ish skin, and she wore a blue cowl that was closely fitted to her skull.

"All right," she said. She did not seem to be speaking to Peron. "Motor control seems to be there. *Command: Let's have three c.c.'s of historex in the thigh.*"

It was the voice that he had first heard, and again it sounded hoarse and oddly mechanical. He saw and heard nothing happen, but after a few seconds there was a brief new ache in his thigh. Then the pain in all his muscles began to decrease. The woman gazed at his expression, and nodded.

"Excellent. *Command: Check the monitors, and if they're satisfactory remove catheters. Gently.*"

Peron stared down at the catheters that ran into his lower body, and made sure that he kept his gaze on them. Again he saw and felt nothing, but after a moment they had vanished. Another second, and the tube into his nostrils was gone. He drew in a long, shuddering breath. The fire in the lungs was still there.

The woman still looked annoyed. "You feel strange and uncomfortable. I know. S-space has that effect on everybody at first. It doesn't last. Just be thankful that you're alive when you ought to be dead."

Alive! Alive. Peron had a sudden flood of memory, carrying him back to the last despairing min-utes on Whirlygig. He had been dying there, resigned to the inevitable, quite sure of his own death—and here he was alive! All the pain washed away in a moment, overwhelmed by knowledge of life. He wanted to speak, to give out a great shout of joy at the fact of simple existence; but again no words would come out.

"Don't try it," said the woman. "Not yet. You'll have to learn how to speak, and it takes a little while. And don't rub your eyes, they're working normally but things look different here. Now, there are things to be done before you're ready to talk. That fool Wilmer certainly gave us all a problem, but I guess we're stuck with it. We can't kill you now. *Command: Bring him a drink. Water will do, but check the ion balances and the blood sugar, and if he needs anything make the necessary additions.*"

She held out her hand, and suddenly it was holding a flask of straw-yellow liquid.

"I want you to try to take this from me. Can you do that? Then drink all of it and try to talk to me."

Peron lifted his arm, and again there was the feeling that the laws of physics had been changed. It took deliberate control to make his hand move in the direction that he wanted. He carefully took the container, brought it back to his mouth, and drank. It was like balm, soothing his throat and making him realize for the first time that he was desperately thirsty. He drank it all.

"Good. *Command: Take it away.*"

The flask was gone. The woman looked a little less irritated.

"Can you speak? Try a word."

Peron swallowed, commanded his vocal chords, and was rewarded with a grunt and a grating cough. He tried again.

"Yaahh. Y-Yaasss." His voice sounded alien in his ears.

"Excellent. Give it time. And listen to me. You have to know just a few things, and there's noth-

ing to be gained by waiting to tell you them. Do
you know who the Immortals are?"

"They vissi—vizzit—Pen'coss. Don' know if 'u-
man—or not. Lave—live—f'rever."

"Wish that were true." The woman gave Peron a
sour smile. "I'm an Immortal. And now, so are
you. But we won't live forever. We'll live about
seventeen hundred years, according to our best
current estimates—if we don't get killed somehow
along the way. That's one thing you have to learn.
You can be killed just as easily now as you could
before. Living in S-space won't protect you. Understand?"

"Unn-derstand." The skin on Peron's face felt as
though it had been stretched tight, and it could
not show the emotion he was feeling. If he was an
Immortal, what had happened to the others? Would
he outlive Elissa by sixteen hundred years? No
good news could make that thought palatable. He
lifted his head—*again, that strange feeling*—and
looked at the woman directly. "What happ'n to
others on Whir'gig?"

"I'm not in a position to tell you that. I told you,
what Wilmer did for you has made more trouble
than he dreamed. Before we are permitted to tell
you more, we have to get approval from Sector
Headquarters, and that means a long trip. We've
been on the way for about five hours already, and
it will be nearly two days before we get there.
Until we do, you'll have to be patient. *My* patient,
as it happens." She gave him her first real smile.
"You can start by resting some. In a few minutes
you'll get a reaction from the historex, and I'm
going to give you another sedative and painkiller
now. *Command: Give this man five c.c.'s of asfanol.*"

Nothing visible, but again a surprise ache of

something in his thigh. Peron wasn't at all ready to go to sleep—there were a hundred questions to be answered, and he wasn't sure where to start.

"Are we going back to The Ship?"

The woman looked startled, then amused. "No. I can't tell you much, but I can tell you that. We're on a longer trip. Sector Headquarters is outside the Cass system—nearly a lightyear away from Cassay and Pentecost."

"And we'll be there in *two days*. So you *do* travel faster than light!"

Now she was looking very uncomfortable. "I'm not supposed to tell you anything—I'm a *doctor*, not a—a damned administrator." There was an irritation at somebody or something in her tone, and Peron filed it away for future reference. "But we don't travel faster than light. In S-space, light travels almost two thousand lightyears of normal distance in one of our years. We're travelling at only a fraction of lightspeed."

Peron was overwhelmed by the thought. Could she be telling the truth? If she were, Sol and Earth itself were only a couple of months away. And if they had been on their journey for five hours already, they must be deep into interstellar space. He was beginning to feel drowsy, but suddenly he had a tremendous desire to see Cassay again. And what would the starscape be like, at this tremendous speed?

"What's wrong?" She had seen his expression.

"Can we look out of here—look at the stars?"

She shook her head. "I sometimes have that wish myself. When you wake up, take a look in the next room. There's an exterior port there. You'll find that things look rather different in S-space. But now, I have to go. My name, by the way, is

Ferranti; Dr. Olivia Ferranti. I will be seeing a good deal of you until we're sure that you are stable here. And I'll be back tomorrow." She gave him a reassuring nod. "Be patient. *Command: Take me to my apartment.*"

"But what—"

Peron didn't bother to finish his sentence. She had gone, vanished instantly into the air. In another thirty seconds the drugs had taken him and he was sound asleep.

The room where he had first regained consciousness lacked clothing, food, or drink. There was a terminal near the table, which must clearly communicate with other parts of the ship, but when he next awoke Peron resisted his first urge, to call and ask for something to eat. He felt ravenous, and still oddly disoriented, but there were other overriding priorities.

All the monitors by the table were still working, but now they received telemetered data originating from small sensors attached to his body. They undoubtedly passed on those signals to some central monitoring computer, but possibly that responded only to emergencies. Peron felt that he should have at least a few minutes before his actions were controlled again. He slid off the table, took a moment to collect his balance, and then headed for one of the room's two doors.

It led to a long windowless corridor. Wrong choice. He backtracked, and found that the other led to a bigger room, with a great transparent port at one end. Peron went to it and stared out.

He had certainly expected something different from the usual starscape seen from within the Cass system; perhaps the familiar constellations, but subtly distorted. But what he was looking at was wholly inexplicable.

Beyond the port, the whole sky was filled with a faint, pearly glow. It seemed to possess no orientation, and everywhere it was of the same uniform brightness. No stars, no nebulae, no dust clouds, no galaxies; the whole universe had disappeared, lost in a diffuse, glowing haze.

Peron felt his head begin to spin. He was in S-space, and it was so far different from anything he had imagined that he had no idea what to do next. If he had been trapped and held prisoner—for that was the way he was beginning to perceive his situation on this ship—in any ordinary environment he could perhaps have gained control and had some say in his own actions. But what could he do here? There was nothing in Pentecost's science that even hinted at the possibility of this. Sy, far more able scientifically than Peron, had scoffed at the very idea.

Peron felt a moment of annoyance. If only Sy could be here now, to see how far his theories would take him. . . .

The rest of the room lacked any furnishings or useful sources of information. There was a set of small and mysterious doors or panels in the base of the wall, each only a couple of feet high, but he could not open them. He turned to go back to the corridor, and was reminded of his own hunger and thirst. He remembered Dr. Ferranti's ability to conjure drink from nothing (And ask Sy to explain *that*, while he was at it!). Could it possibly work for him, too? There seemed nothing he could lose by trying.

"*Command.*" Even though he was alone, he felt self-conscious—what he was attempting was impossible! But it had worked, he was convinced of that. *"Command: Bring me a drink."*

He waited, feeling foolish. And to confirm his feeling, absolutely nothing happened. He tried once more. *"Command: Bring me something to eat."*

Nothing. How could anything else be the result? He must have been hallucinating, to be convinced that Ferranti had magical powers to make objects—including herself—appear and disappear instantly.

Peron had scarcely come to that conclusion when everything about him changed in one brief and bewildering flicker of movement. There was a second of total disorientation. Then he was no longer standing at the entrance to the corridor. Instead he was in a room with pale yellow walls, decorated with elaborate murals and amateurish paintings. He was fully clothed, in well-fitting brown shirt and trousers. His own shoes, last seen when he donned a suit before leaving for Whirlygig, were on his feet. He was seated in a hard chair, with his hands resting firmly on its arms. In front of him was a long, polished desk of silvery metal, its upper surface containing a single, orange folder and one pen.

And sitting behind that desk, looking at him with a slightly bored and definitely supercilious expression, was a wizened, brown-eyed, hairless man. Peron took an instant and inexplicable dislike to him.

Chapter 18:

"I am Captain Rinker, in command of this ship," said the man. "Dr. Ferranti tells me that you are fully stable and adapted to S-space. Is that so?"

"I don't know. I feel no pain, but I certainly don't feel normal."

"That will pass. Anything else?"

"Someone seems to want to starve me to death."

"Your own fault. When you awoke you could have called for food. Instead you chose to pry." Rinker gestured at a wall display that was showing the room where Peron had returned to consciousness. "You were observed. It would serve you right if we did not feed you for a while. But you are lucky. Regulations would not permit us to starve you. *Command: Bring food and drink, suitable for the awakening.*"

A tray appeared instantly, resting on Peron's knees. The clear carafe held the same liquid as he had drunk before, but the plates of food were unfamiliar. There were brown patties with a coarse granular texture, orange-red jelly, and white slabs

189

of smooth creamy consistency. Rinker gestured to them.

"Carry on. You may eat while we talk."

Peron looked around him. There was no other person in the room, and no sign that the door had opened or closed. "How are you able to do that?"

"It is not appropriate that I tell you. Such information will be given to you at Headquarters—if it is given at all." Rinker waved his hand at the display. "Your efforts to use the service system were already noted. To save you further wasted time, I will point out that any more efforts on your part will be just as unsuccessful. Let me also point out that I am under no official obligation to talk to you, or to deal with you in any way except to provide safe transfer to Headquarters. But I want you to know how much trouble you have caused, you and that fool Wilmer."

Peron could not resist the food in front of him. His body insisted that it had been weeks since it had received nourishment. He ate ravenously. The patties had a reasonable resemblance to bread, and although the white material tasted nothing like the cheese that Peron had expected, it tasted good. He stared across the desk at Captain Rinker, swallowed, and spoke.

"I can't speak for Wilmer, but any trouble I caused was not my doing. I would have died on Whirlygig without his help. I don't see why you assign blame to me."

Rinker gave an impatient wave of his hand. "You were marked as a troublemaker before you left the planet. So were your companions on Whirlygig. You were all scheduled for special indoctrination on the ship *Eleanora*, to be kept apart from the other contestants. As for Wilmer, he was supposed to be there as an *observer*—not as a participant. I have warned several times of the danger of using local recruits as observers. They have too many ties to your planet and its people. But my advice was ignored."

"Is Wilmer an Immortal?"

Rinker leaned back in his chair, frowning. His voice rose in pitch. "That stupid term! It is one I never use. Wilmer was recruited to our group, yes. And he shares our extended life span. But he has never left the Cass System, and he certainly knows nothing of our larger mission. Now I must suffer the consequences of his dabbling. For three hundred and sixty of your years, I have visited Pentecost and the Cass System. This is my nineteenth trip. And never has anything gone wrong. I have developed a perfect record in my work. Success is expected of me, and I demand it of myself. But now, thanks to what Wilmer did on Whirlygig, all that has gone. This visit has turned into a disaster. The materials I should be carrying back from the group on *Eleanora* have been left behind; final selection and indoctrination of recruits has been delayed; and I am carrying six additional and unwanted passengers with me to Headquarters, all of whom are tagged as potential trouble. Do you think I should be happy?"

As Peron's hunger and thirst lessened, he felt an increasing curiosity at his surroundings. It was also matched by a growing annoyance. He had done nothing to justify Rinker's tirade. What did the foolish man expect him to do? Ask to be taken back to die on Whirlygig?

He lifted the tray and placed it on the desk in front of him. "I don't say you should be happy.

But you shouldn't blame me for what happened. Why won't you tell me what's going on here?"

"So you can cause more trouble?"

"I'm not going to cause trouble. But naturally I have many questions. I don't ask for your time, but let me at least have access to a terminal and the data banks. And you say that some of the other contestants are here on this ship. I would certainly like to see them."

Rinker stared angrily at the messy tray lying on his clean and polished desk. He gave Peron an unpleasant smile. "I cannot allow you access to the data banks. As I told you, this situation is unprecedented. No one has ever joined our group here without indoctrination. What happens to you can be decided only after we reach Headquarters, and until we arrive there you must do exactly as you are told. You want to see your companions? Very well. *Command: Remove this tray.*"

It vanished instantly.

"*Command: Take us both to the suspense room.*"

This time Peron had a dizzying image of a long corridor and grey walls. It lasted for a fraction of a second. Then the world steadied, and he and Rinker were standing together in front of a bank of waist-high metal doors. Each one formed the entrance to a long, deep container like an outsize coffin. Monitors sat on the transparent top of each box, and all the outputs were collected into a thick optic bundle that ran to a computer terminal. The room was freezingly cold.

"Perhaps this will give you an idea of how seriously I regard this situation." Rinker stepped forward to one of the boxes. "Your companions are here."

"What have you done to them?" Peron felt a

sense of horror. Was Rinker telling him that Elissa and the others were imprisoned in those black, icy caskets?

"They are in cold sleep, and will remain there." Rinker's voice was as chilly as the room. It offered no possibility of discussion. "They are of course in no danger. I run a well-regulated ship, and all the equipment is checked constantly. They will be awakened—a simple procedure—when we reach Headquarters. Then this matter will move to other hands than mine. I will be very glad to see the last of it."

Peron stepped forward to peer in through the top of the nearest chest. Kallen lay inside, swathed up to his neck in soft white material. He looked dead. His eyes were deep-set in his head, his face grey and drained of all color. Peron stepped to the next container. That one held Elissa. He shuddered to see what she had become. Without its usual animation, her face was like a wax model.

"Are you sure that they are all right?" Peron had to ask. "They look—"

"I have no time to waste in repeating myself. They are all right. I have already told you and shown you more than I intended. You will eat your meals with the rest of us, and I will see you then. If you need food before that, use the terminal. *Command: Take him to his living quarters.*"

There was no chance to protest. Rinker and the room with Elissa and the others suddenly vanished. Peron found himself alone with his worry, perplexity and frustration, in a room that held only a bed, a desk, and a terminal.

The Planetfest games had provided periods of terror, exhaustion, suspense and near-despair. But there had been nothing to match the sheer frustration of the next twelve hours. By the end of it, Peron had reached an unvoiced decision: if he was branded as a troublemaker, he was going to earn his label.

He had started out simply wishing to know more about the ship and his environment. That had proved to be far more difficult than he expected. The room he had been assigned opened to a narrow corridor, which soon branched in both directions to larger rooms and other passageways. He had tried each one in turn, making mental notes of any changes of direction.

A pattern quickly emerged. If he went off along the left corridor, he was free to wander as he pleased. He had found a dining-area, and a library whose terminals ignored his requests for information, but readily provided food or drink. It appeared instantly and mysteriously in front of him the moment that his order was placed through the terminal, and was removed just as promptly when he requested that. He had also met some of the other ship's complement, all much more friendly than Captain Rinker. There were only three of them. It seemed to Peron a preposterously low number to control such a large structure. But as Olivia Ferranti pointed out to him when his wandering took him past her living quarters, it was far more people than were needed. Everything was under automatic control; Captain Rinker alone could handle everything. In fact, the rest of them were making their first trip, and had come from Headquarters to the Cass System for their own reasons (which she refused to discuss). She had even offered something like an apology for Rinker's behavior.

"He's unusually valuable. There are not many people who *like* making these long trips, often with no companions. It takes a special temperament. Captain Rinker likes things neat. He can't stand the idea that you've disturbed the pattern of his life."

"But Wilmer did that, not me."

"Maybe. But Wilmer isn't here, and you are. So you're getting it."

"And he's allowed to keep my friends unconscious?"

"He's the captain. He is in control until we reach Headquarters. Then he'll have to explain his actions, but he'll have no trouble doing that—he's following regulations. And honestly, he's not harming your friends at all. Now, I have to go. We can talk a little more if you like at the next meal period. *Command: Take me to the forward exercise facility.*"

And she was gone.

Peron found that he could get as far as the door of the suspense room, but it refused to open for him. And he could issue as many commands as he chose, in any tone of voice, for anything he liked, but they were all ignored.

When he left his room and went off along the right-hand corridor, affairs were even less satisfactory. The left corridor led him to the upper part of the ship, in terms of the effective gravity. The right corridor should then have taken him to the lower part, and it certainly started out that way. But no matter which branch he followed, when he had progressed a certain distance there would be a dizzying flicker—and he would be back in his room, sitting at the desk. Some whole section of the ship, of indeterminate size, was inaccessible to him.

After a dozen fruitless attempts, Peron lay on the bed in his room, thinking hard. It was twelve hours since his meeting with Rinker, but he didn't feel at all tired. Olivia Ferranti had told him to expect little need for sleep.

"One fringe benefit of S-space," she had said. "You'll find you sleep maybe one hour in twenty."

He continued to feel physically peculiar, but she had been right on that, too. After a while he simply adjusted to it. He still had the impression that he was moving his body in a world where the laws of mechanics had been slightly modified, but it was a feeling that faded.

"Do you want to join us for dinner?" The voice came suddenly from the terminal next to his bed. It was Garao, another of the ship's company that he had encountered in his travels around the forward section.

"I don't think so." Then he sat up quickly. "No, wait a minute. Yes, I do. I'll come over." He didn't feel hungry—except for more information. And the only way to get that seemed to be from other people. Direct exploration of the ship had been totally unrewarding.

"No need for that," said Garao. "Hold tight."

There was the now-familiar moment of disorientation. He found he was sitting in the dining area with three of the others. Captain Rinker was not present. As Ferranti had told him, the captain much preferred his own company, and often dined alone.

Everyone seemed to take it for granted that Peron would now eat and drink the same things as the rest of them. When he arrived there were already five or six different dishes on the table—all of them unfamiliar. He found something that looked like a fish fillet, but clearly wasn't. And there were several pseudo-meat products, each flanked by some kind of vegetable. Nothing tasted quite the way he expected—and all the food was cold.

The others seemed surprised when he mentioned that. Ferranti looked at Garao and at the linguist, Atiyah, then shrugged.

"I should have mentioned that to you before. You won't get hot food in S-space. Better get used to it cold."

"But why?"

"Wait until we get to HQ, and ask there." Ferranti was clearly embarrassed by her non-answer. She was sitting next to Peron, so he was faced only with her profile. But her voice showed her discomfort. "I would tell you, but it's against captain's orders. If you like hot food, I can make what we're eating more acceptable. It's easy enough to order spices. *Command: Bring more of these dishes for Peron Turca, but with added hot spice.*"

There was a delay of about fifteen seconds, then additional dishes appeared on the table in front of Peron. He was preparing to help himself to them when he noticed the expression on Garao and Atiyah's faces, across the table from him.

"What's wrong? Isn't it all right for me to eat these?"

"That's not the problem." Garao picked up an empty plate. "*Command: Take this away.*"

Again there was a delay of a few seconds, then the plate suddenly vanished.

"See?" Garao looked gleeful. "It's the same trouble we had on the trip from Headquarters. Seems even worse."

"It is," said Ferranti. "This time it takes twice as long."

"*What* takes twice as long?" Peron felt as though they were speaking in riddles just to confuse him.

"Service," said Atiyah. He was a man of few words. "It should be instantaneous. Let's time the delay. *Command: Bring me a glass of water.*"

They sat in silence, until after about ten seconds a filled glass of clear liquid appeared in front of Atiyah.

Garao nodded. "We'd better notify Rinker at once. He'll have to leave S-space to correct this. Serves the stiff-necked bastard right—him and his 'perfectly-run ship.'"

"And won't *that* make him pleased," said Ferranti. "Already he's complaining what a disaster this trip has been."

"Leave S-space? But where will he go?"

The others looked at Peron for a moment. "Sorry," said Garao sympathetically. "But this will be captain's orders again. We can't include you on this. *Command: Take Peron back to his room.*"

"*Wait a minute.*" Peron was frantic. "Look, to hell with captain's orders. If something is wrong I have a right to know it, too. I'm on the ship as well as you. I want to stay here and find out what's happening."

But the last sentence was wasted. Peron added a string of curses to it. The service delay might worry the others, but it was still too short. He was back in his room again, talking to the empty walls.

Chapter 19:

Peron allowed himself only a few seconds of cursing. Then he ripped off his shoes and ran at top speed along the corridor that led to the upper part of the ship. The monitors would still show his movements, that seemed certain. But now there was an emergency on board, so who would be watching? There would never be a better chance to explore areas that were normally forbidden.

His earlier careful study of the ship's internal layout had not been wasted. He ran fast and silently towards Rinker's living quarters, sure of every corridor. At the branch before Rinker's door he paused and peered around the corner. Was he in time? If Rinker had already left, there would be no way to know where he had gone.

He heard the door slide open and ducked back, then retreated to the next bend in the corridor. No footsteps. Rinker must be heading in the other direction.

He ran lightly back and stole another look along the corridor, just in time to see the disappearing back of Rinker's blue jacket and shiny bald head.

He was heading over to the left, angling away from the dining room.

Peron tried to visualize the geometry. What lay in that direction? All that he could remember was two great storage chambers, each filled with some kind of pellets, and more living quarters. The suspense room lay out at the very end of the same corridor.

Rinker was heading steadily on, hunched over and not looking back. Past the storage areas, past the living areas—what could he possibly want in the suspense room?

Had Peron forgotten some branch in the corridor? He knew he could not ignore the possibility. He took a bigger chance and closed the distance that separated them. He was close enough to hear Rinker's heavy breathing, and to smell the unpleasant musky talc that he used as body powder.

Peron's nose wrinkled. No wonder the man usually made his trips alone!

He hesitated at the door of the suspense room. Rinker had gone inside, but there was no way to follow him in and remain unnoticed.

There was a creaking sound from within. Peron ducked his head briefly into the doorway. Rinker had opened one of the great, gleaming sarcophagi— and now he was climbing inside and closing the door.

As soon as the front panel was completely closed Peron sneaked forward into the room. But instead of going to Rinker's chest he went to one farther along the line. He looked in through the transparent top. Lum lay there, white and corpselike. Peron tried to ignore the massive, still form and looked instead at the walls of the container.

Strange. Although he had not noticed it on his

first visit with Captain Rinker, the box seemed to
have a complete set of controls *inside*, as well as
outside—as though those imprisoned frozen figures might waken, and wish to control the appara-
tus from within. And here was something else, just
as odd. At the far end of the container, leading
only into the blank wall behind it, was another
door, the same size as the one at this end.

A couple of minutes had passed since Rinker
had gone inside and closed the door. Peron stepped
quietly across to stand beside that box. He placed
his ear close to it. There was a hissing of gases,
and the dull thump of a pump. Peron risked a
quick look in through the top. Rinker was lying
there, eyes closed. He looked quite relaxed and
normal, but a network of silvery filaments had
appeared from the walls of the container and attached themselves to various parts of his body.
Fine sprays of white fluid were drifting down from
tiny nozzles to dampen his skin. Peron touched the
surface of the container, expecting the icy cold he
had felt at Lum's casket. He jumped and pulled
his hand away sharply. The surface was hot and
tingling, as though it was sending an electric current through him.

For a couple of minutes the situation did not
change. Then the spray turned off. The nozzles
were drawn back into the side of the container and
the silver filaments loosened and withdrew. Peron
watched and waited. Ten seconds later Rinker's
body seemed to tremble for a moment.

And then the container was empty. In a fraction
of a second, before Peron could even blink, Rinker
had vanished completely.

Peron was tempted to open the door of the container. Instead, he went to an empty one that stood

near to it, and opened that. The internal controls appeared quite simple. There was a three-way dial, a timer with units in days, hours, and hundredths of hours, and a manual switch. The switch setting showed only an N, an S, and a C. The C position was in red, and below it stood a written notice: *WARNING:* DO NOT USE SETTING FOR *COLD* (C) WITHOUT SETTING TIMING SWITCH OR WITHOUT ASSISTANCE OF AN EXTERNAL OPERATOR.

Peron was thinking of climbing inside to take a closer look when he heard a warning creak from the other container. The door was being opened again. He forced himself to move carefully and quietly as he closed his casket. Too late to leave the room—the door was swinging open. Fortunately it came towards him, so that he was hidden temporarily behind it. He moved silently to the shelter of the next box and ducked down behind it.

Rinker had returned. He was slowly heading out of the room, looking neither to right nor left. Peron caught one glimpse of his half-profile, and saw sunken, bloodshot eyes and a pallid complexion. He followed at a discreet distance. The other man walked drunkenly, as though totally exhausted and giddy with fatigue. Instead of continuing to his quarters he went into the dining-room area. Garao, Ferranti, and Atiyah were still there, talking.

And they were still eating dinner. That seemed peculiar, until Peron realized it had been only a few minutes since Garao's verbal command had whipped him unwillingly back to his room.

"All fixed," said Captain Rinker harshly. "There's a defective component in the command translation device. We don't have replacements on board, so I've jury-rigged it for the trip."

"Will it last, or will it fail again?" That was Olivia Ferranti's voice.

"It will fail again eventually. Not for a while, I hope." Rinker gave a great yawn. "That was almost too much for me. It took a long time. I was there nearly five minutes, with no rest. I must go and sleep now."

There was a murmur of semi-sympathetic voices. "Let's hope it doesn't go again during the trip," said Garao—though his tone didn't support his words.

"It won't," said Rinker. "I don't expect any more trouble on this trip."

Peron thought of those words as he tiptoed away along the corridor. Rinker's actions and comments were revealing, and Peron had some faint inkling now as to what was going on.

If he were right, Rinker had more trouble coming than he imagined.

As soon as he was out of earshot of the dining area, Peron began to run again at top speed. The emergency was over—and that meant his movements would be watched again. Would there be monitors, even within the caskets?

He reached the suspense room and went at once to the same casket that Rinker had occupied. The door opened with the same creak, and he climbed inside and lay down. All the controls were within easy reach. He could stretch up his hand and set them with a simple push of a button. The choice was already fixed. He didn't want S, since he was already in S-space; and he didn't want C, since that was the cold sleep of Elissa and the others. It had to be N—but what did N mean?

Peron had been moving at top speed, but now he

hesitated. Suppose the process that took Rinker out of S-space called for other knowledge that Peron lacked? It was clear that the others on the ship had extra powers, since service commands from Peron were ignored. What if the use of this device required those same powers?

Time was passing. At any moment the familiar dizziness might occur, and he would find that he was once more in his room. But still his finger stayed lightly on the button. When he had been absolutely certain of unavoidable death on Whirly-gig he had been able to face it staunchly, with a complete calm. This was different. Whatever Rinker and the others might do to him, he did not believe that they would kill him. But he could die now by his own hand. His next action might prove to be suicide.

Peron took a last look around at the casket walls. *Now, or never.*

He drew a long, deep breath, closed his eyes, and pressed the button marked N.

Chapter 20:

There was no startling moment of change. Peron had expected a twisting surge of nausea, or perhaps some unendurable pain of transition. Instead he felt a cool touch of electrodes at his temples, and the soothing spray of fluid on his skin. He relaxed, and drifted away into a quiet meditation. It went on for a long time, and ended only when he became aware of his own heartbeat, loud in the secret inner chamber of his ears.

A feeling of well-being was creeping over him, as though he were waking from the best sleep of his life. There was a temptation to lie there for a long time, basking in the sensation. But then he became filled with a sudden fear that he had merely fallen asleep, that nothing else had happened. Worried, he opened his eyes and looked around him.

The inside of the casket had not changed its configuration—but, startlingly, it had somehow changed color from a bland buff-yellow to a pale orange. Even his clothing was different, black instead of brown.

He sat up, then steadied himself against one

wall. He had fallen asleep in a one-gee gravity field; now he was in freefall.

The door through which he had entered could not be locked from the inside. What about pursuit? Aware that he was still likely to be followed and discovered, Peron scrambled his way towards the other door. Thank heaven for the freefall experience he had gained after they left Pentecost! He felt a little peculiar now, but there was no vertigo or feeling of nausea.

The door opened readily. He pulled himself through and closed it behind him. There was an outside catch, and he set it so that it could not be opened from within the box. Next he moved along the row of doors, and locked each one in the same way. Then, and only then, did he feel a first moment of safety.

He looked around. He was floating free in a long, turning passageway. It was dimly lit by faint yellow tubes that ran parallel to the walls, and far away in the distance he could hear a low-pitched rumbling and whistling. He headed in that direction.

As the passage turned, he came to a square-sided chamber with a fully transparent external wall. He stood there for a long time, overwhelmed by the sight of the universe outside the ship. The faint, luminous haze of S-space had gone. Instead he was gazing on a glittering sea of stars, as bright as they could appear only from open space. The old familiar constellations were there, just as they had looked from orbit around Pentecost. They gave him an odd feeling of reassurance. He was still alive, and he was back in a universe that he perhaps understood.

While he was still watching, there was a louder rumble in the corridor. A machine was approaching, drifting along the wall on an invisible magnetic track. The main device was small, only as big as his head, but a number of long, articulated arms were tucked away in at the side. He watched it warily.

It moved along quite slowly, at less than walking speed. A few meters away from him it ducked away into a small door in the wall of the corridor. Peron recognized the type of aperture—there were hundreds of them, all over the ship. They were everywhere, from the living quarters to the dining-room to the library, and he had been unable to open any of them. The machine had no such trouble. It slipped through smoothly, and vanished.

Peron continued on his way. He was in a part of the ship that he had never seen before. The passage finally led him to a great chamber, where hundreds of machines were located. Most sat immobile, but from time to time one or more of them would start into action and slide off on some mysterious errand. He followed a couple of them. Each finally passed through one of the small doors that lined each corridor.

Peron decided that he had to find a quiet place to think. He headed farther along the passage, and at last found he was in a different type of chamber. This one was an automatic galley, similar to the one that had served the Planetfest winners on their travels around the Cass System. Peron found a water spigot and drank deeply from it. He reveled in the clean feel of the pure liquid on his tongue and palate. Whatever its other virtues, S-space definitely made food and drink taste less interesting. He took a few moments more to study the arrangement, and noticed that there was processing equipment different from anything he had seen in the other galley. From the look of it, it could produce a standard menu, or something with added and unknown ingredients.

While he was watching, four of the little robots came trundling into the galley area. They ignored him. They were carrying plates, most of which still held the remains of a meal. One of those plates caught Peron's eye. It held the remnants of uneaten spicy food—the same food that had been served to Peron at his last meal in S-space. The surface of the robots was glistening with moisture. Peron went across to one of them and touched it. The metal was icy cold. He put his finger to his mouth and tasted the liquid with his tongue. The droplets were plain water, condensed from the air around him.

He sat down on the floor, put his head between his hands, and pondered. Everything made sense—if he could force his mind to accept one incredible possibility. And it was a possibility that he was finally in a position to check for himself.

Peron stood up. He took the heaviest metal tureen that he could find in the galley, and swung it as hard as he could against the metal wall. It did not bend. He headed back to the chamber where the patient robots sat, and waited until one of them rose from its position. Then he followed it closely as it proceeded along one of the numerous passageways branching off from the central opening.

When the machine turned to move through one of the small doors, Peron was ready. The door opened, and the robot slid through. While the door was still open Peron jammed the sturdy metal container into the gap. There was a squeak of metal and a protesting whine from the door's control mechanism, but the aperture remained open.

Peron crouched down and looked through.

An icy current of air met him from the other side. The temperature there must be very close to freezing. The little robot had gone on its way, and the area beyond was lit only by the dullest of red glimmers of light.

Peron judged the width of the door with his eye. There would be just enough space for him to squeeze through, provided he was willing to risk the skin on his shoulders. He eased off his jacket, pushed it through ahead of him, and wriggled to the other side.

It was even colder and darker than he had thought. He shivered, and pulled his jacket tight about him. Unless he had more clothing, it would not be possible for him to stay there long.

Peron recognized the room that he was in. It was next to Rinker's living quarters. He had been there before, in his original explorations of the ship. But there was one great difference. Instead of a one-gee field he now felt that he was still in freefall.

The little robot had disappeared. As he watched it came into view along the corridor. It was carrying an empty bottle of the fermented drink that Rinker usually enjoyed with his solitary meals. The robot came steadily closer. Again it ignored Peron. It hesitated at the door jammed open by the tureen, then went to another door and calmly passed through it. As it did so, another pair of service robots appeared on the other side, and set to work to free the obstruction and repair the door.

Peron did not stay to observe. He hurried through to Rinker's apartment, where Rinker was sitting in a chair. He was completely motionless, his hand raised and his mouth open. Peron stood and watched for several minutes. Finally the hand inched closer to the open mouth. Peron stepped forward and touched Rinker's cheek. It was like chilled marble. Fingers stabbed to within an inch of Rinker's eyes produced no reflexive blink of the lids.

It was proof enough. Peron hurried out and headed for the suspense room. On the way there he passed the dining area, where the motionless figures of Garao, Ferranti, and Atiyah still sat at table, three perfect sculptures of frozen flesh.

The suspense room was deserted. Peron paused for a long moment in front of the cold sleep caskets. Again he wondered at his motives. To risk his own life was one thing; to put the lives of his friends in jeopardy was another. Wouldn't it be better to wait until the ship arrived at the mysterious Headquarters of the Immortals, and see how the group would be treated there?

He tried to imagine the answers that the others would give. Part of his mind could create a simulated conversation with Lum, Kallen, Sy, Elissa, and Rosanne.

"You're in no danger in the tanks, and I'm not sure just how the revival process works. It looks simple, but suppose there's a hidden snag? Maybe I should just wait and see what happens when we get to Headquarters?"

He thought he could hear their consensus: "Hell, no. If there's one thing none of us can stand it's to have somebody *else* running our lives for us. You know that—why do you think we were considered as troublemakers? Go on. Make trouble. *Get us out of here.*"

He stepped to examine each tank in turn. The

controls were all identical. He could change the
dial setting either to S or N, and there was a table
to indicate the correct procedure for each. The
return from cold sleep to N-state was a fairly long
process. It would take twelve hours. But Peron did
not need to stand guard all that time. He would
forage for warm clothing for everyone—Elissa and
the others were all naked except for the filmy
white covering. Then he could crack open another
door, and return to the warmer area where the
robots lived and the galley was located.

He considered a barricade for the door to the
suspense room, then decided that it would not be
necessary. If things went according to plan his
work would be over before Rinker and the others
could interfere.

Elissa first. He couldn't wait to see her and talk
to her again. It took only a few moments to change
the setting and press the Start command. Peron
peered in anxiously through the transparent top of
the tank. There was a hum of motors within the
casket, and after a few moments a yellow vapor
began to fill the interior. Then Elissa and everything else within were soon invisible. Filled with
trepidation, Peron went on from tank to tank, setting the conditions that should bring all the others
back to consciousness from cold sleep.

The horror had begun for Elissa when she saw
the condition of Peron's suit. It had been shredded
and ruptured by impact with Whirlygig's rough
surface until it must be useless for thermal protection. The outside temperatures guaranteed that he
could not survive.

Before their grief could do more than begin,
Wilmer had taken charge. Even Lum's casual self-

confidence and Sy's remote air of superiority had crumbled and been swept aside by the other's grim certainty. They had done as Wilmer asked—and done it without questions.

First a breathable atmosphere had to be created within the dome. Then Elissa and Kallen had eased Peron gently out of his suit and clothing. His skin had darkened, and veins were prominent against the dusky surface. Elissa bent close. She could see no sign of breathing. She felt for a pulse, but could find no trace. His wrist and throat were ice-cold to the touch of her ungloved hand.

"Give me a hand to turn him over," said Wilmer. "We want him face down. Good. Now you go over there and help Lum with the temperature controls. They have to be precise—and you don't want to watch this."

Elissa had watched anyway, unable to tear herself away. Wilmer removed the gloves of his suit and encased his hands in a fine, glassy material that moulded itself tight to his skin. He flexed his fingers a few times, testing the fit, then took a silver scalpel from his green case. He made careful incisions into the base of Peron's neck and at the lower end of his spine. Fine, gleaming catheters were inserted there. Placed at the entrance of each aperture, they snaked inwards without further action from Wilmer, insinuating themselves deep into Peron's body. Wilmer placed a face mask in position over Peron's nose and mouth, and connected it to a small blue-grey cylinder. He turned a valve, and Elissa heard the hiss of gas.

The temperature in the dome had risen a little. Wilmer opened his faceplate and sniffed the air.

"Warm enough," he said. "I suggest we all open

our faceplates and conserve air in the suits—we may need it."

He took another cylinder from his case. "Here." He handed it to Elissa. "This will improve the atmosphere. Bleed this into the central circulator for the dome, then we can take that face mask off Peron."

"Is he alive?"

"For the moment—but he's still in danger."

Elissa took the cylinder across to the air circulation unit and snapped it into position. She cracked the nozzle. At first it seemed that nothing had happened. Then the chilly air of the dome took on a heavy, perfumed weight, as though the oxygen in it was bleeding away. Elissa turned frowning towards Wilmer. She noticed that he had closed the faceplate of his suit. She wanted to ask him what he was doing, but she could not phrase her thought. The moment stretched. Wilmer was motionless, watching and waiting. There was a final, odd sense of detachment, as though she were rising to the ceiling of the dome and leaving her body behind.

And now ... she was awakening ... to find Peron standing anxiously over her. She blinked her eyes to clear the blurred image.

"Elissa? Are you all right?"

He put his arm around her shoulders and raised her to a sitting position. She shivered uncontrollably, from a mixture of emotion and freezing cold. She looked down at herself. She had been wearing thermal clothing in the dome, now she was naked except for a transparent membrane of fine cloth.

Where was she? How had she come here? She struggled to think clearly. In the moment of waking it was hard to be logical. And what did logic matter? Peron was here, alive. She felt peculiar, chilled but fluffy-headed and giggly. Explanations could wait for a few more seconds. She snuggled into Peron's embrace.

"Here I am," she said. Everything was pleasant and vastly amusing. "But Peron, I'm cold."

"Good, you're waking up." He pointed to an assortment of garments in a heap by their side. "Help yourself to any that fit you. I've got to see how the others are doing."

"Peron!" She shivered, then reached out and gave Peron a hug strong enough to make their ribs creak. "Explain. What's been happening to me?"

"Tell you later." He returned the embrace with interest. "Come on. I may need help to get Lum out. He should have been called Lump."

Elissa rummaged through the pile and found an adequate set of coveralls while Peron opened the door of the next tank and did his best to pull out its occupant. There was a good deal of grunting and swearing. Lum was semi-conscious, and offering plenty of disorganized resistance.

"Here. Let me have a go at him." Elissa moved round to the other side and leaned over. She took hold of Lum's hair and gave it a great tug. He came suddenly upright, his eyes popped wide open, and he yelped in protest.

"No need to do that. I'm awake." His eyes closed again, and he started to sink back. "It's all right, I'm awake, I'll be up in just a minute."

"Pull his hair again, then give him a hand with his clothes," said Peron. "See if you can find anything big enough. Kallen's next, but I bet he'll be easier. Rosanne told me Lum sleeps like a dead man, even under normal conditions."

In a few more minutes Rosanne and Kallen had been brought back to groggy wakefulness. Peron left them sighing and shivering and searching for warm clothes. Sy was processed last of all. He went instantly from sleep to full attention. Even as his eyes popped open he was twisting sideways like a cat, moving his body to a defensive posture.

"Relax," said Peron. "You're with friends."

Sy gave Peron one brief, incredulous look, then stared around him. "Where am I? Last thing I remember we were in the Whirlygig dome. What happened?"

"That's a long story. Get some clothes on, and follow me. I'll explain as we go."

Peron led them to the dining-room, where Ferranti and the others were finally showing signs of movement. Garao was halfway to the door, one foot clear of the floor.

"I wanted each of you to see this to save arguments," said Peron. "Or you might have told me I was chewing dillason weed. Fourteen hours ago I was in that condition. That's S-space. Remember how much we were troubled by the idea that the Immortals could travel to the stars in days?"

"I still don't believe it," said Sy. "They can't exceed lightspeed."

"You're right—but you're wrong, too. Here's a question for all of you. How far does light travel in one second, or in one year?"

There was a brief silence.

"We all know the answer to that," said Rosanne. "So I assume it's a trick question."

"In a way," said Peron. "The answer depends on your definition of a second and a year. We've been thinking about S-space all wrong. It's not some sort of parallel universe, or hyperspace. It's the same space we live in—but S-space is a *state of changed perception.* If you want proof, look at these people."

Kallen had been watching Olivia Ferranti very closely. "She seems to be unconscious," he said softly. "And her skin is cold. But her eyes are open. They're alive, that's clear. Are they hibernating?"

"No. Each of them is fully conscious. In that condition you feel normal except for a few subtle differences. But their metabolisms have been drastically slowed—two thousand times slower than usual. That's S-space, and it changes your perception of everything. In one of our seconds, light travels three hundred thousand kilometers. In one of *theirs*, it travels six hundred *million* kilometers. To us, Sol is eighteen lightyears away. To them, it's only a little more than three light-days. That's why we heard that the Immortals can travel between the stars in days—*their* days. Their time is passing so slowly that what feels like a day to us is less than a minute for them."

Peron went close to Garao and passed his hand slowly in front of the other's face. "See? They don't even know we're here." He moved over to the stationary figure of Atiyah, removed the belt from around the man's tubby middle, and looped it around Olivia Ferranti's neck. "In about twenty minutes he'll notice that his belt is missing. In another hour of our time he'll begin to wonder where it went. It will be an hour more before he can do anything to get it back."

The others made their own inspections, touching skin and fingering hair.

"How did they get this way?" asked Lum.

"The same way that I did, when Wilmer operated on me back on Whirlygig. I know that's not much of an answer, but it's the best one I can give you. There has to be a complicated treatment, but it must be fairly standardized—and it's fully reversible. I've been both ways, and so has Captain Rinker. He had to go back to normal living to fix a mechanical problem with this ship. Let's take a look at the ship now. We'll all need that information later."

Peron led the way back through to the suspense room. As they went he responded to their torrent of questions. The ship they were travelling on was deep in interstellar space, heading for the Headquarters of the Immortals. That Headquarters was far from any sun or planet, a full lightyear away from the Cass System. They were moving at only a fraction of lightspeed—probably no more than a tenth. During their journey, nearly ten years would pass back on Pentecost.

The other Planetfest winners were not on board. Their fate could only be conjectured, but Peron thought they were all still back in the Cass System, probably living on The Ship. That was where the Immortals lived in the Cass System. The other winners would probably become Immortals themselves after some kind of indoctrination. They would prefer to live in S-space for the longer subjective life span it offered, and they would return to normal life, as Wilmer had done, only for special duties.

"How long does an Immortal live?" asked Sy. "It's obvious that nobody can be truly immortal."

"Seventeen hundred years."

There was another long silence. Finally Elissa said: "You mean seventeen hundred *subjective* years? That's two thousand times seventeen hundred ordinary years back on Pentecost—three million four hundred thousand. They live three million four hundred thousand years!"

"Right," said Peron cheerfully. Adjusting to that idea hadn't been easy, and he was glad to see that others had the same reaction. "Of course, that's only a conjecture. As Dr. Ferranti pointed out, they can only make estimates of full life span—because no one has lived it yet. It's only twenty thousand years or so since we left Earth, and no one was living in S-space there."

"But what about side effects?" said Elissa. "When you make such a profound change. . . ."

"I only know of a couple," said Peron. He brushed his hand through his hair. "See? It has stopped growing, and I think I was starting to lose it in S-space. Better get ready to lose those beautiful locks, Rosanne. I think that when you change metabolic rates for a while you become hairless. That's what happened to Wilmer, and the other contestant Kallen met. Back on Whirlygig I couldn't believe it when Wilmer told me that he had been in trouble there three hundred years before. But it makes sense now. That was just a few months in S-space. He was living there until he was with us in the 'Fest. A hundred years on Pentecost would be only a few weeks for him."

"That would explain why we only saw videos of former winners," said Lum. "They didn't come back to Pentecost. But there'd be no problem with videos. They could take them at S-space speed, then speed them up so they'd look normal. Personal appearances would be impossible unless they had moved back to normal time—N-space, you called it."

"And they'll be reluctant to do that," said Peron. "They lose the benefit of extended life expectancy when they leave S-space. You have to eat special food there, and you don't feel quite normal. But people will put up with a lot to increase their subjective life span by a factor of twenty."

. They were again in the suspense chamber. Peron led them into and through one of the caskets, using it as a convenient path to the other parts of the ship. There was a substantial temperature change as they passed through the suspense tank, and they all loosened their warm clothing.

"I'll tell you one thing I still don't understand," Peron said. "When I was in S-space, I felt as though I was in a one-gee environment. Now we're in exactly the same part of the ship, but we're in freefall. I don't see how that can happen."

There was silence for a while, then Kallen made a little coughing noise. "T-squared effect!" he said softly.

"What?"

"He's quite right," said Sy calmly. "Good for you, Kallen. Don't you see what he's saying, Peron? Accelerations involve the square of the time—distance per second per second. Change the definition of a second, and of course you change the perceived speed. That's why they can travel light-years in what they regard as a few days. But you change perceived acceleration, too—and you change that even more. By the *square* of the relative time rates—"

"—which is another reason the Immortals don't go down to the surface of planets," said Lum. "They want to spend their time in S-space to increase their subjective life-spans, but then that forces them to live in a very weak acceleration field. They can't take gravity."

"Not even a weak field," added Rosanne. "They'd fall over before they even knew they were off balance. What did you say the time factor was? Two thousand to one? Then even a millionth of a gravity would be perceived by them as a four-gee field. They *have* to live in freefall. They have no choice about it. But they perceive even a four-millionth of a gee as normal gravity."

Peron looked around him in disgust. "All right. So everybody saw it easily except me. Try another one. Tell me what's going on outside the ship. One reason I thought at first that S-space had to be some kind of hyperspace was the view from the ports. When you look out, you don't see stars at all. All you see is a sort of faint, glowing haze. It's yellow-white, and it's everywhere outside the ship."

This time there was not even a moment's pause.

"Frequency shift," said Sy at once. "Let's see. Two thousand to one. So the wavelengths your eyes could see would be two thousand times as long. Instead of yellow light at half a micrometer, you'd see yellow at a millimeter wavelength. Where would that put us?"

There was a hush.

"The Big Bang," whispered Kallen.

"The three degree cosmic background radiation," said Rosanne. "My Lord. Peron, you were seeing leftover radiation from the beginning of the Universe—actually *seeing* it directly with your eyes."

"And it's uniform and isotropic," added Lum. "That's why it looked like a general foggy haze. At that wavelength you don't get a strong signal from stars or nebulae, just a continuous field."

Peron looked at Elissa. "Don't say anything. You'll tell me it's obvious, too. I guess it is. But it was a lot more confusing when I had no idea I was dealing with a difference in time rates. I couldn't imagine where I might be, for the Universe to look like that. Here. Try your hands at something else. This time I think I know what's going on, but I need help—especially from Sy and Kallen. You're our computer specialists."

He led them back along narrow corridors to the chamber where the patient robots sat in their silent rows. The others watched warily as three of the little machines came to life and glided past them along the passage.

"Don't worry," said Peron. "They don't move fast enough to be dangerous. We can get out of the way, or even move them around if we have to. They're the maintenance crew for the ship. All normal functions are automatic and under computer control. One person can run everything, and even he may be unnecessary except for emergencies. But the robots certainly made my life confusing. When I first found myself in S-space I thought I was going mad. Those machines were a big part of the reason. The other people on the ship could make things happen by magic. They asked for something to be done, or they asked to be taken somewhere, and it was accomplished instantly." Peron snapped his fingers. "Just like that. I tried to do the same thing, and it wouldn't work for me. When I reached this chamber and saw the robots I finally understood what had been happening. The machines respond to commands given by people in S-space. The ship's computer must be voice-coded through the terminals. When a command is given by someone whose voice is recognized and accepted by the system, the computer mobilizes the robots to carry out the instructions. They don't move very fast, but they don't have to. They're quick enough to be invisible in S-space. Even if it takes the robots ten minutes to bring you a drink, or carry you from one part of the ship to another, you don't notice. That's only a fraction of a second as you perceive it."

The others had moved closer to the ranks of robots and were looking at them curiously.

"They look pretty standard," said Sy. "I've never seen this design before, but they're computer controlled. We should be able to understand their instruction procedure."

"But why?" said Rosanne. "Even when we understand it, what are we supposed to do with it?"

"Dig into the coding," said Peron. "Change it. Make it so that *our* voices can give acceptable commands, too. And maybe make it so that the system won't respond to Captain Rinker and the others in S-space."

"But what good will all that do?" asked Elissa. She was looking puzzled.

Lum grinned at her. "Isn't it obvious?" He turned to Peron. "I have it right, don't I? Rinker is correct, Peron, you *are* a troublemaker. You intend to take over this ship. Then we can go and visit Immortal Headquarters—wherever that is—on *our* terms."

Chapter 21:

Olivia Ferranti blinked her eyes. The texture of the illumination seemed a little different, not quite the way that she remembered it before she last went to S-space; and her body was light, floating away, as though she was leaving part of her on the padded floor of the container.

She shivered and slowly sat up, rubbing at her chilled forearms; then she suddenly jerked to full wakefulness. She was being observed. Five faces were peering in warily at her through the transparent top of the suspense tank. She pulled herself forward to the casket's door and eased it open. Peron was standing there, nervously watching.

"You read our message?" he said.

"Of course we did—you were watching us, weren't you?"

He nodded. "We told you to send someone at once. But it seemed to take you an awful long time."

Olivia Ferranti was breathing deeply, adjusting to the familiar but surprising taste of the air in her lungs. She shrugged her shoulders, as much for muscular experiment as for any body message.

"Four days—four days *here*. But we only talked for a few minutes in S-space. I call that a fast response." She looked around her, at Peron and the others. "Relax. I was only sent here to talk. What do you think I'm going to do, knock the lot of you down and tie you up? Any one of you could beat me in a fight. You're the Planetfest winners, remember?"

"We remember," said Peron. "We just want to be sure that *you* do. You and the others. Why are you here, and not Rinker?"

"He made the transition very recently, just a couple of hours ago, when the automatic systems were going wrong. Transitions too close together have bad effects. In fact, frequent transitions shorten subjective life expectancy. And he doesn't trust you, either."

She licked her lips. "I guess he thinks I'm more expendable. Look, I know you're in a hurry to talk, but I'd like a drink of water."

Peron glanced briefly at the others, then led the way back through the winding corridor, taking them once more to the central food processing chamber of the ship.

"He didn't really want anybody to talk to you," said Ferranti as they moved along the corridor. "But he agreed that there was no choice. 'They'll be like a band of wild apes,' he said. 'Fiddling around with my ship! They don't know how anything works—my God, there's no way of knowing what they may do to it and to us!' "

She looked around her at the intent young faces that closely watched her every movement. "I must say that I have to agree with him. I'm sure you're feeling pretty cocky at the moment, with everything under control. But you could kill this ship by pure accident. It's frightening—you're smart, but there are so many things you simply *don't know*."

"So why don't you tell us some of them?" said Sy in a surly voice. "You'll find we're all quick learners."

"I'm not supposed to tell you much—and some things I don't even know myself. And before you get paranoid as to why I'm holding some things back from you, I'll tell you the reason for *that*. There's a sound logic for why you weren't told everything back on Whirlygig."

They had reached the food chamber. Olivia Ferranti bent over a water spigot, took a long, leisurely drink, then sighed and shook her head.

"That's one of the things that I really miss. Water just doesn't taste right in S-space." She turned to face the group. "How much do you know about the history of your civilization on Pentecost?"

"We know that the first settlers came off The Ship," said Peron. "It was called *Eleanora*, and it started out from a planet called Earth, thousands of years earlier."

"That's a beginning." Olivia Ferranti settled herself cross-legged, floating a handsbreadth above the floor, and gestured to the others to gather round her there. "And if you're anything like most of the candidates we get from Pentecost for indoctrination, that's almost *all* that you'll know. So make yourselves comfortable. I need to give you a bit of a history lesson. You may not like some of it too well, but bear with me.

"*Eleanora* was the biggest and most advanced of half a dozen arcologies that were built as colony ships in the Sol System, more than twenty-five thousand Earth-years ago. The arcologies were all constructed in orbits close to Earth. Just as *Eleanora* was close to completion, and the colonists had arrived on board it, the nations down on Earth did what we'd all been afraid they would do for generations. They went mad. Someone pulled the trigger, and after that there was no stopping it. It was a full-scale nuclear war.

"When that war happened, there were about thirty-five thousand people living away from Earth. They were working on mining and construction, or on applications satellites and stations, or they were inhabitants of the colony ships. We were all helpless, watching the world explode before our eyes. And at first none of us knew what to do next. We were numb with shock and horror."

"You said 'we.' You mean you were *there*—yourself?" asked Elissa.

"I was. Me, myself. I was a physician on one of the orbiting space stations." Olivia Ferranti shook her head and rubbed gently at her eyes. She seemed to be staring far beyond the circle of her listeners, out across space and time to the death of a planet. "Initially we just wouldn't believe it. Earth couldn't destroy itself like that. We knew it must have been terrible on the surface, because we had seen the whole globe change in a few hours from a beautiful blue-green marble to a dusky purple-black grape, and the smoke plumes had risen well into the stratosphere. Even so, emotional acceptance was beyond us. Somehow, beyond logic, we believed that the damage was temporary and the surface nations would recover. We waited for radio signals from survivor groups, messages that would tell us that civilization was still going on beneath those dark clouds of dust and smoke. The signals never came. After a few weeks we sent shuttles down into the atmosphere, shielded against high levels of radioactivity and designed to go down below the clouds and examine the surface. There was so much dust in the northern hemisphere that we could see nothing, not even from low altitude. We tried south of the equator, and after a couple of months we finally knew. It was the end.

"We knew we couldn't rule out the possibility of isolated survivors, clinging on to existence down there in the darkness. But as time went by even that hope seemed less and less likely.

"Some plants would survive, we knew that; and we felt sure there would be life in the sea—but we had no idea how much. We tried to calculate what would happen to the whole food chain when photosynthesis was reduced to less than a tenth of the usual value, but we had no faith in our answers. Anyway, they didn't really make any difference. For mankind on Earth, it was the end. And we felt as though it was the end for us, too. We seemed like a handful of mourners, circling the funeral pyre of all our friends and relations.

"We were too shocked to think logically, but we were certainly far more than a handful. As I said, there were thirty-five thousand of us, with slightly-more men than women. And we had ample power and materials available. There was no question that we could survive very well if we pooled our resources and all worked together. We knew it might be centuries before Earth could be revisited and repopulated, but there was no reason why we could not go on indefinitely as a stable, space-borne society."

Ferranti smiled bitterly. "God knows, many of us had said we wanted just that for long enough.

Then when we had no choice, most of us in our dreams imagined ourselves back on Terra.

"There's one good thing about humans; we forget. Despair can't last forever. We pulled ourselves together, little by little, and began to think again. On Salter Station we finally arranged for a radio conference of all the space groups. It was difficult to handle, because one arcology had been out near Mars, and we had long radio lags. But we pulled everyone into the circuits—all the arcologies, the mining groups that had been smelting from the Amor asteroids, and the scientists who had been building the farside station up on Earth's moon. Everything in space had always been controlled from Salter Station, so it seemed natural that we would still be the organizers.

"Natural *to us*, on Salter Station. But others didn't see it that way.

"The arcologies had been set up to be as self-sufficient as possible, with independent power plants and six-nines recycling systems. The other space facilities were different, they were dependent on supplies provided from Earth, or on space-borne resources provided by the mining and extractive industries.

"The first planning session to discuss pooling of resources went smoothly. Everyone participated. But when the time came to act, three of the arcologies backed out. I believe that they each operated independently, without even discussing it among themselves. They were afraid, you see—scared that the *total* group might not be stably self-sustaining, even though they had no doubt about their own ability to survive. There were other reasons, too. From the very beginning the arcologies had been developing their social and political preferences and differences. Like called to like—colonists tended to apply to the same place as their friends, and to avoid a colony where their views would be ridiculed or in the minority. The last thing that *Helena, Melissa*, and *Eleanora* wanted was a merger with Salter Station and the other arcologies. They didn't ever admit that they were not going to cooperate; they simply cut off radio contact and moved farther out, away from Earth.

"The rest of us were angry with them, but we didn't take as much notice as you might think. We had our own hands full without them for the first few years. We had to establish our own system, self-sufficient and as foolproof as we could make it. That took ninety-nine percent of our energies. And the rest went into the work on reduced metabolic survival—what we finally called S-space existence. As a doctor I was naturally interested in that, and after a while I began to work on it exclusively. Within a couple of months of the first experiments with human subjects on Salter Station it was clear that we had something absolutely revolutionary, something that changed all our ideas about perception and human consciousness. But it took several years more before we saw the other implications. With our work, humanity had found the easy way to the stars.

"There was no need for multi-generation arcologies, or for faster-than-light drives—"

"—which seem to be impossible," murmured Sy softly.

"Which *may be* impossible," said Ferranti. "Keep an open mind. Anyway, we didn't need them. The drive system research on Salter Station would allow us to accelerate a ship up to better than a tenth of lightspeed, and that was enough. In Mode

Two consciousness—S-space—a human being could remain fully aware, live an extended subjective life, and travel across the whole Galaxy in a single lifetime.

"That led to a new crisis. Everyone loved the idea of an extended subjective life span—if it were safe. But everyone was terrified of possible side effects.

"We split into two groups. Some of us said, let's move to S-space, and wait there at least until Earth is habitable again. No one knew how long that would be, but in S-space we could afford to wait centuries and perceive them as only a few weeks. Others were afraid. They argued that there were too many unknowns and too many risks in S-space living; until those were pinned down it was better to stay with our normal perception."

Olivia Ferranti smiled ruefully. "As it turned out, both groups were right. Earth recovered slowly. It took more than a thousand years to develop new and stable plant and animal communities. None of us had ever dreamed it would be so long. And at the same time, we were discovering serious physical consequences of S-space living.

"Fortunately we didn't fight over our differences of opinion on the move to S-space. Maybe the destruction of Earth had taught us all something about the need for peaceful resolution of conflicts. We agreed we would pursue both actions. Most people elected to stay as they were, creating a decent society in the spaceborne environment. After a few generations it was clear that a life in space was as satisfying as most of us had ever hoped. By then a few hundred of us had long since moved to S-space, using ourselves as the subjects for experiments that might reduce the risk for those who followed us. While we were doing that we discovered a new mode of metabolic change, this one a true suspended animation. Five of you have personal experience of that cold sleep, here on the ship. We still don't know how long someone can remain safely unconscious in that mode, but it's certainly a long time—thousands of years at least.

"The move to S-space had two other important consequences. First, we realized that we *couldn't* go back down and live on Earth, or anywhere with a substantial gravity field, even if we wanted to. That had been deduced when the experiments were still all on animals, and it was one major reason for moving the work out to orbit and away from the surface of Earth. You see, perceived accelerations—"

"We understand," said Peron. "Kallen and Sy"—he pointed to them—"figured it out."

"Smart." Olivia Ferranti looked at the group appraisingly. "When I'm through, perhaps you'll tell me a little more about yourselves. All I know so far is what I was told by Peron and by Captain Rinker."

"Won't he be wondering what's happening?" said Rosanne. Then she stopped and put her hand to her mouth.

"He might—in a few more days." Ferranti smiled and Rosanne grinned back at her. The initial tension of confrontation was fading. They were all increasingly absorbed in the first-person tale of remote history.

Olivia Ferranti leaned against the wall and pushed back the blue cowl from her forehead, to reveal a mop of jet-black tight curls. "We have lots of time. At the moment, Captain Rinker and the others hardly know I've left."

"But you've got hair!" blurted out Lum.

Olivia Ferranti raised her dark eyebrows at him. "I'm glad to hear that you think so."

"It's what I told them," said Peron. "I thought S-space made you bald."

"It does. Didn't you ever hear of wigs, down on Pentecost? Most of the men in S-space don't worry about it, but I don't care to face the world with a naked scalp—my ideas on the right way for me to look were fixed long before I ever dreamed of S-space. Anyway, I have a lumpy skull that I have no great desire to show off to others." She patted her dark ringlets. "I much prefer this. The nice thing about it is that it will never go grey."

"What else does S-space do to people?" asked Sy. More than the rest of them, except possibly for Kallen who had typically not spoken at all, Sy seemed reserved and unwarmed by Olivia Ferranti's open manner.

"I'm getting there," she said. "Let me tell you that in a few minutes. I want to do this in a logical order, and explain what happened after Earth had been destroyed. It's important that you know, so you'll understand why we behave the way we do in the Cass system.

"While we were still busy working out the stable society for life away from Earth, and some of us were also learning how to live in S-space, we didn't have time to worry about what was happening to *Eleanora* and the other arcologies. And to tell the truth, we didn't really give a damn. They'd selfishly deserted us, said our logic, so to hell with them. As far as we were concerned they could fly away and rot.

"But after a while those of us who were living in S-space—I was one of the first twenty people to take Mode Two hibernation—became pretty curious. You see, we knew we had the stars within reach. We had the drive we needed, and the time we needed. And *Helena*, *Melissa* and *Eleanora* had all headed off outside the Solar System, in different directions. We didn't know how much of the reason for their departure was an interest in exploration, and how much of it was fear of reprisals from us. We weren't planning revenge of any kind, but how were *they* to know that? All three of them had shown signs of paranoia, back when they were first colonized. We got more and more curious to know what had happened to those three arcologies.

"Eventually we equipped four ships with service robots, similar to the ones on this ship, and with limited life-support systems. We didn't need perfect recycling, only enough for a few months of travel in S-space. The final design gave the ships a useful exploration range of up to fifty lightyears. At the slow speed of the arcologies, we knew they couldn't be farther out than that. And the stellar profiles in the neighborhood of Sol gave us a fairly good idea where the colony ships were likely to be headed. Political systems change, but the physical constraints are still there. We thought we'd find them about twenty lightyears out.

"When we had everything ready, our ships set off with their volunteer crews. We had no shortage of people willing to make the trip—I put my own name in, but didn't make it. There were many with better qualifications than mine for interstellar cruising.

"As it happened, we had overestimated the distance they had gone. We had made insufficient allowance for the difficulties that *Melissa* and the others might be having on board. It hadn't been a smooth ride by any means. There had been a civil war on *Melissa*, an economic collapse on *Eleanora*, and a power plant failure on *Helena*. Those variables affected both their speeds and their directions. *Helena* actually reversed direction and started back to Sol for a while, until the trouble was fixed and she could head outwards again.

"Our ships had no trouble tracking and finding the arcologies. After all, they had no reason to expect pursuit, and nothing to be gained by concealing their presence. But when we reached them, we found that no arcology had found a habitable planet, and all three were still in deep interstellar space. After reporting back to us—S-space radio signal time was only a couple of days—it was agreed that we would not establish contact with them. We decided to do nothing, and not to interfere in any way unless an arcology was in actual danger of extinction. They hadn't asked for help, and we didn't want to give it. Your ancestors would be allowed to wander around until either they found a habitable planet, or they decided that a permanent space life suited them better. Then we would reconsider possible contact.

"Our ships left automated tracking probes to follow the arcologies and report on their movements, and headed for home.

"It may seem strange to you that we had so little interest in the arcologies. But we were in no hurry. We could wait in S-space and see what developed. And certainly we had plenty of other things to interest us, because by that time Earth was finally being visited again on a regular basis.

"Still we had doubts that humans could thrive there. The long dust-winter had exterminated ninety percent of the plant species, and all land-based animal forms bigger than the rat—and I mean an *Earth* rat, not one of the thirty-kilo monsters you call rats on Pentecost. We also found that the surviving plants and animals had changed from their old forms. The grasses were unrecognizable. Many of the old food plants tasted wrong in subtle ways, and some had lost all their nutritional values. We all realized that it would take millennia to restore Earth and make it a place worth living. But oddly enough, we all thought it a worthwhile effort—even those who had found life on Earth absolutely intolerable before the holocaust.

"By the time that the Earth visits began we were feeling much more comfortable about S-space. Some of us had been living there for many Earth-generations, and we were all feeling fine—better than fine, because we didn't seem to be aging at all. Our best estimate, based on limited data, was that the aging rate was twenty times as slow *subjectively* as it was in normal living. That extrapolated to a seventeen hundred year subjective lifetime—and even if we were wrong by a factor of two, that was still a mighty attractive thought.

"When our result became known, naturally more and more people wanted to move to S-space. It didn't happen overnight, but as time went by we learned how to make the transitions both ways, with minimal danger. By then we also knew the big problem with S-space existence."

"You keep referring to problems and never telling us about them," said Elissa. "*What* problem?"

"I've not been talking because I'm not *supposed* to talk," said Ferranti. "No one back on Pentecost should know what I'm telling you until they've been through indoctrination, and not one of you has; but you'll realize the problem for yourselves in a minute as soon as we arrive at local Headquarters, so I'm not revealing any great secrets."

Olivia Ferranti moved her thin hands to her cheeks, framing her eyes. "You'll find no children at Headquarters," she said abruptly. "A woman cannot conceive in S-space, or a man produce active sperm. S-space is a wonderful place for an individual, but it's an evolutionary blind alley. Worse than that, anyone who makes frequent transitions between S-space and normal space suffers reduced fertility.

"That presented us with a terrible choice. Did we opt for extended personal life span in S-space, or would we guarantee the survival of the human race by staying in normal space?

"While we were still agonizing over that, we received a signal from the probe that had been tracking *Melissa*. The colony ship was in the Tau Ceti system, and it had finally found a habitable planet. They were exploring it. We eventually found out that they had named it *Thule*.

"It was twelve lightyears from Earth, which made it a four week one-way journey in S-space when we allowed for acceleration and deceleration. I don't think I mentioned it, but no matter how we tried we had been unable to come up with an economical drive that would take us much faster than a tenth of lightspeed. But it wasn't important any more. As you can see, that's good enough when you live in S-space.

"Our ship went out, and in due course it made contact with *Melissa*. That first meeting was traumatic for the *Melissa* inhabitants. They had left Earth twelve thousand years earlier—five hundred generations of shipboard life. Earth was nothing but a distant legend. It was something that was still talked about, but stories of Earth's destruction were regarded as of the same practical importance as tales about the Garden of Eden. When our crew contacted them and claimed to *remember* the death of Earth, that was too much for the Melissans to take.

"After we had learned something of their history since leaving the Solar System, we could see why. They had never had a stable and trustworthy government that lasted for more than a century. We found historical evidence of every form of rule from water-control to neo-Confucianism. When they discovered Thule they were just recovering from the effects of a long dictatorship. Their mistrust and suspicion was considerable. Even the most rational of them found difficulty in believing that our intentions were wholly innocent, nothing more than curiosity to learn how another culture was faring after so long without any kind of planetary home. They would not let us visit their colony on Thule. Putting it mildly, they suspected our motives."

Olivia Ferranti slowly shook her head. "And, of course, they were wholly correct in doing so. Even in s-space, one is not wholly protected from accidents and disease. There would inevitably be deaths, and without replenishment we foresaw our society shrinking—not at once, but over many thousands of Earth years. In *Melissa* and the other arcologies we saw a possible answer.

"Either we were unusually stupid, or we were simply naive. To make the Melissans believe us, and to show how we could be people who actually remembered Earth's final war, we explained about S-space to them.

"They went crazy. They wanted S-space more than anything else in the Universe. You see, we were misled by our own experiences. We had been slow to accept and move to S-space. We didn't realize that our reluctance wouldn't apply to them. They hadn't been there for the early, risky experiments. To them, our existence *proved* that S-space must be safe. So they thought we were deliberately goading them, tormenting them with a look at immortality while refusing to share its secret with them.

"Most of our ship's crew had gone on board *Melissa*. They took them, eight men and six women, and tried to draw the secret of S-space from them by force. It was useless, of course. The conversion equipment was on the ship, as it is on this ship, and the crew had used it to go from S-space to the perception rate of the Melissans. But they didn't know the *theory*, any more than Garao or Captain Rinker know the theory.

"The inquisitors tortured those crew members to death. Only the two who had remained on our ship were able to escape and come back to tell us what had happened.

"That's when we adopted our first rules for interaction with *all* colony ships and colony worlds. We would have limited contact, and it would be handled with great care and with fixed rules. We would never again return ourselves to normal space for the purpose of contact, as was done with *Melissa*. Contact would be done with robots as intermediaries; and we would *never*, under any circumstances, allow ourselves to fall into the hands of the colonists."

Olivia Ferranti shrugged. "There's another rule we've broken on this trip. Well, let's skip forward four thousand years. That's when another of the arcologies, *Helena*, finally found a habitable planet.

They named it Beacon's World, colonized it, and moved on. That's when we learned another lesson. Beacon's World was settled long before we sent a ship to visit it. When our ship finally got there we found that the population had increased from the original few thousand to forty million; but along the way much of their scientific knowledge had been lost, or had degenerated to hearsay and legend.

"We tried to help. We reintroduced the basis for a more advanced technology. They were keen to receive the information from us—but they applied it to weapons development. Then they started a war, between the two major settlement centers on Beacon's World. Our ship and crew felt helpless, watching while they slaughtered each other. But we felt we had to do *something*—it was impossible to stand by, uninvolved, when we knew the information we provided had allowed the conflict to be so savage. The crew of our ship tried a desperation tactic: through our robots, they *ordered* the warring parties to stop fighting—without saying what would happen if the order were disobeyed.

"It worked. The fighting stopped.

"We had learned another important truth. By being 'Immortals,' with a technology and a life pattern that was incomprehensible to the colonists, we could have enormous influence.

"That provided us with our next rule of contact: remain as aloof and mysterious as possible. And if we recruited anyone to join us in S-space—we wanted only exceptional specimens—we would introduce them to our society gradually, through a long and thorough indoctrination.

"Our rules worked very well. People joined us from Maremar and Jade—two other planets settled by *Helena*—and have been working in those systems and at Headquarters for thousands of Earth-years.

"Finally, there was your world. You probably don't know it, but Pentecost is a very recent addition to our planetary visits. We found you only a few months ago, as we perceive time in S-space, and it was a minor miracle that we found you at all.

"You see, *Eleanora* was the unlucky one of the colony ships. The other two arcologies found several planets suitable for settlements. But your ancestors had to wander the interstellar wilderness for over fifteen thousand years, without ever once approaching a habitable world. We know why, now. For the past four thousand Earth-years we've been able to predict pretty well the stellar systems and planets likely to support life. And *Eleanora* just went to the wrong star systems, in terms of our new knowledge. Unfortunately, that same knowledge led us astray in following *Eleanora*, when our tracking probe finally wore out. As it happens, the Cass system is generally *not* suited to life, or the occurrence of habitable worlds. The existence of Pentecost, Gimperstand, Fuzzball, and Glug is an accident, the by-product of resonance locks between planetary orbits.

"We could have found you on Pentecost four thousand years ago if we had thought to look. As it was, we only detected your radio emissions a few hundred years ago. And we finally made contact with you.

"We followed our standard rules. Slow and limited contact, and don't try to change the government of the contacted world. As it happens, Pentecost has had a classical totalitarian regime ever since first contact—a government more concerned to remain in power than anything else, and sublimely disinterested in interstellar affairs. From our point of view, that was perfect. Everything worked according to plan for hundreds of your years—until this Planetfest, when Headquarters was informed that an unusual group of winners was likely. *You* don't know who the winners will be in advance, you see, but our people down on Pentecost had a pretty good idea. We expected trouble, but we didn't know what. Personally, I think *something* would have happened even if Wilmer hadn't taken the action he did on Whirlygig. Your profiles are all too far away from the standard patterns. But that's my speculation. The main thing is, something *did* happen. And "—Olivia Ferranti looked at the intent young faces around her and shook her head—"here we are. We have to decide what will happen next.

"I'll accept that you have control of the ship. And I hope you'll accept my word when I tell you your control could be dangerous, with the limited knowledge you have. The present situation is bad for everyone, including you. So let me start the ball rolling for more discussions, by telling you that I was sent here with a proposition from all of us—even including Captain Rinker."

The group around her came to life. They were suddenly fidgeting, looking at each other questioningly. For over half an hour their present situation had been pushed into the background by interest in the fate of others. The return to the present was an uncomfortable one.

Peron met the eyes of each of them in turn. Finally he nodded.

"We've nothing to lose by listening to you—just remember that we have physical control of you and of the ship. So all right. We'll listen. What's your proposition?"

Chapter 22:

Slowly, millimeter by infinite millimeter, Olivia Ferranti's eyes were opening. A thin line of white had appeared behind the long false eyelashes. It broadened, to become a slender crescent. The lids crept apart, at last to reveal dilated pupils and the luminous brown irises, flecked with gold.

"That's it," said Peron finally. "She's in S-space. At last. There's no way that anyone could fake an awakening like that. Let's get back to the chamber and talk."

Every one of the six had known that a discussion was urgently needed; but the urge to watch Olivia Ferranti had been irresistible and tacitly admitted by all.

They had gathered around the great tank as she prepared to enter. They watched in silence while she, impressively calm, went inside. And as soon as the heavy casket door slid into sealed position she lay back, stared up at them through the transparent upper surface, and gave a little wave of her fingertips. Then she reached for the interior control panel and hit the key sequence to initiate her return to S-space.

After a few seconds, clusters of contact sprays moved to drift a fine fluid vapor over her limbs and body, while delicate catheters snaked from the casket walls and insinuated themselves gently into the orifices of her head and trunk. A dense yellow-green vapor sluggishly filled the interior of the tank, rising after a few minutes to hide Olivia Ferranti's still form in a soft-edged shroud.

There was little to see after that, but they had stood waiting for almost two hours, exchanging brief phrases in hushed tones. Only when the air in the casket finally cleared and Olivia Ferranti began to stir again to slow consciousness were they able to think of other matters.

And now, watching her eyes creep open, they all felt a renewed and ridiculous sense of urgency. Logic said that another day or two of their thought and discussion would pass unnoticed to Rinker and the others in S-space, but the sense of haste went beyond logic. That feeling dimmed a little as they moved back to the computer chamber, and found the control settings and service robots exactly as they had left them.

"So what do you think?" said Peron abruptly, as they settled down in a close circle by the gently flickering displays of the main computer console.

"I believe her," said Rosanne at once.

"I don't," added Sy promptly. "She was lying to us."

"Lum?"

"Some of each." Lum massaged his full cheeks with one hand, and furrowed his brow. "Mostly I believe her. She kept pretty close to the truth, but

I think she exercised selective memory. She left some things out."

"She sure did." Sy's thin face wore a scowl. "Things she didn't tell us. I could list ten of them. What happens if we reject their suggestion? Who makes the rules that decide what we ought to know, and when? What's supposed to happen if a Planetfest winner doesn't swallow the party line? Where do *they* go? One thing's for sure, they don't go back home to Pentecost. I wonder if they have convenient 'accidents' in the Cass system—we know there's ample scope for that around the Fifty Worlds."

"We're getting ahead of ourselves," said Lum. He wriggled uncomfortably inside his jacket, a brown garment too tight in the chest and short in the sleeves. "Let's take Ferranti's story one piece at a time, and see what we agree on. Anything?"

"I thought her history lesson sounded genuine," volunteered Elissa.

"So did I," said Peron.

"More to the point," said Lum, "I can't see what advantage she would gain by lying. And I believe her when she says that we are now on our way to their headquarters. But some of her other statements struck me as false. For one thing, I don't really believe that we're a danger to the ship and to ourselves, just because we're strangers here and in normal space. We didn't get through the Planetfest trials without learning caution. We know how to be careful, and we look before we leap. I think she said we were in danger because they *want* us in S-space, where they can keep an eye on us. They want to be in control. Well, we can't afford that. Sy, how's the reprogramming going for the service robots?"

"Done. They'll obey our voice commands now. But Kallen and I have a question. Do we want it so the computer will activate the service robots in response to our voices, and no one else's? Or should we leave it working for Ferranti and the others, too?"

"Must it be one or the other?" said Lum. "Couldn't you set a trigger, so that we can cut the others out of control if we choose to, based on our voice command? Then we'd be quite safe."

Sy raised his eyebrows inquiringly at Kallen, who pursed his lips and massaged his scarred throat.

"Think so," he said after a moment. "I'll try it."

"All right." Lum nodded. "Before you do that, let's think a bit more about what we were told by Ferranti. What about their headquarters? According to her, it's about a lightyear away from Pentecost. But why put it there? If the rest of her story is true, there are *fewer* colonies near the Cass System than anywhere else. It would make more sense to locate Immortal Headquarters near Tau Ceti, or some other star with more habitable planets."

"I can answer that," said Peron. "When I was first awakened, Ferranti referred to *Sector* Headquarters. That means there ought to be others, in other systems. Remember, according to Ferranti *all* the colonies are twenty lightyears or less away from Sol. For S-space travel, that's only at most a five week trip. I'll bet there are several Sector Headquarters, one near each stellar system that was colonized."

"So where is General Headquarters?" asked Elissa. "Is there one?"

"I'll bet there is," said Lum. "Even the Immortals would need some sort of overall organization of resources. And didn't you get the feeling that at the headquarters we are headed for most of the rules are *followed*, not made?"

"So where is the central one?" repeated Elissa. "Where's Main Headquarters?"

Lum put his hands up to his head and rubbed at his thick shock of mousy-brown hair. "Lord knows. We have to rethink *everything*, if travel to the stars is so easy for them. Headquarters could be a hundred lightyears away from here. That's only a six month trip in S-space. But it wouldn't make much sense. Even in S-space, it would be hard to manage an organization where messages take weeks to get around the system."

"You're making it hard," said Sy softly. "Think simple."

"You mean Sector Headquarters is the only one?"

"No. Think Sol."

The others looked at him, then at each other.

"He's right, as usual," said Peron. "All the ships started from Earth. It was the center of the sphere of expansion, so it's still the natural hub for coordinating colonies and Sector Headquarters. Main Headquarters ought to be Earth."

There was another silence.

"*Earth!*" said Rosanne at last. Her voice was hushed, and the word came from her lips like a benediction. "If General Headquarters is back on Earth, maybe we can go there. . . ."

"Not actually *on* Earth," said Lum. "We know you can't go down to a planet's surface if you live in S-space."

Kallen was shaking his head. "No. Can't live on planet. We could *visit*." He looked greatly excited.

"He's quite right, you know," said Sy. "We all agree that anyone in S-space wouldn't be able to keep their balance in anything more than a micro-gravity field. But perception and physical tolerance are nothing to do with each other. Your body could stand gravity all right. You'd have to be supported and restrained, but you could visit the surface of Earth—or of Pentecost—living in S-space."

"That would be enough," said Rosanne suddenly. "Even a short visit, in S-space or in normal space. I want to go to Earth, see where everything began. We've talked about it and thought about it so much. Can you imagine flying down through the atmosphere, and walking on Earth's surface?"

"Steady on," said Peron. "Don't get carried away. Sol is eighteen lightyears from here. I know that's only a few weeks travel in S-space, but it's nearly two centuries back on Pentecost. Everyone we know there would be long dead before we even reached Earth, let alone came back to Cass."

Rosanne shrugged. "I can't speak for you, but I already said goodbye to all my best friends. It's curious, but I think we were set up for it. We said our farewells before we lifted off from Pentecost. Remember, they encouraged us to do it, and we thought it was in case we died in the off-planet trials? But it makes sense. If winners go through indoctrination and move to S-space, they would outlive all their contemporaries on Pentecost in just a few S-space weeks. Do you realize that the people we left back home have already aged five years since we last saw them?"

"I've been thinking of that," said Lum. "I'm not like you, Rosanne, I really miss some of the friends I left—and I'd like to see them again sometime. That's something else we ought to be worrying about. We've been dealing with Olivia Ferranti on the 'united we stand' basis, as though we all have identical objectives and want the same things. But we don't. I know you all well enough to be sure that's not true. We should get our personal preferences out on the table, so we'll know what we're bargaining for with the Immortals."

"But what are our options?" said Elissa. "We can go to Headquarters, I suppose, and live in S-space there. Or we could return to Cass and live on The Ship, and work with the government of Pentecost. But I'm sure they won't let us go back down to the surface of Pentecost, and live the way we used to do, even if we want to. We know too much. Maybe they'd let us go to one of the other colonies. Or maybe we can go to Earth."

"That's why I'd like to know what we *want*," said Lum. "We each have our own desires and priorities—but what are they?"

"Why don't you start?" said Rosanne. "It's your question, and it gives the rest of us more time to think."

"Fair enough." Lum took a deep breath. "I've known what I want ever since the moment when I found out there are other planets and colonies, and a way to reach them in a reasonable time. Ferranti mentioned at least seven inhabited planets, and I'll bet there are more. I want to move to S-space, and see *everything*. I'd like to visit every planet, and every arcology, and every headquarters. If I could do it, I'd like to see every planet in the Galaxy—even if most of them prove to be like Glug."

Rosanne nodded. "I don't know if that's all possible, but at least you're voting for a move to S-space—otherwise you'd be dead long before you reached your first colony. Sy? What about you?"

"Wandering around forever isn't for me." Sy was smiling, but there was something in his look that suggested his disdain for Lum's travel plans. "I want to visit Immortal Headquarters—whichever one is the most appropriate, wherever their science is farthest developed. What we learned on Pentecost is probably generations out of date. After that, I'd like to visit the galactic center."

"That's thirty thousand lightyears!" said Peron.

"Sure it is. I don't mind. If I have to go back to cold sleep for a while to get there, I'll do it. The rest of us have all been under once, and it wasn't a bad experience."

Rosanne was staring at him and shaking her head. "Sy, I worked with you on the Planetfest trials, and I know you're pretty much all right— but you're certainly *weird*. The galactic center!"

He grinned back at her. "So? Let's hear from somebody normal, then. Where do you want to go?"

"Well. . . ." She hesitated. "I like the Cass system, and I liked Pentecost. But I agree with Elissa, they wouldn't let us go back there for a long time. So forget that. I'd certainly like to see Earth—who wouldn't? Apart from that I suppose I'm a lot like Lum. I want to see lots of other places, wander around the colonies and the habitable planets, see what's there. . . ."

Elissa winked at Peron. *I told you so*, said her look. *I win that bet. Rosanne's a lot more interested in Lum that she'll ever admit.* "What about you, Peron?" she said loudly.

Peron looked as perplexed as he felt. "I'm not at all sure, and I just wish I knew. I want it *all*—to be back home on Pentecost, to travel, and to take a really close look at the Immortals."

"You're not much help!"

"I know. I suppose the best answer is that I can't say for the long term. But for the moment I want to know more about S-space, and the only way to do that is to move there for a while. Olivia Ferranti makes me feel like a child in the cradle. She didn't exactly say it, but she must think we're upstart babies. When I think of all that she has seen and done, and the things she told us about. . . ."

"Not to mention all the things she has seen and done, and *not* told us about," said Sy drily. "Kallen, it's your turn."

The tall youth nodded. He stood silent for a while, as though organizing his words.

"Rosanne told Sy he was strange," he said at last. He smiled shyly. "I am afraid that she will judge me even more so." He cleared his throat, and spoke louder than any of them had heard before. "Back on Pentecost, I lay awake at night with my own dreams. I wondered what we are, as a species, and what in time we might become. It has always seemed to me that humans are best regarded as a transitional stage, something between animals and what may come after. I speculated. What will that next phase be? The question always seemed an unanswerable one; but no longer. I want to see the future—the far future. And like Sy, I will be happy to return to cold sleep in order to accomplish that." He smiled again. "*After* I have had a good look at S-space, but not before."

"I always told the others you were the dreamer," said Elissa. "The far future? You're worse than Sy. Let's see, what conclusions do we have? We're quite a mixed bag. We've got two votes for the colonies, and for taking the grand tour; one for science and the galactic center; one for the future;

and one who's not sure just what he wants. What else? We all think we're not getting the whole story, and that Olivia Ferranti knows things about S-space life that she hasn't told us. Nobody relishes the notion of spending a long time at local Headquarters, but we know we'll have to start there. And I gather we're all itching to take a trip to Earth if we can find a way to do it. That's my summary. Anything missing?"

"At least one thing," said Peron. "There's still one person we've not heard from. What about *you*, Elissa—what do you want to do?"

She gave him a peculiar stare. "You mean, where will I go? Peron, you're a bone-headed idiot and a blind tardy. Are you trying to embarrass me?"

To Peron's surprise there was a burst of laughter and incoherent comments from the other four.

"You name it, Peron!" said Lum.

"Name it. Name what?"

"Anything you like."

"Lum's right," said Elissa. She moved across to Peron and hugged him, while the others cheered.

"You name it." She ran her knuckles along his ribs. "Shake me loose—if you can. I'm going where you're going, and it would be kind of nice if you'd make up your mind and tell me where that is. But you don't have to do it now, because it looks like we all agree on the next step. We go to S-space, then to Earth. Think it's feasible?"

"We'll have to do some arm-twisting," said Lum. "But we have an awful lot of power so long as one of us is here in normal space. Do you realize that a tiny boost from the engines of this ship, one we wouldn't notice, would make it impossible for anyone in S-space to stand up? You can bet that *they* all know it—they must be wondering what we might do next."

"So let's tell them we're ready for the next round of bargaining," said Peron. "And let's insist that it be done here, not in S-space. That's going to make any of them uncomfortable, and eager to get back to their usual environment. Agreed?"

The others nodded.

"I can hardly wait to see S-space," added Rosanne. "I hope that Kallen and Sy changed the control program correctly. I like the idea of all my wishes being granted."

PART III

THE PATH TO GULF CITY

Chapter 23:

Peron was drowsing when the alert sounded. For a couple of minutes he struggled against awakening, trying to merge the soft, blurred tones into the fabric of his dreams.

roomb . . . roomb . . . roomb . . . roomb . . .

He had been back on Pentecost, back when the idea of competition in the Planetfest had itself been like a dream. Twelve years old; the first tests, part of the State-wide evaluation of every adolescent. The blindfold maze was presented to them as no more than a game, something that they could all enjoy. He had scrupulously obeyed the rules, mapping his path by ears alone, following the soft, purring will-o'-the-wisp tone of the muted bell.

It was seven more years before he understood the hidden purpose of the maze test. Sense of direction, yes. But more than that. Memory, courage, honesty, and a willingness to cooperate with other competitors when single talents could not provide a solution. It was *direct* preparation for Planetfest, though no one ever admitted it.

So how was Sy performing in the maze? That

was a mystery. Sy was a loner. He didn't seek partners, even when the task looked impossible for a solo performer.

Peron, hauled back to full consciousness, realized that he had been confusing past and present. Sy was here, now, on the ship. When Peron took the maze test, he had never heard of Sy.

But it was still a good question. How *had* Sy found his way through the preliminaries for Planetfest? That was a puzzle to be filed away and addressed later. Meanwhile, that insistent tone was continuing, summoning Peron to action.

. . . roomb . . . roomb . . . roomb.

He sighed. So much for sleep. He had been trying to push the S-space sleep requirement down to its lower limit, to less than one hour in twenty-four. But he had been overdoing it. He stood up unsteadily, noticing that Elissa had already left their living quarters, and made his way to the central control chamber.

Olivia Ferranti was already there, gazing out of the port. Elissa and Sy were at her side, staring out into the formless sea of milky-white that sat outside the ship in S-space.

Except that it was no longer formless. Dark, complex shapes were there, drifting past the window. Peron saw a tracery of wispy rectangles, joined by braided lines of silver. Attendant on them, although not connected to them, were veined doublet wings like giant sycamore seeds.

Olivia Ferranti acknowledged Peron's arrival with no more than a brief nod.

"Remember what I told you when we were heading for Sector Headquarters?" she said. "I'm not sure you believed me. There's one of the reasons why Rinker didn't want you messing with his ship. Look at the power drain."

On the main console, every readout showed energy consumption up near the danger level. Peron glanced at the indicators for only a moment, then his attention was irresistibly drawn back to the shapes outside the port.

"What are they?" he said. "Are they taking our power?"

Olivia Ferranti was keying in a signal to the communications module. "They certainly are," she said. "That lattice shape is a Gossamere—one of the surprises of interstellar space. You'll never find one within a lightyear of a star. The strangest thing about them is that they're quite invisible in ordinary space, but so easy to see here in S-space." She indicated the screen to the left of the port where a frequency-shifted image was displayed, allowing them to see outside the ship at the wavelengths of normal visible radiation. It showed only the star field of deep space. Sol was the nearest star now, nearly three lightyears ahead and no more than a faint point of light.

"We don't know how the Gossameres do it," went on Ferranti. "But they maintain themselves at less than one degree absolute, well *below* cosmic background temperature, without emitting radiation at any frequency that we've been able to detect. And they suck up all the power that a ship can give out. If you didn't know that and were in charge of a ship, you could get into terrible trouble."

"But what *are* they?" repeated Peron. "I mean, are they intelligent?"

"We don't know," said Ferranti. "They certainly respond to stimuli. They seem to interpret signals we send them, and they stop the power drain on us as soon as they receive a suitable non-random message. Our best guess is that the Gossameres are not intelligent, they're no more than power collection and propulsion systems. But the Pipistrelles—those bat shapes that you can see alongside the Gossamere—they're another matter. They ride the galactic gravitational and magnetic fields, and they do it in complex ways. We've never managed a two-way exchange of information with them—they never emit—but they *act* smart. They really use the fields efficiently to make minimum time and energy movements. That could be some kind of advanced instinct, too, the way that a soaring bird will ride the thermals of an atmosphere. But watch them now. What does this mean? Are they saying goodbye? We've never been sure."

She had completed the signal sequence. After a brief delay, one of the Pipistrelles swooped in close towards the ship. There was a flutter of cambered wings, a dip to left and right, and a final surge of power drain on the meters. Then the panels and filaments of the Gossamere began to move farther off. The silver connecting lines shone brighter, while the whole assembly slowly faded. After a few minutes, the winged shapes of the Pipistrelles closed into a tighter formation and followed the Gossamere.

"We had ships drift helpless, with all power shut down for months, until we learned how to handle this," said Ferranti. "We even tried aggression, but nothing we did affected the Gossameres at all. Now we've learned how to live with them."

"Can you bring them back?" asked Sy.

"We've never found a way to do it. They appear at random. And we encounter them far less often now than when our ships first went out. We think that the 'power plant failure' on *Helena* when the arcologies first set out was probably an encounter with a Gossamere. When the colonists turned off the plant to repair it, they couldn't find anything wrong. That's typical of a Gossamere power drain. They certainly don't seem to *need* our energy, but they like it. The science group in the Jade sector headquarters argue that we're a treat for the Pipistrelles, a compact energy source when they are used to a very dilute one. We're like candy to them, and maybe they've learned that too much candy isn't a good thing."

She switched off the display screen and rose from her seat at the port. "Stay here if you like, and play with the com link. Maybe you can find a way to lure them back. That would certainly please our exobiologists and communications people. I wanted you all to see this, and absorb my message: you can't learn all about the Universe crouching in close by a star. You have to know what's going on out in deep space."

"What else *is* going on?" asked Elissa. She was still peering out into the milky depths of S-space, watching as the final traces of the Pipistrelles slowly faded from sight.

"Here?" said Ferranti. "Nothing much. On the other hand, we're not in deep space. Sol is less than three lightyears from here—we'll be there in less than a week. Now, if we were in *deep* space, with no star closer than ten lightyears. . . ."

Olivia Ferranti stopped abruptly. She had seemed about to say more, but thought better of it. With a nod at the others, she turned and left the control room.

*　　*　　*

"So what do you make of *that*?" said Elissa.

Sy merely shook his head and offered no comment.

"She's telling us there are more surprises on the way," said Peron. "I like Olivia, and I think she's doing her best for us. She knows there are still things she's not supposed to reveal to us, so she gives us hints and lets us work on them for ourselves. That was another one—but I don't know how to interpret it. Damn it, though, I wish that the others were here. I'd like Kallen's comments on the Gossameres. Do you think we made a bad mistake, splitting up like that?"

Peron had been asking himself and the other two that question ever since they left Sector Headquarters. It had seemed like a small thing at the time. Given their experiences after they left Whirlygig, the briefings from the Immortals had been boring rather than thrilling. They had learned about S-space for themselves, the hard way, and what should have come as revelations came merely as confirmation of known facts. The personnel at Sector Headquarters were minimal, little more than a communications and administrative group, and almost all the information was provided through education robots and computer courses—neither of which had been programmed with interest as a dominant factor. As Rosanne had put it, after a long and tedious series of humorless computer warnings about the physiological dangers of frequent movements to and from S-space: "You mean they had to bring us a whole lightyear for *this*? Maybe when you're an Immortal you don't live longer—it just *seems* longer."

One of their negotiated conditions with Captain Rinker for return of ship control to him had been a freedom to travel after their training and indoctri-

nation. At first he had indignantly refused to consider such a thing. Unprecedented! He at last
grudgingly agreed, after Kallen had sent several
thousand service robots to Rinker's living quarters. They cluttered up every available square foot
of space, moved randomly about, refused to obey
any of Rinker's orders, and made eating, walking,
or even sleeping impossible.

When the indoctrination was finally over, each
of them was bored and restless. And when they
learned that two ships would be arriving at Sector
Headquarters within one S-space day of each other,
one bound for Earth directly, and the other proceeding there via Paradise, they had split into two
groups. Kallen wanted to visit the investigating
group of Immortals orbiting Paradise, while Lum
and Rosanne were curious to take a trip down to
the surface of the planet itself. The computer had
contained a brief description of events that led to
the extinction of the colony on Paradise, but as
Lum had pointed out, that stark recitation of facts
was unsatisfying. A healthy, thriving population of
over a million humans had died in a few days,
with no written or natural record to show how or
why. If it could happen so easily on Paradise, why
couldn't it happen on Pentecost, or anywhere else?

Since the whole detour would amount to no more
than a week of S-space travel, Elissa, Peron and Sy
had taken the ship direct to Sol. Kallen, Rosanne,
and Lum went to Paradise. And as Lum had cheerfully pointed out as they were leaving, they would
never be more than an S-day apart through radio
communications. They could talk to each other
any time. Except that their ship's equipment
seemed to be in continuous higher-priority use. . . .

Now, Peron at least was regretting their decision to separate. And Sy was looking unusually thoughtful and withdrawn, even for him.

"Perhaps I have everything backwards," he said at last. "When I said that I wanted to visit the galactic center, I assumed that it would be the place to find new mysteries. Maybe not. Perhaps the true unknown is elsewhere. Should I be looking at nothing, at the regions *between* the galaxies?"

He stood up abruptly and followed Olivia Ferranti out of the control chamber, leaving Peron and Elissa looking at each other uncertainly.

"More questions," said Elissa.

"I know. And nobody willing to provide us with answers. I'll tell you the biggest mystery of all. The society of Immortals has a complicated structure. They have the network of ships linking all the inhabited worlds, they have an elaborate recruiting system to bring people like us into S-space, and they have definite rules for encounters with other societies—even human ones. Lord knows what they'd do if they met aliens who were obviously intelligent and lived close to stars. But with all that, we never seem to get any closer to the Immortals who are in charge of the whole organization."

"Maybe their society doesn't operate like that— perhaps it's a true democracy."

"I don't believe it." Peron leaned across and put his arm around Elissa's shoulders. "Just think about it for a minute. *Somebody* has to develop rules and procedures. Somebody has to monitor them. Somebody has to arrange for food supplies, and energy, and travel, and construction. You have to have leaders. Without that you don't have democracy— you have anarchy, and complete chaos. Where is their *government*?"

Elissa was absently rubbing the back of Peron's right hand, as it lay across her shoulder. "Didn't we conclude that it's on Earth, or at least in orbit somewhere in the Sol System?"

"We did. But I don't believe it any more. I told Olivia Ferranti that we want to meet the leaders of the Immortals. She won't talk about that, but she insists we'll really enjoy the visit to Earth. How could she possibly say that, if we might be heading for a confrontation there?"

Elissa shook her head. She did not speak, and after a couple of minutes moved out of Peron's embrace and quietly left the control cabin.

Peron was left alone, gloomily staring out into the pearly blankness of the S-space sky. It felt like only weeks since he was walking through the sticky marshes of Glug, or contemplating the dangers of a landing on Whirlygig. To him, and to Sy and Elissa, it *was* weeks.

But back on Pentecost, new generations of contestants had won and lost at Planetfest. By now, Peron's name, along with Kallen, Lum, and the others, was no more than a footnote in an ancient record book. And Wilmer, or some newly trained Immortal, would be down on the planet's surface, observing the new contestants and reporting back on their behavior.

And everyone they had known on Pentecost, except for Wilmer, was now long dead. Peron wondered about the great centuries-long project to reclaim the southern marshes of Turcanta Province. Was that finished now, with real life agricultural developments replacing the futuristic artists' drawings that had illustrated a geography lesson when he was back in school? And what other planet-shaping projects had been developed since then?

He and Elissa had talked of their decision, and there were no regrets. With what they had learned, there could have been no turning back to a planet-bound 'normal' life on Pentecost. The idea of visiting Earth had filled them all with energy and enthusiasm; and he and Elissa were ridiculously happy together. And yet. . . .

Peron had a premonition of other travels and troubles ahead, before the true secret of the Immortals was revealed.

Chapter 24:

Deceleration: procedures, Part I.

The deceleration phase of an interstellar journey is normally passed in cold sleep. While the human passengers are unconscious, on-board computers perform the task of matching velocity and position with the target. They awaken the sleepers only upon final arrival.

The alternatives to cold sleep are limited: a move to normal space, followed by full consciousness during lengthy deceleration and final maneuvers; or an immobilized and dizzying ride in S-space. Neither is recommended. . . .

Without discussion, Sy had chosen cold sleep during their approach to Sol. He was planning on using suspended animation techniques extensively in his future travels, and he was keen to gain more experience with it as soon as possible.

Peron and Elissa had far more difficulty making a decision. After dreaming for so long of a return to Sol and to Earth, the idea that they would close their eyes, then suddenly find themselves *there*, was not at all attractive. It missed the whole point of the trip. Earth was a legend, and every experience connected with it should be savored. They had studied the Solar System during the journey from Sector Headquarters, and now they wanted to witness the whole approach. But that meant over a month of subjective travel time during deceleration, or a nauseating hour of slowing and orbit adjustment, tightly strapped in and unable to move a muscle. . . .

They had discussed it over and over, and at last made their decision. Now they lay side by side, tightly cocooned in restraining nets. As a special favor, Olivia Ferranti had placed screen displays so that Peron and Elissa would have frequency-adjusted views both ahead of and behind the ship as it neared Sol. They had entered the nets before deceleration began, when they were still nearly fifty billion kilometers from Sol and the Sun was nothing more than an exceptionally bright star on the displays.

At first, they both felt that all their studies would be wasted. The Sun had grown steadily bigger and more brilliant, gyrating across the sky as their trajectory responded to the System-wide navigation control system. But it looked disappointingly like any other star. In the last five minutes of travel they caught a glimpse of Saturn, and had one snapshot look at the ring structure; but it was a long way off, and there was little detail to be seen of surface or satellites. All the other planets remained invisible.

They could not talk to each other, but they independently decided that the nausea and discomfort were definitely not worth it. Until, quite suddenly, Earth showed in the screen off to one side. The planet rapidly swung to loom directly ahead for the last stages of their approach.

And their sufferings were suddenly of no consequence.

They had been conditioned by the ship's stored viewing tapes to expect a blue-green clouded marble and attendant moon, hanging isolated in space. Instead, the whole sphere of Earth shone girdled by a necklace of bright points of light, whirling around the central orb like an electron cloud about the central nucleus. There were so many of them that they created the illusion of a bright, continuous cloud, a glittering halo about the planet's equator. As they watched, smaller units darted like fireflies between Earth and the orbiting structures.

Space stations. They were at all heights, some almost grazing the atmosphere, an entire dense ring at synchronous altitude, others wandering out beyond the Moon. And to be visible from this distance, many of them must be kilometers across. Peron and Elissa were looking at the result of twenty-five thousand years of continuous development of earth orbit. The asteroid moving and mining operations that began at the dawn of Earth's space age had yielded a rich harvest.

Before Peron and Elissa had more than a minute or two to absorb the scene, they were homing in on one of the larger structures. It was in synchronous orbit, hovering above a great land mass shaped like a broad arrow head. A shining filament extended downwards from the station towards Earth, finally to vanish from sight within the atmosphere.

Their final approach was compressed to a few S-seconds of blurred motion, twisting a way in through a moving labyrinth of other spacecraft and connecting cables and tunnels. All at once they were docked, and the ship motionless. They were trying to release themselves from the cocoons when a man materialized in the cabin and stood looking down at them.

He was short, pudgy, grey-haired, and precisely dressed, with elaborate jewelled rings on most of his fingers. He wore a flower in his lapel—the first blossom of any kind that they had seen since they left Pentecost. The stern look on his face was contradicted by a pattern of laughter lines around his button-bright eyes and small mouth.

"Well," he said briskly, after a thorough inspection of Peron and Elissa. "You look normal enough. I've been waiting for your arrival with some interest. Neither of you appears to be quite the degenerate monster that sector reports suggest, and Olivia Ferranti speaks well of you. So let us proceed on the basis of that assumption. *Command: Remove the cocoons.*"

The restraining nets vanished, and the little man calmly extended a hand to help Elissa to her feet.

"My name is Jan de Vries," he said. "It is my melancholy duty to approve—or veto—all trips to and from Earth by certain persons living in S-space. You *do* still wish to visit Earth, I suppose, as you had requested?"

"Of course we do," said Elissa. "Will you be going down there with us?"

De Vries looked pained. "Hardly. My dear young lady, my duties are various and sometimes odd, but they have not to date included the function of tour guide. I can, however, dispose of certain formalities for you that would normally be handled otherwise. When were you last in normal space?"

"Not since we were on the way to Sector Headquarters," said Peron. He was becoming increasingly uneasy. He had been preparing himself for a great clash with the secret rulers of the Immortals, and instead here he was chatting with some apparent bureaucrat.

"Very good," said de Vries. "Then you can be prepared at once for your visit to Earth. By the way, you will find that the robot services ignore your commands until we have your voice patterns keyed into the station's computer. That is part of a larger data transfer. It will be complete upon your return here, and we will talk again then. But for the moment you will need my assistance. *Command: prepare them for the standard Earth visit.*"

"But we don't—" Peron stopped. De Vries had disappeared. Then the walls spun about Peron and he caught a glimpse of a long corridor. As the scene steadied again he felt a sharp pain in his thigh. Suddenly it was as though he were back on Whirlygig, experiencing that familiar and disquieting fall into blackness.

His last thought was an angry one. *It wouldn't happen again, he had sworn it—but it was happening now! Things were out of control. And he had no idea what came next.*

Peron and Elissa emerged from the suspense tanks together, into a room filled with a noisy, excited crowd. They knew at once that they were again in normal space—S-space couldn't offer the sharpness of vision or the bright colors. There was an exhilarating taste to the air, and a feeling of well-being running through their veins. They looked around them curiously.

A loud, metallic voice was booming out directions. "Single file into the cars, please. Take your seats, and don't overload them—there will be another one along every ten minutes."

The crowd took little notice, pushing and surging forward down a long broad hall towards a loading area.

"Peron!" Elissa reached out and grabbed hold of his arm. "Keep a grip. We don't want to be separated now."

It was like being in a river and swept along by the current. With no effort on their part, they found themselves carried forward into a semi-circular chamber, and seated on soft benches covered with a warm velvety material. On either side people were grinning at them and staring out of the half-circle of the ports.

"Look down!" said a woman next to Elissa. Her accent had peculiar vowel sounds to it, but it was easy to understand. "It'll give you the shivers. No wonder it's called Skydown."

Elissa followed the other's gesture, and found that the floor beneath their feet was transparent. She was looking directly down towards Earth, following the line of a giant silvery cylinder. As she watched, the doors of the chamber closed and they began a smooth, accelerated descent, their car riding an invisible path along the side of the cylinder.

"Peron." Elissa leaned close to him so that he could hear her above the clamor. "What's going on here? Look at them. They're like the mob at the end of Planetfest. And where are we going?"

Peron shook his head. "It's our own fault. I realized it as soon as we came out of the tanks there—we should have known we're no different from anyone else. Don't you see? *Everybody* from the planetary colonies and arcologies has been told about Earth since they were small children. They all want to visit. No wonder de Vries was amazed when you asked if he was coming with us—I bet people who live in the Sol System get tired of explaining things to the simple-minded visitors. Better face it, love, we're just part of the tourist crowd."

Elissa looked around her at the restless, exuberant travellers. "You're right—but they're all having fun. You know what? I feel wonderful. I'm going to postpone solving the mysteries of the universe until we get back into orbit." She grabbed Peron's arm and pulled him closer. "Come on, misery. Let's get into the spirit of it. Remember, a week down on Earth will only be five minutes in S-space—they won't even notice that we've gone."

They bent forward to look down through the floor. Although the cylinder was rushing past them as one continuous blur of motion, Earth was not perceptibly closer. It hung beneath them, a glittering white ball blocking out over fifteen degrees of the sky.

"I wonder how long the journey will be," said Elissa. She reached out to the miniature information outlet built into the arm of her seat, and switched it on. "Speed, please, and arrival time."

"Present speed, forty-four hundred kilometers an hour," said a cheerful voice. The vocal reply system had been chosen with as pleasant and soothing a tone as possible. "Arrival will be three hours and forty-one minutes from now. We are still in the acceleration phase. We have thirty-three thousand four hundred kilometers to go to touchdown."

"Where will we land?"

"Half a degree south of the equator, on one of the major continents."

Peron was still staring down at the globe beneath them. "This doesn't look the way I expected it to—it's too bright. Why so much cloud cover?"

There was silence for a split second, as the on-board computer called back up to the synchronous station above them for assistance with the answer. "There is less cloud cover than usual today. You are probably mistaking snow cover for cloud cover."

"But that would mean there's snow over two-thirds of the surface!"

"Correct." Again the machine hesitated. "That is not unusual."

"Earth was not snow-covered in the old days—is this a consequence of the old war?"

"Not at all. It is a result of reduced solar activity." The information system hesitated for a moment, then went on: "The amount of received radiation from the Sun has declined by half a percent over the past fifteen thousand years. The increased glaciation is apparent even from this distance. It is predicted that this Ice Age will persist for at least ten thousand more years, to be followed by an unusually warm period. Within fifteen thousand years there will be partial melting of the polar ice caps, and submergence of most coastal lands."

Elissa reached out and switched off the set. She looked at Peron. "You don't mind, do you? I had the feeling it was just getting into its stride. I hate being burbled at—whoever programmed that sequence needs brevity lessons from Kallen."

Peron nodded his agreement. The view below was enough for their full attention. From the poles almost to the tropics, blue-white shining glaciers coated the land areas. The old outline of the larger land masses was unchanged. Soon Peron could see where the Skyhook was tethered. It met the surface on the west coast of the continent that had been known as Africa. They were descending rapidly towards that touchdown point, a couple of hundred kilometers from the place where the region's mightiest river flowed to the Atlantic Ocean.

"We ought to decide what we really want to see," said Elissa. "If we have a choice, I don't care to travel around in the middle of a mob of sight-seers."

"So let's see what the options are. Can you stand to have the information service on again for a couple of minutes?"

He touched the switch and spoke into the tiny microphone.

"Will we be free to move as we choose when we reach the surface?"

"Of course." The cheerful but impersonal voice answered at once. "There will be air and ground vehicles at your disposal, and personal information systems to go with you and answer any questions. Your account will automatically be charged for services."

Elissa looked at Peron. To their knowledge, they had no credit account of any kind. They might have to fight that one with Jan de Vries when they returned from Earth.

"Do you have a site selected?" went on the service computer. "If so, we can schedule something to be available at once upon touchdown."

"Wait a minute." Peron turned away from the microphone. "Elissa? Let's get away from everybody for a while. Maybe we'll take a look at one typical Earth city, then let's see some wild country."

At her nod, Peron relayed their request to the machine. There was the longest silence so far.

"I am sorry," said the voice at last. "We cannot grant your request."

"It is not permitted?" said Elissa.

"It would be permitted. But the environment you describe no longer exists."

Elissa showed her astonishment. "You mean—there is no natural country left, anywhere on Earth?"

"No," said the voice. Peron imagined he could hear an element of surprise in the overall joviality of the machine's tones. "There is natural country, plenty of it. But there are no towns or cities on Earth."

Chapter 25: *Earth*

The steady march of the glaciers had been more effective in the northern hemisphere. In Africa, Australia, and South America, the great oceans had moderated temperatures and checked the spread from polar regions. Occasional snow-free pockets could be found as far as forty degrees south of the equator. But in the north, the glaciers ruled everywhere past latitude thirty-five.

Even at Skydown the temperature was chilly. Peron and Elissa emerged from the cable car at the foot of the Beanstalk to bright sunshine and clear skies, but they stood in a blustery east wind that encouraged warm clothing. While most of the visitors headed for a briefing on the sights of Earth, the two took an aircar and flew north.

They spent the first evening on the lush southern shore of the Mediterranean Sea near the ancient site of Tripoli. The information service computer informed them that they had reached the border for true forest land. Farther north, in what had once been Europe, only stunted stands of spruce and juniper persisted, clinging to south-facing slopes.

Night came quickly, sweeping in with a scented darkness across the white sandy beach. The aircar contained two bunks, but they were on opposite sides of the cabin. Peron and Elissa chose to sleep outside, protected by automatic sensors and the car's warning system. Holding each other close beneath a moonless sky, they watched the wheel of unfamiliar constellations. Against that slow-moving backdrop, the space stations swept constantly overhead, one or more of them always visible. Sleep would not come easily. They whispered for a long time, of Pentecost, Planetfest, and Whirlygig, and of the accident to Peron that had plunged them across lightyears and centuries.

The night was full of unfamiliar sounds. There was wind rustling in tall trees, and the steady beat of waves on the seashore. Somewhere to the south a group of animals called to each other, their voices tantalizingly familiar, like humans sobbing and crying out in some foreign tongue. When Peron at last fell asleep, it was to unpleasant dreams. The voices called to him still through the night; but now he imagined he could understand their lamenting message.

Your visit to Earth is a delusion. You are hiding from the truth, trying to put off unpleasant actions. But they cannot be put aside. You must return to S-space . . . and go farther yet.

The next morning they took to the air again and headed north and east into Asia. Two days' travel convinced Peron and Elissa of two things. Apart from the general location of the land masses, Earth bore no resemblance to the fabled planet described in the old records of Pentecost and the library records on the ship. And there was no chance that they would choose to live on Earth, even if it were to be colonized again in the near future. Pentecost was more beautiful in every way.

They left the information service on all the time. It described a link between the old, fertile Earth of legend and the present wilderness.

The post-nuclear winter had been the first cause of the trouble. It was far more influential as an agent of change than the Ice Age that now held Earth in a frozen grasp. Immediately after the thermonuclear explosions, temperatures below the thick clouds of radioactive dust dropped drastically. Plants and animals that fought for survival in the sunless gloom of the surface did so in a poisoned environment that forced rapid mutation or extinction.

In the air, the birds could not find enough food over the land. A few remaining species skimmed the surface of the tropical seas, competing with sea mammals for the diminished supply of fish. Their high energy need killed them. The last flying bird on Earth fell from the skies within two years of the thermonuclear blast that obliterated Washington. The penguins alone lived on, moving north from the Antarctic to inhabit the coastlines of South America and Africa. Small colonies of emperor penguins still clung to the shores of the Java Sea and Indonesia.

The larger surface animals—including all surviving members of *homo sapiens*—were early victims. Long life spans permitted the build-up of lethal doses of radiation in body tissues. The small burrowers, driven far underground to live on deep-lying roots and tubers, fared much better.

One circumstance had assisted their survival.

The hour of Armageddon came close to the winter solstice in the northern hemisphere, at a time when many animals were fat for the winter and preparing for hibernation. They had burrowed deeper and settled in for the hibernal sleep. The ones too far north had never wakened. Others, returning to consciousness in a cold, dark spring, foraged far and wide for food. The lucky ones moved steadily south, to the zone where a pale, sickly sunlight still permitted some plant growth. Of all Earth's land mammals, only a few small rodents—mice, hamsters, ground squirrels, and woodchucks—lived on to inherit the Earth.

Their competition had been formidable. The invertebrates were fighting for their own survival. Insect life dwindled at first, then adapted, mutated, grew, and multiplied. They had always dominated the tropical regions of Earth; now the larger ants and spiders, aided by their formidable mandibles and stings, strove to become the lords of creation.

The mammals took the only paths left to them. The invertebrates were limited in maximum size because of passive breathing mechanisms and their lack of an internal skeleton; and they were cold-blooded. The rodents grew in size to improve their heat retention, developed thick coats and hairy paws, and moved away from the equator to regions where there was no insect competition. Some of them were totally vegetarian, browsing on the sparse, chlorotic plant life that still grew in the dust-filtered twilight. They developed thick layers of blubber, for food storage and insulation. The other survivors became super-efficient predators, preying on their herbivorous relatives.

As the nuclear winter slowly ended the insects

moved north and south again, away from the tropics. But the mutated mice and woodchucks were
ready for them. They had increased in size and
ferocity, to become a match for any pre-civilization
wolf; and now they wore thick coats of fur and
protective fat that rendered impotent the fierce
mandibles and poison stings. The insects were a
new convenient source of protein. The carnivores
followed them back into their tropic habitats, and
on to the southern regions.

The changes to animal life on Earth were easiest
to see; but the changes to the vegetation were in
some ways more fundamental. The grasses were
gone; in their place a dwarf form of eucalyptus
covered millions of square kilometers with flat,
bluish-green leaves. Waving fields of corn and wheat
would never be seen again on Earth. Their nour-
ishing seeds had been replaced by the red clusters
of berries that hung from every euclypt stem. After
being assured that it was safe to do so, Elissa
sampled a couple. They were filled with a fatty
syrup, and at their center sat an oval, impenetrable seed. The seeds, berries and roots of the euclypts
sustained a thriving animal community beneath
the foot-high canopy of their leaves, where in the
blue-green gloom devolved mice fought finger-long
giant ants for the best food and living space.

As they travelled on across the natural face of an
Earth where no vestige of human works remained,
Peron became gradually more silent and withdrawn.
Elissa assumed that it was a reaction to their surroundings. She was reluctant to interfere with his
thoughts. But as they skirted the barren western
seaboard of South America, where the continuous
line of glaciers stretched down to the Pacific, Pe-

ron's need to discuss his worries became overwhelming.

They had landed in the Andean foothills to watch sunset over the Pacific. Neither spoke as the broad face of Sol, red in the evening twilight, sank steadily past a thin line of clouds far out over the western ocean. Even after the last of the light had faded, they could turn to the east and see the sun's rays still caught by the summits of high, snow-covered peaks.

"We can't stay here," said Peron at last. "Even if we liked it better here than on Pentecost, even if we thought Earth was perfect, we'd have to go back—to S-space."

Elissa remained silent. She knew Peron. He had to be allowed the time to work his way into a subject, without pressure and with minimal coaxing. That was the way that he had first managed to speak to her of their own relationship—and the way that she had finally learned of his continued doubts over leaving his family to take part in Planetfest.

The last of the light vanished, leaving them sitting side by side on the soft earth next to the aircar. Stars were appearing, one by one, twinkling brightly in the crisp night air.

"We've had a great time here," Peron went on at last. "But for the past two days I've had trouble getting a thought out of my head. Remember the colony of mouse-monkeys, the black ones with the fat tails?"

Elissa squeezed his hand without speaking.

"You asked me how the head of the colony could control the others so easily," he continued. "He didn't seem to fight them, or bully them, or try to dominate them at all. But they climbed the trees, and brought him food, and groomed him, and he didn't even have to move to live in comfort. Well, for some reason that reminded me of something my father said to me when I was only ten years old. He asked me, who controlled Pentecost? He said that was the third most important question to answer in a society, and the most important ones were, *how* did they control, and *why* did they control? If you knew all three, masters, mechanisms, and motives, you were in a position to make changes."

"Did he ever tell you the answers?"

"No. He never knew them. He spent his life looking. The answers were not on Pentecost—we know now that the true controllers of Pentecost are the Immortals, with the cooperation of a nervous planetary government. They control through superior knowledge, and they use the planet—so they say—as a source of new Immortals. Those ideas were beyond my father's imaginings. But he was right about the important questions."

Elissa stirred at his side. She was lightly dressed, and the air was cold on her bare arms, but she was reluctant to suggest a move.

"I finally tried to ask the important questions myself," said Peron at last. "Not about Pentecost—about the Immortals themselves. They have a well-developed society. But who runs it? How, and most of all *why*? At first I thought we had the answer to the first question: the Immortals were run from The Ship. As soon as I was in S-space, I found that wasn't true. Then I thought we would have the answer at Sector Headquarters. But we learned that was false—Headquarters is nothing but an administrative center with a switching station and cargo pickup point for travelling starships. So what next? We decided control had to be back at Sol, and we came here. But we have no more answers. Who runs the show in the Sol system? Not Jan de Vries, I'll bet my life on it. He's a good follower, but he's not a leader. And even if we find out *who*, that still leaves how and why."

"So what do you want to do?"

"I don't know. Look harder, I suppose. Elissa, we've been on Earth for nearly five days now. How do you feel?"

"Physically? I feel absolutely wonderful. Don't you?"

"I do. Do you know why?"

"I've wondered. I think maybe part of the reason is our ancestry. We come from millions of years of adaptation to Earth as the natural environment— gravity, air pressure, sunlight. We *ought* to feel good here."

"I know all that. But Elissa, I think there's another reason. I think everything is relative, and we had spent over a month in S-space before we came here. I'll tell you my theory, and it's one that makes me uncomfortable. I think that S-space isn't right for humans, in ways that we haven't been told yet."

"Even though we will live many times as long there? I don't just mean long in S-time, I mean live *subjectively* longer. Doesn't that suggest S-space is good for our bodies?"

Peron sighed. Elissa didn't know it, but she was presenting arguments to him that he had wrestled with for days, and found no satisfactory answers.

"It looks that way. It seems logical: we live longer there, so it must be good for us. But I don't believe it. Think of the way you *feel*. S-space didn't give you the same sense of vitality. Think of our lovemaking. Wasn't it wonderful on Pentecost, and hasn't it been even better the last few days on Earth?"

Elissa reached out and ran her fingers gently up Peron's thigh. "You know the answer to that without asking. Be careful now, or you'll give me ideas."

He placed his hand gently over hers, but his voice remained thoughtful and unhappy. "So you agree: some things just don't feel right in S-space. We've known that, deep inside, but I assumed it was all part of the readjustment process. Now I feel just as sure that's not the case, and everybody who has lived in S-space for any length of time must know it, too."

Peron rose slowly to his feet. Elissa followed suit, and they both stood there for a few moments, shivering in the seaward nightwind sweeping off the snowy eastern peaks.

"Suppose you're right," said Elissa. "And you have me fairly well persuaded. What can we do about it?"

Peron hugged her close to him, sharing their warmth. But when he spoke his voice was as cold as the wind. "Love, I'm tired of being manipulated. I'm tired of blind guesswork. We must go back to orbit now. We must stop allowing ourselves to be fobbed off with sweet reasonableness and bland answers, from Olivia, or Jan de Vries, or anyone else. And we have to push as hard as we can for the *real* answers about S-space civilization: *who, how, and why.*"

Chapter 26:

At Elissa's insistence, they set a meeting with Sy as their first priority on returning to orbit and to S-space. She agreed with Peron's ideas, but she wanted Sy's unique perspective on them.

Their journey back up the Beanstalk took place in a totally different atmosphere from the trip down. The cable car was as crowded as ever, but the travellers were subdued, the mood somber. After a few days on the surface, everyone had sensed at some deep level that Earth was now *alien*—a world so affected by Man's wars and changing climate that permanent return there was unthinkable. Humanity had left its original home. There would be no going back. The travellers looked down at the planet's glittering clouds and snow cover, and said their mental farewells.

Olivia Ferranti had mentioned that few people made more than one visit to Earth. Now Peron and Elissa knew why.

When they arrived at the set of stations that formed the upper debarkation point of the Beanstalk, Elissa queried the information system for

Sy's location. While she did so, Peron prepared to transfer them back to S-space. It proved surprisingly easy. Since almost everyone returning from a visit to Earth moved at once back to S-space, the procedure had been streamlined to become completely routine. Peron gave their ID codes, and was quickly offered access to a pair of suspense tanks.

"Ready?" he said to Elissa.

She was still sitting at the information terminal. She shook her head and looked puzzled. "No. Not ready at all. Hold off on booking us into the tanks."

"What's the problem? Can't you find Sy?"

"I found him—but he isn't in S-space any more. He moved to normal space even before we did."

"You mean he went down to Earth, too?"

"Not according to the information service. He's been here all the time we were on Earth. And he left S-space a quarter of an S-hour before we did—so that means he's been in normal space for over twenty days!"

"What's he been doing?"

Elissa shook her head again. "Lord knows. That information isn't in the computer bank. But he was last reported on one of the stations here in the synchronous complex. If we want to get our heads together with his, there's no point in going to S-space yet."

Peron cancelled the suspense tank request. "Come on then. I don't know how to do it, but we have to discover some way to track him down."

That task proved far easier than Peron had imagined. Sy had made no attempt to conceal his whereabouts. He had lived in one room for the whole time, with an almost continuous link to the orbiting data banks and central computer network. He was sitting quietly at a terminal when Elissa and Peron slid open his door.

He took his eyes away from the screen for a second and nodded to them casually. "I've been expecting you for a few days now. Give me a moment to finish what I'm doing."

Elissa looked curiously around the small room. It was a one-fifth gee chamber, with few material signs of Sy's presence. The service robots had cleared away all food and dishes, and there were no luxury or entertainment items. The bed looked unused, and the small desk top was completely empty. Sy was neatly groomed, clean-shaven and dressed in tight-fitting dark clothes.

"No hurry," she said. She sat herself down calmly on the bed.

"Got a message from Kallen," said Sy, without taking his eyes off the screen. "Lum and Rosanne are delayed, won't be here as soon as they thought. How was Earth?"

"Thought-provoking," said Peron. He seated himself next to Elissa, and waited until Sy had completed data storage, signed off, and swung to face them. "You ought to make a trip there, Sy. It's something you'd never forget."

"I thought of it," said Sy. "Then I decided I had higher priorities. Plenty of time for Earth later—it won't go away."

"But what are you doing here, in normal space?" asked Elissa. "According to the information service, you've been here forever."

"Twenty-six days." Sy grinned. "You know what's wrong with S-space? You can't get anything done there in a *hurry*. I had things I wanted to do, and things I wanted to know—fast—and I wasn't sure that our Immortal friends would give permission.

So I came here. I've been here for only nineteen minutes of S-time. By the time they register the fact that I've gone, I'll be all finished."

"I had the same feeling," said Peron. "We're too slow in S-space. We have a lot less control over what happens to us there. But finished doing what?"

"Several things. First, I've been testing Kallen's Law—my name for it, not his. Remember what he said? 'Anything that can be put *into* a data bank by one person can be taken *out* of it by another, if you're smart enough and have enough time.' That's one problem with a computer-based society, and one reason why computers were so tightly controlled on Pentecost: it's almost impossible to prevent access to computer-stored information. I decided that if there were another Headquarters for the Immortals, and one that they preferred not to talk about, there must be clues to its location somewhere in the data banks. Well-hidden, sure, but they should be there. Is there a secret installation, and if so, where is it? Those were two questions I set out to answer. And I had another thing that worried me. When we met the Gossameres and Pipistrelles, Ferranti said that the Immortals couldn't really communicate with them. But she *did* communicate with them, even if they didn't send a message back. And I couldn't be sure that was true, either. Suppose they did send a message? We don't know what the ship was receiving. I'm afraid I don't have an answer yet to that one. I've been working here flat out, but it takes time."

"Do you mean you *have* answered the other questions?"

"Think so." Sy cradled his left elbow thoughtfully in his right hand. "Wasn't easy. There's a pretty strong cover-up going on. None of the data that's available for the usual starship libraries will tell you a thing. I had to get there by internal consistency checks. What do you make of these data base facts? First, the official flight manifests show one hundred and sixty-two outbound trips initiated from Sol in the past S-month. The *maximum* fuel capacity of any single ship is 4.4 billion tons. And the fuel taken out of supplies in the Sol System in the past S-month is eight hundred and seventy-one billion tons. See the problem? I'll save you the trouble of doing the arithmetic. There is *too much* fuel being used—enough for a minimum of twenty-six outbound flights that don't show on the manifests."

"Did you check other periods?" asked Peron.

Sy looked at him scornfully. "What do you think? Let's go on. This one is suggestive, but not conclusive. The navigation network around the Sol System is all computer-controlled, and it's continuously self-adapting to changing requirements. Generally speaking, the most-travelled approach routes to Sol are the ones with the most monitoring radars and navigation controls. The information on the placement of radars is available from the data banks, so you can use it to set up an inverse problem: given the disposition of the equipment, what direction in space is the most-travelled approach route to and from Sol? I set up the problem, and let the computers grind out an answer. When I had it I was puzzled for days. The solution indicated a vector outwards from Sol that seemed to lead *nowhere at all*—not to any star, or towards any significant object. It pointed at nothing. I was stuck.

"I put that to one side and chased another thought. Suppose there were a hidden Headquarters somewhere in space. It would communicate with the Sol System not just with the ships—they only travel at a tenth of lightspeed—but with radio signals, too. There are thousands of big antennae and phased arrays scattered all around the Sol System, and the computers keep track of their instantaneous pointings. So I accessed that pointing data base, and I asked the computer a question: of all the places that the antennae and arrays point to, what direction was pointed to *most often*? Want to guess the answer?"

"The same one as you got from the navigation system solution," said Peron. "That's wild. But damn it, how does it help? You have the same mystery."

"Not quite." Sy looked unusually pleased with himself. For the first time, Peron realized that even Sy liked to have an appreciative audience for his deductions.

"You're right in one way," went on Sy. "I got the same answer as from the navigation system solution. I had a vector that pointed to nothing. But there's one other thing about the antennae. The computer points them all very accurately, but of course they're scattered all over the Solar System, from inside the orbit of Mercury out past Saturn. So if you want to beam a message to a precise *point* in space, rather than merely in a specified *direction*, each antenna would be aimed along a slightly different vector. In other words, the computer pointing must allow for *parallax* of the target. So I took the next step. I asked if there were parallax on the previous solution, for the most common antennae pointings, and if so, what was the convergence point? I got a surprising answer. There *is* parallax—it's small, only a total of a second of arc—and the convergence point is twenty-eight lightyears from Sol, in just the direction I'd determined before. But when you check the star charts and the positions of kernels and hot collapsed bodies, there's nothing there. *Nothing.* The antennae are aimed at the middle of nothing. I called that place Convergence Point, just for lack of a better name. But just what place is it?—that was the question. And that's where I stuck again, for a long time. Know what finally gave me the answer?"

Elissa was sitting on the bed, her expression dreamy. "Olivia Ferranti. Remember what she told us—'you can't learn all about the Universe crouching in close by a star.' And you, Sy, you said maybe you should be looking at *nothing* to find new mysteries, rather than at the center of the Galaxy. Convergence Point is a nothing point."

Sy was looking at her in amazement. "Elissa, I was asking a rhetorical question. You're not *supposed* to give me the right answer. How the devil did you work it out?"

Elissa smiled. "I didn't. You gave it away yourself. You'll never be a good liar, Sy, even though your face doesn't give you away. It was your choice of words. Even before you knew the distance, the twenty-eight lightyears, you said several times that the antennae were pointing 'at nothing.' But you couldn't know there was no dark object there, if you went out far enough. And from your voice, it was the 'nothing' that was important, not the co-ordinates of the target point."

Sy looked at Peron. "She's a witch. If she reads you like that, you'll never keep any secrets from her. All right, Elissa, take it one step farther. Can you tell me what's so special about that particular nothing?"

Elissa thought for a few moments, then shook her head. "No data."

"That's what I thought, too. How can nothing be special? But then I remembered what else Olivia Ferranti said: 'you have to know what's going on out in deep space.' So I asked myself, what *is* deep space? I went back to the star charts and the kernel coordinates, and I asked the computer another question: Give me the coordinates of the point of open space within one hundred lightyears of Sol that is *farthest from every known material body*. Uncertainties in our knowledge of distances make the answer slightly ambiguous, but the computer gave back only two candidates. One is ninety-one lightyears away; half a year's trip, even in S-space. The other is—no prizes for guessing—just twenty-eight lightyears from Sol, in the right direction. Convergence Point is a real nothing point. Communication time: five S-days."

Sy called a holographic starscape display on to the space in front of them. He moved the 3-D pointer to an empty location within the star field. "Would you like to visit the real power center of the Immortals? Then I say that's where you want to be. Nowhere Station. S-space travel time: less than two months."

Elissa looked puzzled. "But Sy, *why* would anyone build a Headquarters out there, in the middle of nowhere?"

Sy shook his head. "I can't answer that."

Peron was still staring at the display. "We may have to go there to find out. And it won't be easy. You can be sure that the Immortals don't want us there—they don't even want us to know the place exists. You've solved the 'where' puzzle, Sy, I feel sure of it. But that just leaves a bigger problem:

how can we find a way to make the trip, when the whole system is set up to prevent it?"

Sy looked smug. "I told you I've been working hard. If we want to make an S-space trip out to Convergence Point, I've identified the major problems we'll have to solve. Solving them, now—that's another matter, and I'll need help."

He called out a numbered list onto the display. "First, we have to find the departure time and place of the next starship to Convergence Point. Second, we have to find a way to get ourselves onto that departing starship—preferably in a way no one else will notice. Third, we have to explain our absence, so that no one wonders where we have gone. Fourth, we'll have to do something with the ship's crew. Fifth, before we get there we'll need a plan of action for what we'll do when we reach Convergence Point. Where do you want to begin?"

"Can't we put the crew in cold sleep and take them with us?" asked Elissa.

"That's my thought. It won't do them any harm, and it's a lot better than leaving them somewhere in the Sol System. I'm confident that we can handle the mechanics of the ship—the service robots do almost everything, and we learned the rest on our trip from Cassay. The other problems are not so easy. I'd like your thoughts."

"The third one—explaining our absence," said Elissa. "All we need is enough time to get us well on our way to our real destination. Once we're gone, they'll never catch us."

"That's true. But we don't want them to know where we're going. If they find out they'll send a radio signal to warn Headquarters we're coming their way."

"Why should they learn where we're heading? Jan de Vries already implied that we're more of a nuisance to him than anything else. If we can show we've departed for a plausible place, I don't think he'll take much interest. Pentecost would be a natural—it was our home. The most I would expect him to do would be to warn them to watch for our arrival. Can you do a fake data bank entry, indicating that we are shipping out for Pentecost?"

Sy shrugged. "I can try. One nice thing about the information system, it doesn't *expect* the sort of changes we'll be making. The logic is protected against the usual screw-ups and programmer meddling, but not against systematic sabotage. I'll do it. I've learned the software pretty well in the past few weeks."

"Well enough to answer your first question?" asked Peron. "You said it, Sy—the information about starship departure has to be in the data banks somewhere. It's just a question of finding it. But if anybody can pull it out, you can."

Sy grimaced. "Not without a long, horrible grind."

"It would be for me or Elissa—but you'll come up with a smart approach to it."

"Cut out the flattery."

"I'm serious. And if you can do it, find out when and where, I think I have the key to the problem of how we get on board the starship."

Sy frowned. "Do you, now? What have I missed?"

"You lack one piece of information. Elissa and I learned this the hard way, and we can vouch for it: there is no way that the crew will stay in S-space for the acceleration phase of their journey. It's just too damned uncomfortable. They'll be in cold sleep when the journey begins. See what that means?"

He pulled the terminal entry pad closer. "Let me sketch an approach. Then we can look at some timings."

"T MINUS 4 MINUTES, COUNTDOWN PROCEEDING," said a disembodied voice.

"—FUEL MASS CHECK IN PROCESS."

"—THRUST PROTOCOL COMPLETE."

"—CARGO CHECK PROCEEDING."

"—OUTBOUND TRAJECTORY CONFIRMED AND APPROVED."

The mechanical voices chimed in one after another. Ward Lunga, ship's pilot, lay quietly in the suspense tank. He was watching the displays, chatting to co-pilot Celia Deveny and listening with half an ear to the robotic checklist. Full attention was unnecessary. Anomalies would be separately flagged and reported to them.

"T MINUS 180 SECONDS, COUNTDOWN PROCEEDING," said the voice.

"—MECHANICAL SYSTEM CHECKS COMPLETE."

The starship *Manta* floated in stable orbit about Sol, hovering at a Saturnian Trojan Point. Final count-down for departure was nearly complete. The nav displays showed a thrust profile that would carry the *Manta* from the middle Solar System direct to Gulf City, twenty-eight lightyears away. The ship still floated in freefall, but in three S-minutes that would be changed to an accelerated outbound trajectory.

"ELECTRICAL AND ELECTRONIC SYSTEMS CHECK COMPLETE."

"—FUEL MASS CHECK COMPLETE."

The final few hundred million tons of fuel had now been transferred; the mobile tank was swinging away under robot control towards Sol.

"ANOMALY! CARGO PORT ANOMALY," said a voice suddenly. "CARGO PORT SEVEN OPEN."

Lunga grunted in surprise. "Damn. All that cargo should have been in and secured by now. *Command: display Port Seven.*"

Two views of Cargo Port Seven showed on the displays. Lunga looked at them closely. "Bloody thing looks shut to me. Everything else reports normal—see anything odd there, Celia?"

"Not a thing." She threw a pair of switches. *"Command: repeat status check, Cargo Port Seven."*

"CARGO PORT SEVEN CONDITION: CLOSED AND NORMAL. ALL CARGO DELIVERY PODS MOVING NOW TO SAFE RANGE. ALL CARGO SECURE AND BALANCED."

"—T MINUS 120 SECONDS, COUNTDOWN PROCEEDING."

"—TRANSITION TO COLD SLEEP BEGINS IN THIRTY SECONDS UNLESS ALTERNATE SIGNAL PROVIDED TO CENTRAL CONTROL."

Ward Lunga's finger hovered over the button. He hesitated. Unless he took action in the next half minute, the system would initiate the crew's descent from S-space to cold sleep. *"Command: repeat all checks and report any anomalies in condition."*

There was a fraction of a second's pause. "ALL CHECKS REPEATED. NO ANOMALIES OBSERVED, ALL SYSTEMS ARE READY FOR FLIGHT DEPARTURE."

"—T MINUS 100 SECONDS, COUNTDOWN PROCEEDING."

Lunga moved his hand away from the abort button. He took a last look at the displays, then lay back full-length in the suspense chamber. He started to sit up again, then changed his mind and allowed his body to relax in the tank. The gentle hissing of vapors that would initiate the first phase of cold sleep was already beginning. Time to let the computers and the robots take over, and wake again at Gulf City. . . .

Outside the tank, three figures flickered through the interior of *Manta*. Peron, Sy, and Elissa were moving cautiously, but to an observer in S-space they went too fast for the eye to follow—the six hundred meter length of the ship from cargo hold to control room was traversed in less than an eighth of an S-second, in a flashing blur too rapid for comprehension. The biggest obstacle to even greater speed was the service robots, trundling haphazardly along in their assigned tasks at a slow walking speed.

Ninety-nine S-seconds before launch, they were standing outside the suspense chamber. As a first priority, there must be enough spare tanks to accommodate three extra travellers in cold sleep. If not, there was still time to recall a cargo pod and make their exit from the *Manta*.

"T MINUS NINETY SECONDS"—the three intruders were now familiar with all the main controls of the ship, had assured themselves of the ship's immediate destination, and confirmed the trip travel time to the fraction of a second.

"T MINUS EIGHTY SECONDS"—after a meal and a four-hour rest period, Sy, Elissa and Peron adjusted the cold sleep settings for the ship's crew, and prepared three unoccupied suspense tanks.

"T MINUS SEVENTY SECONDS"—Sy sent coded messages to Kallen, Lum and Rosanne, one to Earth and one to Paradise, explaining what was happening.

"How confident are you that they'll know there's a hidden signal?" asked Peron.

"If Kallen receives it, no question." Sy had smiled grimly. "Sometimes I think he's as smart as I am. If they can't find a way to follow us, I expect they'll send us a message. Want to bet on it with me?"

"Not today."

"T MINUS SIXTY SECONDS"—every contingency had been checked. Now it was time to settle into their cold sleep chambers, next to the crew members.

"These tanks are set to wake us one S-minute before arrival at Gulf City," said Peron. "They'll still be asleep. Sy, are you sure you changed the deceleration profile so that we'll be in freefall when we wake?"

"Trust me."

Peron lay in his suspense tank; for the thousandth time his mind ran over the same event sequence. The three of them had reviewed it together until it was totally familiar to each of them.

Arrival time minus one S-minute: They would wake in normal space during the ship's final approach to Gulf City. One S-minute would give them a little more than one normal day for possible changes to final plans. The Immortals in Gulf City should be in S-space, and unable to formulate a timely response.

Arrival in Gulf City; next came control of the service robots. Control of Gulf City itself would follow. . . .

The cold sleep vapors were hissing about him, and he could feel the cool and unpleasant touch of catheters on his arms and chest. Nothing more to be done now; except to sleep, and wake at Gulf City.

Peron closed his eyes. . . .

Chapter 27: *Gulf City*

. . . and opened his eyes, to the immediate knowledge that something had gone terribly wrong.

He should have been in normal space. He was not. The blurred outlines of the objects around him, and their muted colors, told him at once that he was in S-space. And he was no longer in the snug confines of the *Manta's* suspense tanks.

He tried to sit up, but could not do it. He was secured by broad straps to the bed that supported him. Worse, he had no feeling or muscular control below the neck. He turned his head desperately from side to side and saw that Elissa lay on his right, with Sy just beyond her. Sy was already fully conscious, and looking about him thoughtfully. Elissa's eyes were just beginning to blink open.

Where in Heaven's name were they? He craned his head forward, and as he did so there was a soft whir of machinery. The bed he lay on was tilting to a semi-upright position, and he was gradually able to see more of his surroundings.

He was in a long, grey-walled room with no

windows. Bare shelves lined the walls, and the only other furnishings were three hard-backed chairs, arranged to face the beds. The whole room had a seedy look, of an area poorly maintained. On the chairs, eyeing him curiously, sat three people: a short, powerfully-built man with hot, tawny eyes, and two women; one black-skinned, tall, and angular, but at the same time graceful, the other tiny, plump, and fair. Peron guessed that the women were in their thirties, the man a few years younger.

"Very good," said the shorter woman unexpectedly. "All present and correct. I think we may begin."

Peron caught his first glimpse of her eyes, and it was like a plunge into cold water. They were brown and wide-set, and in them was a disconcerting power and intensity. He felt as though she could see right through him. The forehead above the alert eyes showed a faint but extensive pattern of fine white scars, running up into the hairline.

"You are probably feeling quite surprised," the woman went on. She turned her attention to Sy, and stared at him closely. He gazed back, the usual expression of cynical abstraction on his face.

"Or maybe not," she said at last. "But maybe a little disoriented. So let me begin by telling you that you are exactly where you wanted to be. This is Gulf City—your 'Convergence Point,' which I rather like as a fitting name for this location. This is also our main Headquarters. You have arrived. No longer will you need to imagine other gates still to be passed through."

Peron looked at Sy, but the other remained silent. He would be performing his own evaluation, and until that was complete he was unlikely to speak.

"What happened?" said Peron at last. As usual in S-space, speech was a problem. And there was something in the woman's super-confident tones that was irksome. "How did we get here?"

"You found your own way here," said the woman. "Everything else is of lesser importance. Jan de Vries told us about the three of you, and said you had the potential; but we were all surprised—and delighted—at how quickly you came. Only one or two people finagle their way to Gulf City every Earth-year. Three at once is a bonanza."

"You mean you *wanted* us to come?"

"Anyone who can find their way to Gulf City is welcome. There is a natural selection process at work—if you lack the necessary qualities, you will never overcome the intellectual and physical barriers, and you will never reach this place."

"You were playing with us," said Peron bitterly. He was feeling sick with the sense of failure. "Watching all our moves. When we thought we were so clever sneaking aboard the *Manta*, you knew we were there all along."

"We did not." The woman's voice carried conviction. "The crew of the *Manta* is in cold sleep recovery—they still have no idea of your presence on board their ship. Your actual departure from the Sol System also went unobserved. And you made a team of technicians there work for many weeks, eliminating the data system weaknesses that you discovered and ingeniously exploited. You walked through the Sol checkpoints and safeguards. Jan de Vries was appalled at how inadequate you made them seem. You should certainly feel no shame. But we find it expedient to employ our own security system in Gulf City. As I'm sure you know, S-space inhabitants are highly vulnerable to actions in ordinary space. We inspect all approaching ships ourselves, during deceleration, long before they are allowed to dock here."

Peron realized that Elissa was now fully conscious next to him, and listening intently. "Just who are you?" he said. "And what do you mean, you want us here? *Why* do you want us?"

"One question at a time." The woman smiled, and it transformed her face. She no longer looked austere and unsympathetic. "Introductions first: you are Peron of Turcanta, Elissa Morimar, and Sy Day of Burgon." Her eyes went again to Sy, and there was another long moment of locked gazes. "The Pentecost trouble-makers—but also the first people from your planet ever to reach Gulf City. My congratulations. As for us"—she touched the stocky man lightly on the shoulder—"this is Wolfgang Gibbs, Manager of Gulf City. This is Charlene Bloom, my special assistant. And I am Judith Niles." She smiled again. "I am Director General of Gulf City, and of all Immortal operations. Lie quiet for one moment longer."

She moved forward and looked at their faces. Then she studied the dials set into the heads of the three beds for a second or two, and nodded. "I think we can return you to free mobility. The precautions were for your sakes as much as ours. *Command: release these three.*"

The straps around Peron at once went loose, and after a second he felt a painful tingling in his limbs and the return of full sensation there. He slid forward and stood, making sure of his balance.

"You are impatient for answers," went on Judith Niles. "As I would be. Very well, we will not disappoint you. Wolfgang, will you begin the explanations and tour? Please summon me at the appropriate time."

She touched a setting at her belt, and vanished. A moment later, and Charlene Bloom was gone also. Wolfgang Gibbs stood looking quizzically at Sy, Elissa and Peron.

"Well. That's real nice." He sniffed. "Yeah. JN says you can go free, then she and Charlene go back to work—so I have to handle you on my own when you go homicidal. All right, then, I'll trust you. If you feel up to a little walk, we'll take the old guided tour."

Wolfgang Gibbs turned casually and ambled towards the door of the room. After a single look at each other, the other three followed.

"We could use the service robots to move us around," Gibbs said over his shoulder. "I'd normally do that. But if we did you'd get no feel for the Gulf City layout. Better to do it on your two feet, then you'll know where everything is for future reference. We'll begin with the outside."

"Where are you taking us?" said Elissa, falling into step at his side, while Peron and Sy trailed along behind.

He looked at her appreciatively. To Peron's annoyance he seemed to be making a close inspection of her face and figure. "Lookout Point. It's the place where the galactic observations are done— the whole galaxy and beyond. We do a lot of listening and looking in Gulf City. That's why we're here, lightyears from anywhere you'd ever choose to be. You'll notice a lot less service robots here than usual, and less mechanical gadgets. We put up with the mess. When you've come all this way to find a quiet place to listen, you don't want to clutter up the observational signals with your own electronic garbage."

He led the way along a radial corridor that ran for more than a kilometer outwards. The size of Gulf City began to make an impression on the other three. By the time they reached Lookout Point they were moving in total silence, making mental notes of everything they saw. The whole of Gulf City was girded with antennae, telescopes, interferometers, and signal devices. Dozens of exterior ports showed the same blank white of S-space, but screens on the interior walls performed frequency conversions and display. They could observe open interstellar space as it looked at every wavelength range, from hard X-ray to million kilometer radio waves.

Wolfgang Gibbs paused for a long time in front of one screen. "See that?" he said at last. He tapped the display, where a faint, crablike shape showed dark against a lighter background. "That dark, spirally blob? That's one of the main reasons we're here at Gulf City. We've been watching them for fifteen thousand Earth years. I've been studying them myself for half that time—I came here four S-years ago, with Charlene Bloom."

"What are they?" asked Sy. His taciturn manner was gone, and there was a febrile excitement in his voice. "That screen shows signals at ultralong radio frequencies—I didn't know anything radiated there, except the Gossameres and Pipistrelles that we saw on the way to Earth."

Wolfgang lost his detached and casual manner. He looked hard at Sy. "Quite right, sport. We started with the same idea. But now we think half the Universe communicates on those long frequencies. Like our friend there. We call that a Kermel

Object, but that's only a name. It's still a major mystery. We think it's a sort of big brother to the Gossameres. They all send signals to each other, multi-kilometer wavelengths."

The displays showed a full three hundred and sixty degree field of view. Sy moved quickly from one to another, checking for the dark, spidery shapes. "The screens show Kermel Objects in all directions," he said. "How far away are they?"

"Good question," said Wolfgang. "A long way—a damned long way. We estimate the nearest one at two thousand lightyears, and even that nearest one is out of the plane of our galaxy. They're not galactic objects, generally speaking—they're intergalactic objects. Unless you get to a quiet place like this, you can't hope to detect them at all. Come on. You'll have plenty of opportunity to find out more about the Kermels, but for now I want you to get the ten-cent tour. I'll tell you one more thing, though: you're looking at possible intelligence there—and it's an intelligence that seems to be older than this galaxy."

He continued around the outside of Gulf City, making a circuit that was more than three miles long. Sy did not speak again. Elissa asked questions about everything, and Gibbs did his best to answer. Once inside Gulf City, any secrecy towards outside inquirers appeared to vanish.

They saw billions of cubic feet of power generation equipment, and massive drives sufficient to allow Gulf City to cruise where it chose in interstellar space. There were food production facilities enough to feed tens of thousands, lying near the center of the structure. Most of them stood idle. According to Wolfgang Gibbs, the current population of Gulf City approached seven hundred, though the original capacity was more than ten times that.

Finally, after showing them corridor after corridor of living accommodation, Gibbs stopped and shrugged his shoulders. "It will take you a month to see everything, but you should have enough for a first impression. Take a break, and make yourselves comfortable here. All these suites are fully equipped. The information system will tell you most things about the city that I haven't covered. I'll make sure the service robots will accept your voice commands—but don't expect instant response, we're always short of service. We have an appointment in JN's office in three hours. I'll see you there."

"Where is that?" asked Elissa.

"Ask the info-system if you want to go there on foot. If you're feeling lazy, just give the command. If you want me, use the call system." Wolfgang Gibbs winked at Elissa, manipulated a control on his belt, and vanished.

"So. What do you think?" asked Peron.

Elissa looked up at the ceiling. They were alone at last. Sy had left them a few minutes after Wolfgang Gibbs, saying he needed time to think. Peron and Elissa had wandered for a while along the endless corridors, poking their heads into kitchens, entertainment areas, and exercise rooms. All were deserted. Finally they found a set of living quarters that appealed to them, and decided they might as well move in. Now they were lying side by side on a huge, cloud-soft floor area.

"Think we're being monitored?" she said at last.

"When in doubt, assume yes. But does it make any difference?"

"I guess not. But I think we're going to see sparks

fly here at the next meeting. Did you notice the way that Sy and the Director General looked at each other?"

"Judith Niles? It was hard to miss it. She's probably used to a lot of respect here. You know old Sy, he'd be rude to the devil."

"I told him to go easy." Elissa laughed. "He said she was arrogant."

"Coming from Sy, that's a bit much. What does he think *he* is?"

"I told him that. He says that maybe he has 'the natural suspicion of youth for age' but that she has the 'intolerable arrogance of unquestioned authority.' According to Sy, she's surrounded by yes-men and yes-women, and she thinks she knows all the answers."

"When in fact, he does?" Peron was irritated. He was still slightly jealous of Sy—particularly when Elissa sounded admiring.

"No. He says he has a hundred unanswered questions, but he didn't want to go into them with Gibbs. He's waiting for a shot at Judith Niles."

"So am I. But there's really only one question to be asked. Why does Gulf City exist?"

"You heard what Wolfgang said; to study the Kermel Objects."

"Sure—but that's nonsense." Peron rolled over to face Elissa. "Look, I can imagine a group of pure scientists arguing that it was worth the enormous effort of setting up a research station out here in the gulf, to decide the nature of the Kermel Objects. But you've met Judith Niles. Can you see her swallowing that argument? She'd throw them out of her office in two minutes. I think Sy will ask her the main question—and rather him than me. But if he doesn't, you and I must do it."

Peron sounded unhappy but resolute. Elissa said no more, but she snuggled closer to him and took him in her arms.

Almost a mile away, in a secluded area on the other side of Gulf City, Wolfgang Gibbs was engaged in his own secret meeting with Charlene Bloom. They lay side by side in an empty room, in darkness and with all monitors turned off.

"You noticed the difference, didn't you?" he said softly. "I think we caught a new breed of fish this time. Sharks, maybe, instead of guppies."

"I agree. JN certainly thinks so, too. You could feel the tension between all four of them. Especially with the dark-haired kid, Sy—he didn't give her an inch. I'm not sure I want to be at the next meeting. She'll have her hands full."

"I sure as hell hope so." Wolfgang Gibbs smiled bitterly in the darkness. "You know the trouble with the two of us, Charlene? We're outgunned. JN's the boss, and we know it, all three. We just can't argue with her, even when we're on the right side of the issue—she has too much firepower. I'm sick of this place, and I'm beginning to hate S-space life, but I still can't tell her I want out."

"You mean *leave*? Leave Gulf City and JN completely?" Charlene Bloom pulled away from him. "We couldn't do that. We've all been together since the beginning."

"Yeah. And that's too long. Over fifteen years, most of them in S-space. God, Charlene, don't you think we need a new look at things here? And I don't believe we can provide it. Maybe those three kids can. You and I should be off, out to pasture, running a planet contact group, or a Sector Headquarters. Maybe we should go to Pentecost, where they came from."

"Did you tell them about their three friends?"

Gibbs scowled and shook his head. "Not yet. I couldn't do it. They're expecting them to roll up here at Gulf City. I'm leaving it to JN to break the news. They'll hear it soon enough. That's going to be hard for them."

There was a long silence.

"Wolfgang?" said Charlene at last.

"Yeah."

"I'm sorry you feel the way you do." Her voice was unhappy and tentative. "I know it's frustrating here, sometimes. But I've been very happy, all these years. I know my limitations. I could never have done what Judith has done, pulling us together and holding us together. Nor could you. And you can say what you like about living in Gulf City, but we're working on humanity's biggest problem. If we don't find a solution, I think it's the end of the road for *homo sapiens*. And if you're making a sacrifice, JN is making one that's just as big."

"I know it. But she's calling the shots. Suppose we're off on the wrong tack? JN thinks we're making progress, but as far as I'm concerned we're in just the same position as when Gulf City was created—that's over fifteen thousand Earth-years ago. What have we accomplished in all that time? And how long do we have, before it's all over?"

Charlene did not reply. Wolfgang had sometimes spoken of breaking away from Gulf City, but never before in such strong terms. If he went, what would she do? She could not bear to lose Wolfgang, but also she could not desert her work and Judith Niles.

She was glad of the darkness. And she was more than ever dreading the results of the coming meeting.

Chapter 28:

Sy hesitated for maybe a minute after leaving Peron and Elissa. Then he moved fast. During their tour of Gulf City they had seen a dozen suspense chambers for movement to and from S-space. Now he headed for the nearest of them and unhesitatingly lowered himself inside one of the tanks. He performed a final check of the monitors to confirm that he was alone and unobserved, then lay back in the casket, and initiated the process that would take him to normal space. His eyes closed. . . .

. . . . and opened—to find Judith Niles calmly peering in at him through the tank's transparent cover. She had an unreadable smile on her face, and when he was fully awake she opened the door and helped him out. He looked at her warily.

"Come on," she said. "You and I need to talk, just the two of us. I think my office will feel more comfortable than the chamber here." And without looking at him she turned and led the way.

She took him towards the main labs of Gulf City, in the very center of the station. Sy soon found himself in a well-appointed set of rooms, with pictures on the walls, shelves of genuine books, and serried ranks of monitors. She waved at them.

"First lesson. I'll be throwing a lot of lessons at you. Don't *ever* assume that you are unobserved in Gulf City. I learned the art of monitoring from a master—the only master I've ever known. From here you can watch everything." She initiated a suite-spin to give an effective gravity about half that of Earth, then sank into an armchair and tucked her feet in under her. She gestured Sy to take a seat opposite. There was a long silence, during which they performed a close inspection of each other.

"Want me to do the talking?" she said at last.

Sy shook his head. "You first, me second. You know I have questions."

"Of course you do." JN leaned back and sighed. "I wouldn't be interested in you if you didn't. And I think I have some answers. But it has to be a two-way street."

"What do you want from me?"

"Everything. Cooperation, understanding, brain-power, new ideas—maybe partnership." She was staring at him with peculiar intensity, eyes wide and unblinking beneath the scarred forehead. "It's something I haven't had in all the years since we left Earth. I think you can be a full partner. God knows, we need it. We're dying for lack of fresh thoughts here. Every time a new arrival finds a way to Gulf City, I've waited and hoped." Her expression had changed, become almost beseeching. "I think you're different. We can read each other, you and I. That's rarer than you know. I want you to help me recruit your companions, because I'm not sure I can do that. They're a stubborn pair. But you think in the same way as I do. I suspected you would come here, to normal space, because it's exactly what I do myself, when I need quiet time, time to think. You heard that it's bad to go from normal space to S-space and back too often?"

Sy nodded. "That's what Olivia Ferranti told us. She believes it, but I'm not sure I do. I've seen no evidence of it."

"I don't think you will. If there are bad effects, they are very subtle." Judith Niles smiled again, an open smile that lit up her face. "But a system in which people pop into normal space to think too much is hard to control. You don't take other people's word for much, do you?"

"Should I?" Sy's face was expressionless. "Look, if this is to be more than a waste of time, let's get to specifics. You're right, I came here to think before we met with you again. I needed time. Gulf City seemed like a big charade—a place without a plausible purpose. If you want my cooperation, and the cooperation of Peron and Elissa, begin by telling me what's really going on here—*tell me why Gulf City exists*."

"I'll do better than that." Judith Niles stood up. "I'll show you. You can see for yourself. I don't often have a chance to brag about the work we've done here, but that doesn't mean I'm not proud of it. Put this suit on—we'll be visiting some cold places."

She led the way down a long corridor. The first room contained half a dozen people, all frozen in postures of concentration around two beds occupied by recumbent forms.

"Standard S-space lab." Judith Niles shrugged. "No big mysteries here, and no justification for

Gulf City. We still conduct sleep experiments in S-space, but there's no reason except my personal interests why this has to be here. This is my own lab. I started out in sleep research, back on Earth—it led us to discover S-space. The main center for sleep research is still back in the Sol System, under Jan de Vries. The best protocol we know reduces sleep to about one hour in thirty. Our end objective is still the same: zero sleep."

She closed the door. Another corridor, another lab, this one entered through a double insulating door. Before they went inside, they sealed their suits.

"Temperature here is well below freezing." Niles spoke over the suit radio. "This one should be more interesting. We discovered it about seven thousand Earth-years ago. Wolfgang Gibbs stumbled across the condition when we were exploring the long-term physiological effects of cold sleep. He calls it T-state."

The room had four people in it, each sitting in a chair and supported at head, wrists, waist, and thighs. They wore headsets covering eyes and ears, and they did not move.

Sy moved forward and looked at each of them closely. He touched a frozen fingertip, and lifted the front of a headset to peer into an open eye. "They can't be in S-space," he said at last. "This room is too cold for it. Are they conscious?"

"Completely. These four are volunteers. They have been in T-state for almost one thousand Earth-years, but they feel as though they entered it less than five hours ago. Their subjective rate of experience is about one two-millionth of normal, roughly one thousandth of the usual S-space rate."

Sy was silent, but for the first time he looked surprised.

"Mind-boggled?" She nodded. "We all felt the same when Wolfgang showed us. But the real significance of T-state won't be obvious to you for a little while yet. It's hard to grasp just how slow time passes here. Let me tell you how Charlene Bloom put it when she and I had our first one-minute experience of T-state: in the time it takes a T-state clock to strike the hour of midnight, Earth would pass through two whole seasons, from winter to spring to summer. A full life on Earth would flash by in half a T-hour. We have no idea of the human life expectancy for someone who remains in T-state, but we assume it's millions of Earth-years."

"Why the headsets?"

"Sensory perception. Humans in T-state are blind, deaf and dumb without computer assistance. Our sense organs are not designed for light and sound waves of such long wavelength. The headsets do the frequency adjustment. Want to try T-state?"

"Definitely."

"I'll put you on the roster to spend a few minutes there. That's enough. Remember the time rate difference—one T-minute costs most of a day in S-space, and nearly four Earth-years." Again Judith Niles turned to leave the room. Sy, after a final glance at the four cowled and motionless figures, followed her outside and along another long and dimly-lit corridor. He noted approvingly that her energy and concentration remained undiminished.

They finally approached a massive metal door, protected against entry by locks that called for fingerprint, vocal, and retinal matching. When Sy was at last cleared by the system and stepped inside, he looked around him in surprise. He had expected something new and exotic, perhaps another frozen lab, full of strange experiments in time-slowing or suspension of consciousness; but this room appeared to be no more than a standard communications complex. And a dusty, poorly maintained one, at that.

"Don't judge by appearances." Judith Niles had seen his expression. "This is the most important room in Gulf City. If there are any secrets, they're here. And don't think that human nature changes when people move to S-space. It doesn't, and most individuals never question *why* things are done the way they are in our system. If they do question, they are shown what you are about to see. If not, we don't force the information on them. This is the place where the oldest records are accessed."

She sat down at the console and performed a lengthy coded entry procedure. "You should try cracking this, if you think you're a hot shot at finding holes in system software. It has six levels of entry protection. Let's feel our way into the data base gradually. This is a good place to begin."

She entered another sequence. The screen lit with the soft, uniform white glow characteristic of S-space. After a few moments there appeared on it a dark network of polyhedral patterns, panels joined by silvery filaments. "You've seen one of these yourself, I gather. Gossameres and Pipistrelles— probably the first alien intelligence that humans discovered. We ran into them twenty thousand Earth-years ago, as soon as deep space probes began with S-space crews; but we're still not sure if we're meeting intelligence. Maybe it depends on our definition of intelligence. Interesting?"

Sy shrugged in a non-committal way.

"But not that interesting?" Judith Niles touched the control console again. "I agree. Abstractly interesting, but no more than that unless humans learn to set up a real dialogue with them. Well, we tried. We located their preferred output frequencies, and we found that simple signal sequences would drive them away and discourage them from draining our power supplies. But that's not much of a message, and we never got beyond it. The Gossameres and Pipistrelles proved to be a kind of dead end. But they served one enormously important function. They alerted us to a particular wavelength region. We began to listen on those frequencies anytime we were in deep space and thought there might be a Gossamere around. And that's when we began to intercept other signals on the same wavelengths—regular coded pulses of low-frequency radiation, with a pattern like this."

On the screen appeared a series of rising and falling curves, an interlocking sequence of complex sinusoids, broken by regularly spaced even pulses.

"We became convinced they were signals, not just natural emissions. But they were faint and intermittent, and we couldn't locate their sources. Sometimes, a ship on an interstellar transit would pick up a signal on the receiver, long enough for the crew to lock an imaging antenna onto the signal source direction. They might receive a faint source image for a while, then they would lose it as the ship moved on. It was tantalizing, but over the years we built up a library of partial, blurred images. Finally we had enough to plug everything into a computer and look for a pattern. We found one. The 'sightings' took place only near the midpoints of the trips, and only when the ships were far from all material bodies and signal sources. The signals were received only when we were in deep space—the deeper, the better.

"By then we knew we were seeing something different from Gossameres and Pipistrelles. The new sources were very faint and distant, and the reconstructed image outlines showed a hint of a spiral structure, nothing like those paneled polyhedra. But we were still too short of information. It seemed a fascinating scientific mystery, but not much more. That was when Otto Kermel proposed a series of missions for a long-term search and study of the objects.

"I don't deserve any credit at all for what happened next. I thought his idea would go nowhere, and gave him minimal resources and support. He did all the pioneer work on his own. We gave him the use of a one-man ship, and he went away to a quiet location about seven lightyears from Sol. He argued that the absence of electromagnetic and gravitational fields was essential to studying the objects. Although his first objective was communication with them, he found that a round-trip message to even the nearest of them took two S-years. That limited him, but during his studies he discovered lots of other things.

"First, he found many Kermel Objects, all around the Galaxy. The signals we intercept are not intended for us. We were eavesdroppers on transmissions between the Kermels, and those signals between them are numerous. Based on the length of those transmissions, Otto concluded that the Kermel Objects are immensely old, with a natural life-rate so slow that S-space is inadequate to study them—in thousands of Earth-years, he was receiving only partial signals. Otto claimed that he could partially decode their messages, and he believed that they have been in existence since the formation of the Universe—since *before* the Big Bang, according to one of his wilder reports. He a suggested that they propagate not by exchange genetic material, but by radio exchange of gen...c information. We have not been able to verify any of those conjectures, and Otto could not provide enough data for convincing proof. What he needed was the T-state, and a chance for more extended study periods on a time scale appropriate to the Kermel Objects. But by an accident of timing, he departed for a second expedition just before the T-state was discovered. And he has never returned.

"By the time he left, though, we had changed our ideas about the practical importance of studying the Kermel Objects. We decided that it is central to the future of the human species. We have continued his work, but without much of his data base. Take a look at this."

Judith Niles projected another scene onto the display. "Does it seem familiar?"

Sy studied it for a second or two, then shrugged. "It's a picture of a spiral galaxy, looking down on the disk. I've no idea which one."

"Correct. There's no way you'd recognize it, but it's this galaxy, seen from outside. That signal was recorded by Otto Kermel, from one of the Objects sitting way up above the galactic plane. And as part of the same signal, this image came with it." At her keyed command, another picture appeared split-screen, side by side with the first one. It was the same galaxy, but now the star patterns were shown in different colors. "Keep watching closely. I'm going to zoom."

The star fields expanded steadily as the field of view moved in to focus on one of the spiral arms. Soon individual stars could be distinguished on the screen.

Judith Niles halted the zoom. "Once you look at individual stars, you can see what's going on. The stars in the right hand image have been color-coded according to spectral type. And by looking at the stars in our own stellar neighborhood, it was easy for us to read the code. For instance, Sol is a G-2 V star, and G-types show in pale green. Red giants are magenta, O-type supergiants are purple, red dwarfs are orange-yellow. There was another important piece of information in the image. By looking at the distribution of stars in some of the main stellar clusters, we could determine the date. All the evidence was consistent, and told us that the image represented the situation seventy thousand Earth-years ago. When Otto Kermel received another signal of the same type, he thought at first that it was just a copy. But it wasn't. Here it is."

She brought another image on the screen, overwriting the first one. "For one thing, the stellar distribution indicates a different date. This image shows our arm of the galaxy as it *will be* in about forty thousand Earth-years. Take a good look at it—it's the most important picture in human history."

Sy stared at the screen in silence for a couple of minutes. "Can you display the color key for spectral type?" he said at last.

Without speaking, Judith Niles flashed a color code onto the screen header. Sy was silent again for an even longer period.

"Where's Sol?" he finally asked.

Judith Niles smiled grimly, and moved the screen cursor to indicate one star in the field. "That's Sol, forty thousand years in the future. Now you see why we're here in Gulf City."

"Red dwarf. Wrong spectral type. The whole spiral arm is *full* of red dwarfs—far too high a proportion of them." Sy turned his attention again to the first image. "This is impossible. It wasn't that way seventy thousand years ago, according to the image. And there's no way that stellar types could change so much, and in such a short time. You must be misinterpreting the data."

"That's what we thought—at first. Then we began to compare recent star catalogs with ones made in the earliest days of stellar astronomy. There's no mistake. The main sequence stars centered on this region of the spiral arm," she moved the cursor to a place about three thousand lightyears closer to the galactic center "—have been changing. What used to be spectral classes G and K are becoming class M."

"No way!" Sy shook his head vigorously. "Not unless all the astrophysics we knew back on Pentecost was nonsense. It takes hundreds of millions of years *at least* to move from one spectral class to another, unless there's a cataclysmic change like a nova."

"You know the same astrophysics as we do. And we can only think of one mechanism for change. Class G and class K stars have surface temperatures between about four and six thousand degrees. Class M are more like two to three thousand. You *could* get those changes in stellar type—if somehow you could artificially damp the fusion reaction in the stars. Lower the internal energy production, and you would lower the overall temperature."

Sy looked frustrated. "Maybe—but can you suggest any process that could possibly do that? I know of none."

"Nor do we. No *natural* process. That keeps leading me back to one unpleasant conclusion. The information we've received from the Kermel Objects is true—we've done other checks on changes in stellar types. And there's no natural way for these changes to happen. So: either the Kermel Objects *induce* the changes; or some other entity, living in our spiral arm of the galaxy, prefers stars of lower temperature and luminosity."

"You mean something or someone is inducing reduced fusion reactions through the spiral arm—intentionally."

"I mean exactly that." Judith Niles' forehead filled with frown lines, and she suddenly looked a dozen years older. "It's a frightening conclusion, but it's the only one. I don't think the Kermel Objects are doing this, even though they seem to know a lot about it. We have some evidence that suggests they understand the whole process, and they certainly seem able to predict the rate of change in the spiral arm. But I believe the action doesn't originate with them. What we're seeing is the work of another species, one more like ourselves—one that has no use for the deep space preferred by Gossameres or Kermel Objects. These other creatures want to live near a star. A red, low luminosity star." She cleared the display, leaned back, and closed her eyes. "A long time ago humans talked of terraforming Mars and Venus, but we never did it. Just too busy blowing ourselves up, I guess, ever to get round to it. Now maybe we've met someone more rational and more ambitious than we were. What we are seeing is *stellaforming*. And if it goes on, and if we don't understand it and find out how to stop it, in another hundred thousand years this whole spiral arm will have no G-type stars. And that will be the end of human planetary colonies. Finis."

Judith Niles paused. She switched off all the displays.

"And we think the Kermel Objects hold the key," she said softly. "Now do you see why we're living out here in the middle of nowhere, and why S-space and T-state are so important? In normal space, a hundred thousand years used to seem like forever. But I expect to be alive, a thousand Earth-centuries from now."

Sy wore an expression that Peron and Elissa would have found unfamiliar. He seemed uneasy, and lacking in confidence. "I read it wrong. I thought the only reason for being here in Gulf City was safety from outside interference, and control of S-space. The whole advantage of being an 'Immortal' was presented to us as increased subjective life span—but now I wonder about that."

"You are right to do so. We have life-extension methods available—ones that came out of S-space research—that can allow increased life span in normal space. And probably let the subject enjoy life more keenly, too. But you can't solve the problem thrown at us by the Kermel Objects unless you can work on it for a long time. That means Gulf City, and it means S-space." She stood up. "Will you work with me on this? And will you help me to persuade your friends to do the same?"

"I'll try." Sy hesitated. "But I still need to think.

I've not had the thinking time that I wanted when I headed for the tanks."

Judith Niles nodded. "I know. But I wanted you to do your thinking with a full knowledge of what's going on here. You have that. I'll head back now. This chamber is self-locking when you leave. And as soon as you're ready to do it, let's meet again with your friends." Now she hesitated, and her expression matched Sy's for uneasiness. "There's something else to be discussed, but it's on another subject. And I want to do it when all of you are together."

She gave him a worried smile and headed for the door. For the first time, Sy could see her as a lonely and vulnerable figure. The power and intensity of personality were still there, unmistakable, but they were muted, overlain with an awareness of a monstrous unsolved problem. He thought of the splendid confidence with which the Planetfest winners had lifted off from Pentecost. They had the shining conviction that any problem in the Galaxy would fall to their combined attack. And now? Sy felt older, with a great need for time to think. Judith Niles had been carrying a killing load of responsibility for a long time. She needed help, but could he provide it? Could anyone? He wanted to try. For the first time in his life, he had met someone whose intellect walked the same paths as his own, someone in whose presence he felt totally at ease.

Sy leaned back in his chair. It would be ironic if that satisfaction of mind-meeting came at the same time as a problem too big for both of them.

An hour later Sy was still sitting in the same position. In spite of every effort, his mind had driven back relentlessly to a single focus: the Kermel Objects. He began to see the Universe as they must see it, from that unique vantage point of the longest perspective of evolutionary time. With the T-state available, humans had a chance to experience that other world-view.

Here was a cosmos which exploded from an initial singular point of incomprehensible heat and light, in which great galaxies formed, tightened into spirals, and whirled about their central axes like giant pinwheels. They clustered together in loose galactic families, threw off supercharged jets of gas and radiation, collided and passed through each other, and spawned within themselves vast gaseous nebulae.

Suns coalesced quickly from dark clouds of dust and gas, blooming from faintest red to fiery blue-white. As he watched in his mind's eye, they brightened, expanded, exploded, dimmed, threw off trains of planets, or spun dizzily around each other. A myriad planetary fragments cooled, cracked, and breathed off their protective sheaths of gases. They caught the spark of life within their oceans of water and air, fanned it, nurtured it, and finally hurled it aloft into surrounding space. Then there was a seething jitter of life around the stars, a Brownian dance of ceaseless human activity against the changing stellar background. The space close to the stars filled with the hummingbird beat and shimmer of intelligent organic life. The whole Universe lay open before it.

And now the T-state became essential. Planet-based humans, less than mayflies, flickered through their brief existence in a tiny fraction of a cosmic day. The whole of human history had run its course in a single T-week, while mankind moved out from the dervish whirl of the planets into the space surrounding Sol. Then S-space had given the nearer stars; but the whole Galaxy and the open vastness of inter-galactic space still beckoned. And in that space, in T-state, humans could be free to thrive forever.

Sy sat back in the chair, drunk with his new vision. He could see a bright path that led from mankind's earliest beginnings, stretching out unbroken into the farthest future. It was the road to forever. And it was a road he wanted to take, whatever the consequences.

Chapter 29:

Elissa was the last to arrive at the meeting. As she hurried into the long conference room to take her seat she glanced around the table, and was struck at once by the odd seating arrangement. Judith Niles sat alone at the head of the table, head bowed forward and her eyes on the control console built into the table in front of her. Sy sat to her immediate right, and Peron next to him, with an empty chair between them. Peron looked a little uncomfortable, while Sy was obviously a million miles away, absorbed by some private concern. Wolfgang Gibbs and Charlene Bloom occupied seats on the opposite side of the table. They were sitting very close together, but well away from the rest. Wolfgang was scowling, and chewing moodily at a fingernail, while Charlene Bloom glanced from one person to another with rapidly blinking eyes. Elissa looked at her closely. Extreme nervousness? It certainly appeared that way, but for no obvious reason. And the whole room was unnaturally quiet, without the normal casual chit-chat that preceded even a serious meeting. The overall atmosphere was glacial and tense.

Elissa paused, still standing. She had a choice. Sit opposite Sy, and thus be between Wolfgang and the Director? Or next to Sy and Peron; or at the other end of the table, facing Judith Niles. She headed to sit next to Sy, then on some obscure impulse changed her mind and went to the end chair directly opposite the Director. Judith Niles raised her head. Elissa underwent a brief scrutiny from those intense eyes, then the Director nodded briefly in greeting. She seemed as remote and preoccupied as Sy.

"To business," Judith Niles said at last. "I gather that Sy briefed both of you on our meeting and conversation?"

Peron and Elissa looked at each other. "In detail," said Elissa. She waited for Peron, but he did not speak. "However, we still have questions," she went on.

Judith Niles nodded. "I am sure you do. Perhaps it is best if you first listen to what I propose. That may answer many of your questions for you. If not, we will consider them later."

Her words were couched as a suggestion, but her tone of voice showed she expected no argument. No one replied. Wolfgang ducked his head and seemed to be studying the granular plastic table top, rendered a soft continuous blur by the oddities of S-space optics. Charlene looked expectantly around the table at the others, then back to the Director.

"It is interesting that the arrival here of the three of you should coincide with a decision point in my own thinking," went on Judith Niles. "Although I could argue that your presence in Gulf

City precipitated that point. By now you know something of our history here. For fifteen thousand Earth-years, research work here has continued without a break: monitoring messages from the Kermel Objects; developing new techniques for slowing of consciousness, designed to make us better able to match the Kermel transmission rates; and making many attempts at direct communication with them. Failed attempts, I should add. But we have had some successes. We are assured now of the extreme age of the Kermels; we have learned how to present signals received from them reliably, as one, two, or three dimensional arrays; we have confirmed by independent methods that the changes in stellar types in this spiral arm of our galaxy are real; and finally, we are beginning to see hints of methods to slow subjective experience rates even further, beyond those of T-state.

"These are all major advances. Yet you do not need me to point out that they will all be of no value unless we can learn how to inhibit the stellaforming of G type stars. We face the possibility of greatly extended life spans, with no place to live except far from our home stars. If that happens, we will also face the extinction of all our planetary colonies. And that is an intolerable thought, even if we forget recruitment needs from normal space to S-space.

"Before you arrived, the senior staff of Gulf City, and in particular Wolfgang, Charlene and I, had worried long and hard about the slowness of our progress. I decided some time ago that the pace of our efforts had to be picked up—by whatever methods. This is an absolute necessity. And to accomplish it, I have resolved to take an unprecedented step. You, the three of you, are uniquely central to that step."

Elissa and Peron looked at each other in surprise, then both turned to Sy. He was unmoved, his usual cool self.

"Hear me out," went on Judith Niles. "Why you? Because you have not yet become locked into our existing ways of thinking about the problem. We must find totally new avenues, create new thought patterns, and explore different options; but we cannot do that—we are too wedded to our existing exploration, and too fixed in the pattern of past analyses. Stay here for a few months, and you will have the same problem. That is why I propose a change at once, before you harden into our ways and ideas.

"What I am suggesting is revolutionary. I expect to establish a completely new facility, similar to Gulf City but in a separate location. It will have independent management, and independent research staff. The location that I have as first choice is eighteen lightyears from here, and almost twelve lightyears from Sol. It does not have quite the same degree of isolation from interference as this site, but signals received here from Kermel Objects will naturally be available to the new facility. There will be cooperation, but strictly limited interchange of information. We cannot afford to inhibit each other's research.

"And now, here is my specific proposal: you three are invited to go to that facility, with the best support that we can offer from anywhere in our network of colonies and stations. You will not merely be *participants* in the facility's research; you will in practice direct it, setting directions and allocating resources." She smiled. "I am sure you feel suspicious. Why would I, without taking leave of my senses, entrust a huge new undertaking to three near-strangers? I will tell you. Your performance to date has been highly impressive, but my real reason is far more compelling: we are becoming desperate here. *Something* must be done, and something new has to be tried."

She looked along the table. "You are silent. I am not surprised. I would be silent also. But when you have questions, I will do my best to answer all of them."

Sy did not move. He had been nodding his head a tiny fraction as she spoke, but now he was motionless. Wolfgang and Charlene were looking at Peron and Elissa, and avoiding Judith Niles' eye. Charlene looked tenser than ever.

"Why us?" said Peron at last. "Why didn't you do it with the last group of people to find their way to Gulf City?"

"For two simple reasons. First, I did not feel they could do it—I feel that you can. And second, I had not yet reached my own flashpoint. Now I feel a great need for action. Our present approach is too slow, and we must have at least two facilities working in parallel."

Peron looked at each participant in turn, taking his time, then finally turned back to Judith Niles. "When do you propose this would begin?"

She smiled with her mouth, but her eyes remained tense. "I am now about to fail one test of a good manipulator. Take it, if you will, as evidence of the depth of my concern on this issue. The process for creating the second facility has already begun. A station from Sol is now on the way to form the facility's nucleus, and other equipment is in shipment from three Sector Headquarters. It will be ready for operation as soon as you arrive there. If you agree, I hope that you will begin your journey at once. You can become familiar with details of equipment on the way there."

Peron nodded. "And what experiments would we do?"

"You will tell me that—remember, too much direction from here and the second facility becomes useless." She smiled again, and this time there was real humor there. "Talk to Wolfgang and Charlene, if you want to know how much it costs me to remove myself from the direction of the new effort. All my working life I have insisted in hands-on knowledge of any experiments under my control. Now I am promising to turn my back on you."

Judith Niles touched the controls on the table top, and the room began to darken. Behind her, panels in front of the big display slid open, and a flickering pattern showed on the screen.

"You will need time to make a decision. I expect that, but I also urge you to minimize that time. The most important job in human civilization is waiting for you. And for that reason, I do not hesitate to use unfair tactics of persuasion. I have one more argument to present to you. If you are the people that I believe you to be, it cannot fail to sway your opinions.

"A few days ago we received at Gulf City a video message from one of our Sector Headquarters, out near the planet of Paradise. It was sent via Earth, and addressed to you. It appears to be in clear form—though I know your penchant for hiding coded messages in with clear ones. The clear message is quite enough. Watch closely."

The screen behind Judith Niles now showed the

image of a man. He was a stranger to Elissa, grey-bearded and balding, with a prominent nose, pale grey eyes, and a craggy, lined face. A faint scar ran across his forehead, diagonally from the upper right to his left eyebrow. He grinned, looked directly into the camera, and raised his hand in greeting.

"Hello again. Greetings from Paradise—or near it."

Elissa heard Peron gasp, at the same moment as she felt her own rush of recognition. There could be no mistaking that strained, husky voice and precise diction. "It's Kallen!" said Peron. "My God, Sy, that's Kallen."

"Yes, quite right," said the face on the screen, exactly as though he could somehow hear the comments in the conference room. He grinned again. "This is Kallen, the one and only. Long time no see. But now get ready for a bigger shock."

The camera field of view slowly panned across from him to a large photograph, then zoomed in to take a close-up of a group of eight people. In the foreground, sitting cross-legged on cushions, were two teenage girls. Behind them, on a bench, were two men and two women in early middle age, and an elderly couple stood at the back in the center of the picture. The old man was white-haired and stooped, with heavy shoulders and a substantial paunch. The woman, also white-haired, was thin and wiry. Everyone was smiling.

"More greetings," said Kallen's thin voice. "And also a farewell. From Lum and Rosanne, their children, and their oldest grandchildren. There are four little ones, not in the picture. They are all still living on Paradise at the time I send you this message. When you receive it, they expect to be long dead." He shrugged. "Sorry, friends, I know we told you that we'd follow you to Earth in a few S-days. As you can see, it didn't quite work out that way.

"I expect that this will take a while to reach you. I know you're not on Earth, even though this message will be routed that way. But I've heard more than you might think about what you've been doing. Sy will tell you that nothing in the Universe can travel faster than light, but let me tell *him* that doesn't apply to rumors. There are great rumors about you three, and what you did to Sol's data bases and computer network—I wish I'd been there to help cheat the system. Don't give up on me, though. I expect that I'll see the three of you eventually.

"Rosanne and Lum asked me to give you their love, and to tell you not to grieve on their behalf. I pass that message, and agree with the sentiment." Kallen smiled. "I suspect that you are feeling horrified with the way that Lum and Rosanne look in this picture, and probably horrified also with the way that I look. But don't make the mistake of feeling sorry for them, or for me. Their lives have been the most rewarding of anyone I know. They lived happy, and they're happy now. And if you think of us as old people, remember that we think of you as children. Smart children, sure, and we love you like our own sons and daughters; but still children. Don't confuse calendar time and experience. When two or three hundred Pentecost years flash by in a month of S-space, you don't get the knowledge of life that comes with thirty years of living. You all have a lot of real living to do.

"I promised Lum and Rosanne that I would tell you what happened here. I'm back in S-space, in orbit around Paradise. I've been here for twenty-five Earth-years. But I couldn't persuade them to join me. Sy, do you remember the arguments we had, after Planetfest was over, on the strongest force in the Universe? Well, I can tell you now, it's not gravitation, or the force governing hadronic interactions. It's a force unique to living organisms. When Lum and Rosanne went down to Paradise, it was a frightening world, where all the humans had died. They wanted to stay there long enough to study the problem thoroughly. And after a few months, Rosanne became pregnant. They wanted the baby, but they knew they couldn't raise a child in S-space. And the idea of leaving their children was unthinkable to them. They stayed, to raise the family. *That's* the strongest force. After a while I joined them, down on the surface. I was there when each of the children was born.

"We were trying to find out what had killed off the previous colony on Paradise, and we had the best possible incentive. Unless we found an answer, we could go the same way, along with the children.

"I won't bore you with details. It took nearly thirty years, and we felt like giving up a dozen times. But we found the answer. Paradise has a benign protozoan parasitic life form, part of the intestinal flora and fauna that help the animals there to digest cellulose. It usually stays in the alimentary canal, but a few organisms make their way into the blood stream. No problem. The animals remain healthy, and don't even know the bugs are there. The colonists found that the organisms were inside them soon after they arrived, but all the tests showed that they were just as harmless to humans as they were to the native animals. Paradise has a wonderful climate, and fertile soils.

The human colony was doing fine, thriving and growing. Until they decided it would be less effort to import food synthesizers, and make most of their food rather than growing it.

"And since humans can't digest cellulose, the synthetic foods didn't contain it. An alternative indigestible material was used to provide food bulk. Most inhabitants of Paradise, including everyone in the cities, turned to use of the synthetics. Still everything seemed to be going well, and they were all in good health. But the internal parasites were suddenly deprived of food, and when that happened many of them migrated out of the alimentary canal and into the bloodstream. They starved and died there. Those deaths seemed to produce no ill-effects on the human hosts—they weren't even aware of it. But one of the decomposition by-products of the parasites has a structure very similar to a human neuro-transmitter. So far as we can tell, human intelligence all over Paradise suddenly dropped, fifty to a hundred points, from normal range to sub-moron. And it happened quickly. The city dwellers became ferocious animals, not smart enough to operate their own signalling system and call for advice and assistance. And they turned on the few people outside the towns, and killed them as they found them. By the time the next ship touched down on Paradise, it could find no survivors. And since the cause of the problem was still unknown, the ship did not stay long.

"Well, I've said enough to make my point. Paradise is a safe, habitable planet again. I helped a little, but it was really Lum and Rosanne who cracked the problem, and pointed out the simple solution: adequate cellulose in the diet. And that's related to the message that they want to send to you. Back on Pentecost, and later when we were looking at the Fifty Worlds, we had long debates on the usefulness of our lives. Lum and Rosanne feel they found the answer. They wouldn't put it this way, but they saved a world. Don't waste your life on small problems, they say. Find the biggest challenge that you can, the hardest one, the most frustrating one, and hit it with everything you've got."

Kallen paused. "See, I've changed, too. Thirty years ago, the speech I've just given was a month's supply of words. But I'm finished. I told you not to grieve for Rosanne and Lum. I meant it. If you ever have the satisfaction of finding a problem as big as the one they found, and solving it, you'll have answered our old question about the meaning of our lives."

Kallen's face went solemn, and he looked into the screen for a long time without speaking. "I'd like to see you all again," he said at last. "But the odd thing is, I know exactly what you look like. You haven't changed a bit since we said goodbye at the Cass System Sector Headquarters. Whereas I. . . ." He shrugged, and ran his hand across his balding head. "Goodbye, old friends, and good luck. And seek the highest, whatever you do."

The picture on the screen dissolved to a formless flicker of white, then that too faded to leave the room in darkness.

"Bless them," said Judith Niles softly. "I never knew Lum and Rosanne, but I grieve with you to know that they are dead. They were just the minds and spirits that we need for our problems here. Seek the highest, the hardest, the most frustrating. If you wanted a one-line description of the Kermel

Objects and stellaforming, those all apply. I wish we had Rosanne and Lum with us, but there will be others. Kallen may find his way here. He said as much, and from what I have heard of him from Paradise Station, he'll be hard to stop once he makes up his mind to get here."

"Impossible to stop," said Peron softly. "I just wish he were here with us now."

"But he is not." The lights in the conference room slowly came back to normal intensity, and Judith Niles gave her full attention to Elissa and Peron. She looked from one to the other, meeting their eyes. "You heard your friends. I don't see how you can resist that message. They saved a world. You have a chance to save every planet that can support human life. Don't you feel as though they could have been speaking to you about the exact problem we have here, and telling you to undertake it?"

Elissa looked around her. Sy was nodding. She realized that his decision had been made before he heard the message from Kallen—perhaps before this meeting began. She turned to Peron. He was wavering, half-persuaded but still uncomfortable. Elissa was on her own.

"NO!" The word seemed to burst from her, surprising her with its force and intensity. "No, that's not the answer. You're missing the point."

There was a ghastly silence. Everyone looked at her in astonishment—even Peron, and she had hoped that he would understand at once. "Can't you see it?" she went on. "You've missed the real significance of their message."

"I very much doubt it," said Judith Niles curtly. Her face was calm, but the scars were prominent on her forehead. "It was clear enough. Work on major problems, and do not let yourselves be distracted with trivia."

"Yes, certainly—tackle big subjects, there's no question about that. But look behind the message, at the facts. The problem on Paradise had been known for *five thousand* Earth-years, and no one had come near a solution. Until our friends came along, people were studying it *from S-space*, and that gave only a couple of S-years of effort. Now look at our situation. We have fifty thousand Earth-years to learn how to control the changes in stellar types—maybe a hundred thousand years if we are lucky. With that much time available, the human race should be able to solve anything, any problem you care to mention. *But not if you work it in S-space.* That moves at a snails-pace—and we need fast action."

"But the messages from the Kermel Objects are absolutely vital." Judith Niles was leaning back, a perplexed look on her face. "They're quite inaccessible from normal space."

"Of course they are—and somebody must be in S-space or T-state to receive them. But the analysis of those messages must go as fast as possible. That means we must be in normal space. You have to change your system, change it completely. Tell the planet-dwellers the problem, and make them the key to its solution. *That's* the rest of the message from Kallen and the others, the part you've been ignoring."

Elissa leaned forward across the table, her full attention on Judith Niles. "You want us to work on the central problem? I'd love to, there's nothing in the Universe that I'd like better. But *in normal space.* I know I may never see the solution if we do it this way. But I'll take my chances, because I feel sure that my descendants will find the answer, maybe a thousand Earth-years after I'm dead. That's enough to make it all worth it for me." She looked at Peron, and drew encouragement from his expression. He was nodding vigorously, his earlier uncertainty gone.

"I agree completely with Elissa," he said. "Though I didn't see it until she pointed it out to us. Let's go ahead just as you suggest, and set up your second facility. But in *normal* space. You'll feed us the best information you can collect in Gulf City, as you get it. We'll be turning that to new theories, two thousand times as fast as you could ever do it in S-space."

Judith Niles had listened closely, but now she was frowning and shaking her head. "It sounds good. But it would never work. Both of you, listen to what else your friend Kallen said: 'You lack experience.' It will take many years to acquire it. You need the interaction with us, here in Gulf City—and you could never gain the benefit of our experience if you were in normal space and we stayed in S-space. The information exchange problems are enormous. I said I would leave you free to undertake experiments in the second facility, but you would still have access to us, to talk to and exchange ideas. No." She shook her head. "It sounds good, but it wouldn't work."

"I agree with Elissa," said Wolfgang Gibbs suddenly from the other side of the table. He stopped, as though amazed at his own outburst. When he continued he addressed his words to Judith Niles, but he kept his eyes on Elissa and Peron, as though drawing support from them. "She's right. We'll be able to progress thousands of times as fast in normal space as in S-space—not to mention T-state, and you know that's my own special baby. I've worried the problem for months and years, wondering how to make better progress. But I never thought of two facilities, one in S-space and one in normal space. To us, used to the way things are here, normal space is almost the unthinkable thought. Shorter life span, planet-grubbing, probably never seeing a solution. But I bet it will work."

He paused, hesitated, looked at Charlene and Elissa, then at Judith Niles. His face was pale, but there was only conviction in his voice. "Your point about experience is a valid one. There is no substitute for years of practical experience of our work here. But I have that. If you go ahead and set up a second facility, in normal space, then I am volunteering to go to that facility."

"Wolfgang!" said Charlene Bloom. The word came from her unbidden. She bit her lip, and looked down. They were revealing too much—too much new hope in his voice, and too much raw pain in her own.

Judith Niles was sitting bolt upright in her chair. Elissa's support had come from the place she least expected it. "And you, Charlene?" she said calmly. "Since we all appear to have formed our opinions by now."

Peron looked at the Director and marvelled. Like Sy, she appeared able to move instantly from one position to another, and be ready at once for the next stage of discussion. It was as though her analysis of Elissa's and Peron's remarks had been performed automatically, subconsciously, needing no time for assimilation and full reflection.

"I'll stay here," said Charlene after a few seconds. She turned to look at Wolfgang, and her voice was despairing. "My work is here, in Gulf

City. I couldn't do it in another facility. But Wolfgang, if you go—who could do your work on T-state?"

Judith Niles looked at Sy, who gave a fractional nod of his head. "We have a volunteer for that," she said. "Sy is keen to explore T-state—and beyond. So now. . . ."

She leaned back in her chair and closed her eyes again. "Now comes the difficult question. You are proposing a radically different approach. Am I persuaded that it will work?"

"*Wrong question*," said Peron.

She opened her eyes and smiled at him. "True. I stand corrected. We cannot know in advance what will work, and what will fail. The right question, then: do I think a second facility in normal space has a better chance to succeed than one in S-space? The answer: maybe. Just maybe. I thought of many options, but I never seriously considered the Mayfly solution."

"You can't afford *not* to try it," said Peron. "Even if you reject it, we'll attempt it."

"I know. Bad position for a boss, right?" She smiled, then turned to Wolfgang. "And do you know what you are volunteering for? We can give you an extended life span in normal space, but you will still be dead in much less than one S-year."

"Give me credit for something, JN." Wolfgang's moment of defiance had brought him a new confidence. "I know exactly what I'm offering to do. I'll go to normal space, and I expect that I'll die there. So what? I saw that message from Paradise, too. And now I think about it, I never really wanted to live forever. I just want to live *well*. Sy can do my work here at least as well as I can, probably a damned sight better. Let's get on with it, I say."

He did not wait for an answer from Judith Niles. Instead he turned to Charlene and took her hand in his. The room went silent, with everyone watching closely. Charlene's mind flashed across the centuries, to the time back on Earth when Wolfgang had horrified her by secretly stroking her thigh in JN's presence. But this time she did not flinch when Wolfgang touched her gently on the shoulder. Her vision was clouded with tears. She moved to meet him when he leaned forward to kiss her, and put her arms around his neck. The final words had not been spoken, but she knew that the decision was already made.

The departure for a second facility could not happen immediately. She and Wolfgang would see each other many times before there was another parting, formal and final.

But this moment was unique. This was their first goodbye.

Epilogue:

Five minutes. Five minutes remain. And after that? If I were sure of the answer, a forty billion year journey could have been avoided.

Five minutes . . . to the moment of the monobloc.

The Kermel Objects are all around me, crowding in as the Universe dwindles. They are finally silent; even the low frequency transmission has subsided to nothing. And the Kermels have changed in appearance during the past two hours. There is a pulsation now at their centers, like a slow, strengthening heartbeat; and the outer tendrils have been steadily contracting, to tighten about the darker center. I feel as though I am witnessing a parody of galactic evolution, atramental spiral arms drawing close, knotting into the cores. The innermost regions are totally black. They look like holes in the Universe.

Beyond them, everything grows brighter and brighter. I see it only as it is filtered through the protective layers of the Kermels, but every few moments there is a flare of blue, then a scintillation so fierce I cannot look at it. It is a beauty that the Universe perhaps sees once only. . . .

Four minutes. We are approaching the final singularity. The total radius of the Universe is now less than eighty million kilometers. Another two hundred seconds, and the point of infinite compression will arrive.

Five seconds before that, the diameter of the Universe will be less than the size of a Kermel Object. And then?

The end of the journey; faster and faster.

If there is to be a singularity, the moment of final annihilation must occupy zero time.

And my mind wanders. It insistently pokes a fact forward, an element of mathematics learned long ago and thought long-forgotten. *In the neighborhood of an essential singularity, a complex variable assumes all possible values.* If that has relevance here, approaching the ultimate singularity of our Universe, then three minutes from now anything will be possible. As chaos grows out of order, nothing is forbidden.

My three companions are silent, overwhelmed by the sights around us. They are content to watch the displays, while I record this final message—to whom?

There is another change. The stars went long ago, vanished into the glowing bubble around me. Now there should be no residual structure to space. But the Kermel Objects persist. They take on darker and darker shades, standing solid against the golden-blue dazzle of cosmic collapse.

Witness the anomaly. The brightness grows, the Universe shrinks towards its final point; but the Kermel darkness is undiminished.

The black spirals surrounding me draw tighter,

tearing open sharp-edged holes of shadow, quenching the inferno, gobbling up energy. They provide my shield from an intolerable glare. Without their protection I would long since be burned alive; instead, the temperature in the ship remains constant. The temperature of the Universe—if temperature still has any meaning—is trillions of degrees.

I know what science and logic tell me to expect. At the final mini-microsecond, in the terminal instant of un-creation, everything disintegrates. Nothing can survive infinite temperature, infinite pressure, infinite density. All will be gone, all consumed. . . .

. . . unless, perhaps, consciousness can transcend the limitations of physics?

I do not know. Less than one minute from the end, the nature of reality still eludes me.

The sky is infinite contrast now, swelling black and impossible radiance. Twenty seconds to the monobloc. There is no time left for time. *Fifteen seconds*.

This is Sy Day, once of Pentecost and now of everywhere. In the final moments of infinite light, I proclaim my faith:

I have made no error. I have interpreted the message of the Kermel Objects correctly.

The end is the beginning. There will be tomorrow.

More SF/Fantasy from Headline:

SHADOWS

Darkest fantasies by masters of the macabre including STEPHEN KING

EDITED BY CHARLES L GRANT

Imagine a collection of nightmarish tales as dark as a
freshly opened grave.
So terrifying that they scatter dreams like leaves before
a midnight wind.
So macabre that they freeze the blood. So horrific that
Evil itself turns away.
Imagine. Now open and read.

FICTION   0-7472-3002-1   £2.50

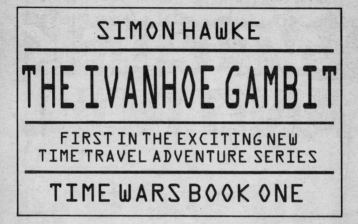

SIMON HAWKE

THE IVANHOE GAMBIT

FIRST IN THE EXCITING NEW TIME TRAVEL ADVENTURE SERIES

TIME WARS BOOK ONE

Lucas Priest is a Sergeant Major in the US Army Temporal Corps. But fighting the Time Wars isn't an easy way to make a living – not when you have to sail with Lord Nelson, battle Custer at Little Big Horn and spend a year pillaging with Attila and his infamous Huns.

Now a demented scheme to impersonate the King of England in the twelfth century is threatening to change the course of history. Two army teams have already failed to intercept the madman.

So Lucas and his band of men clock back to try and prevent an irreversible split in time. They are the last hope for the future of the world. . .

0 7472 3059 5   £2.50

From the depths
of hell, from the
darkest nightmare
it comes . . .

THE POWER

IAN WATSON

An ancient Power awakes . . .

A modern evil mushrooms into apocalypse . . .

Cocooned in a nightmare world, the village of Melfort
waits, as The Power feeds on the death and destruction,
fuelling its gross appetite . . .

And the dead rise up . . .

0 7472 3041 2   £2.50

WINNER OF THE WORLD FANTASY AWARD

Dan Simmons

Calcutta – a monstrous city of slums, disease and misery, clasped in the fetid embrace of an ancient cult.

Kali – the dark mother of pain, four-armed and eternal, her song the sound of death and destruction.

Robert Luczak – caught in a vortex of violence that threatens to engulf the entire world in an apocalyptic orgy of death.

The song of Kali has just begun . . .

"*Song of Kali* is as harrowing and ghoulish as anyone could wish. Simmons makes the stuff of nightmare very real indeed."
Locus

0 7472 3044 7   £2.95

Headline books are available at your bookshop or newsagent, or can be ordered from the following address:

Headline Book Publishing PLC
Cash Sales Department
PO Box 11
Falmouth
Cornwall
TR10 9EN
England

UK customers please send cheque or postal order (no currency), allowing 60p for postage and packing for the first book, plus 25p for the second book and 15p for each additional book ordered up to a maximum charge of £1.90 in UK.

BFPO customers please allow 60p for postage and packing for the first book, plus 25p for the second book and 15p per copy for the next seven books, thereafter 9p per book.

Overseas and Eire customers please allow £1.25 for postage and packing for the first book, plus 75p for the second book and 28p for each subsequent book.